W9-AKV-360

"What's that?"

Lane's voice brought Nora out of her reverie. She'd been drifting in the dreamworld that exists only for lovers.

Suddenly the bedroom door burst open and a hundred pounds of dog launched itself across the room. Nora only had time to fling the bedclothes over her and Lane's naked bodies before Chauncy landed on the bed like a giant cannonball.

"What the...?" Lane's voice was muffled. In her haste, Nora had thrown the covers over his head.

"Welcome to Chauncy's world," she said, trying not to laugh as she watched him struggle to get free.

Throwing back the covers, Lane stood up. He looked down at the dog who had wormed his way up beside Nora. "Didn't we talk about this, old man?"

Dear Reader,

If January puts ideas of "getting away from it all" into your mind, our Superromance authors can help.

Lynn Erickson's adventurous and very twentieth-century heroine, Tess Bonney, finds herself face-to-face with *The Last Buccaneer* when she is transported through time to the Spanish Main.

Out on the west coast, Nora Carmichael's ordered life is suddenly thrown into chaos when her apartment is invaded by *The Dog from Rodeo Drive.* Author Risa Kirk gives Lane Kincaid, her wonderful hero, the formidable task of convincing Nora that both he and the puppy are perfect for her.

In Boston, Stephanie Webb and her boss, Ben Strother, reluctantly join forces to bring their parents together, but their parents, it seems, have plans of their own. They arrange a vacation in Hilton Head so that their stubborn children will give in to the inevitable—*their* mutual attraction. *The Parent Plan* is a must for Judith Arnold fans!

Media personality Patrice Sullivan returns to North Carolina for her zany daughter's wedding and finds her "ex" as sexy and infuriating as ever. Peg Sutherland's *Simply Irresistible* is just that—a touching and lighthearted romp that stitches together a relationship clearly never meant to end.

In the coming months, in addition to more great books by some of your favorite authors, we've got some new talents to showcase. There's lots of excitement planned for 1994, so go ahead and get away from it all—and then come back and join us for all the fun!

Marsha Zinberg
Senior Editor

THE DOG FROM RODEO DRIVE

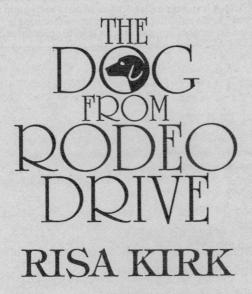

RISA KIRK

Harlequin Books

TORONTO • NEW YORK • LONDON
AMSTERDAM • PARIS • SYDNEY • HAMBURG
STOCKHOLM • ATHENS • TOKYO • MILAN
MADRID • WARSAW • BUDAPEST • AUCKLAND

If you purchased this book without a cover you should be aware that this book is stolen property. It was reported as "unsold and destroyed" to the publisher, and neither the author nor the publisher has received any payment for this "stripped book."

ISBN 0-373-70579-4

THE DOG FROM RODEO DRIVE

Copyright © 1994 by Janis Flores.

All rights reserved. Except for use in any review, the reproduction or utilization of this work in whole or in part in any form by any electronic, mechanical or other means, now known or hereafter invented, including xerography, photocopying and recording, or in any information storage or retrieval system, is forbidden without the written permission of the publisher, Harlequin Enterprises Limited, 225 Duncan Mill Road, Don Mills, Ontario, Canada M3B 3K9.

All characters in this book have no existence outside the imagination of the author and have no relation whatsoever to anyone bearing the same name or names. They are not even distantly inspired by any individual known or unknown to the author, and all incidents are pure invention.

This edition published by arrangement with Harlequin Enterprises B. V.

® and TM are trademarks of the publisher. Trademarks indicated with ® are registered in the United States Patent and Trademark Office, the Canadian Trade Marks Office and in other countries.

Printed in U.S.A.

ABOUT THE AUTHOR

This is Risa Kirk's tenth Superromance novel. Once again, the California author, who has published several mainstream novels, reveals her understanding of the special relationship between people and their pets. This book, says Risa, "was inspired by the arrival of Rhett, our new Australian puppy, who started out small and is still growing..."

Books by Risa Kirk

HARLEQUIN SUPERROMANCE

238—TEMPTING FATE
273—DREAMS TO MEND
300—WITHOUT A DOUBT
361—PLAYING WITH FIRE
408—UNDERCOVER AFFAIR
441—SEND NO REGRETS
476—MADE TO ORDER
542—WORTH THE WAIT

Don't miss any of our special offers. Write to us at the following address for information on our newest releases.

Harlequin Reader Service
P.O. Box 1397, Buffalo, NY 14240
Canadian address: P.O. Box 603,
Fort Erie, Ont. L2A 5X3

CHAPTER ONE

NORA CARMICHAEL knew exactly when her quiet, structured life had begun to unravel. It wasn't when she'd first been introduced to filmdom's reigning superstar Lane Kincaid...or even when her actress mother, Theodora DeVere, breezed back into town to do a new film. Oh, no, it hadn't been as uneventful as *that,* she thought. The day her life *really* changed was the day she found a puppy on Rodeo Drive.

She didn't even know what she was doing on the famous street late that fateful afternoon. She rarely came to Beverly Hills; she wouldn't even have been in the area if she hadn't had to meet a client. She couldn't explain the impulse she'd had to park her car and stroll down the street to look in the windows of the exclusive stores. The names sounded like a roll call of the luxuriously expensive: Louis Vuitton, Chanel, Gucci, to name only a few.

She'd just stopped to marvel at one display that offered some board game made of solid gold when she thought she heard something behind her. She wasn't afraid, not here, even though it was after five, and the normally bustling street was almost empty. With all these expensive goods in sight, she was sure there were security guards lurking every two feet. But then it came again. This time it sounded like a *whine*. She turned and looked around. There, right behind her, no bigger than a cantaloupe and similarly shaped, was a puppy. At first she didn't believe what she was seeing. Foolishly, she blinked, but when she looked again, it was still there, looking up at her with sad little eyes.

Thinking that the dog had gotten away from its master or mistress, she glanced around, but the person closest to her was a blond woman whose hat and stiletto heels matched her obviously expensive outfit perfectly.

"Excuse me," Nora called.

The woman turned. Stiffly, she said, "Are you speaking to me?"

Her cheeks reddening at the woman's tone, Nora pressed on. It seemed silly to ask, but she couldn't just leave the puppy in the street, so she said, "I...er...this little dog seems to be lost. Would you know... I mean, have you seen anyone looking for a puppy?"

The woman stared at her as though Nora were out of her mind. Then, at Nora's helpless gesture, she glanced down her perfectly chiseled nose at the dog. Her nostrils actually pinched. "I can't help you," she said haughtily.

"But—"

Still gazing distastefully at the little creature, who had crept closer to Nora and was now cuddling against her leg, the woman sniffed. "Obviously, it's a stray that doesn't belong *here*. Why, anyone can see that it has no pedigree."

Nora looked down at the pup with its fuzzy reddish coat and floppy black ears framing an adorable face.

Its paws seemed a little too big for its small body, but then, she didn't know too much about dogs and in any case, she thought impatiently, that wasn't the point. Chagrined that the puppy seemed to have adopted her, she looked up again, intending to ask the woman's advice about what to do. To her dismay, the stranger was already walking away, leaving her alone with the dog.

Now what? she wondered. She looked down again. The puppy stared up at her so trustingly that she had to bend down and pick it up. As soon as she did, it began wriggling in her arms, struggling to lick her face. The small sandpaper tongue felt so strange that she laughed. Then, quickly, she frowned.

"Oh, no, you don't," she said, holding the now-ecstatic little creature away from her. "Don't think you're going to ingratiate yourself with me that way. I've never had a dog, and I'm not starting now. Do you hear me?"

The puppy tipped its head at her. Seeing its expression, she added, "Don't look at me like that, I'm telling you. You'll be better off with your own family. I'm sure they have kids who love you and who will take care of you—"

She stopped. Embarrassed at the thought that someone might hear her talking to this cuddly little thing, she looked around. She knew that stores, especially ones like these, frowned on animals, but she had no choice. Resigned, she went through the nearest door.

"Excuse me," she said to the salesperson who swooped down on her. "Would you know anything about this little puppy? I found it just now on the walk outside, and—"

"I'm sorry, miss, we don't allow dogs in the store," the clerk said. "You'll have to take it outside."

"But I think it's lost—"

"Lost?" The clerk shook her head. "Oh, no, not here on Rodeo Drive. We don't allow animals to...*roam* here at will." She looked disapprovingly at the puppy, who was now nestled against Nora's neck. "And we certainly don't see dogs like *that* around here."

By this time, despite herself, Nora was feeling protective. She held on to her temper and thanked the clerk for her help. Outside again, she tried two more passersby, and then three more stores, with the same result. When she finally realized that no one knew, or cared, where the puppy had come from or what would happen to it next, she went back to her car and got in. Trying to decide what to do, she put the puppy in her lap, but when she felt its sad little eyes on her again, she sighed.

"Please don't look at me like that," she repeated. "We're going to the shelter, and they'll find you a good home. I promise."

As if deliberately trying to make her feel like a monster, the dog curled up into a little ball, right in the lap of her cream-colored skirt. She couldn't believe that she, who was always so meticulously groomed and perfectly in charge of herself and everything around her, was allowing a dog to ruin one of her good suits, and she debated briefly about putting the puppy on the back seat. Then she felt impatient again. *Come on Nora. Just get to the shelter. They'll take care of everything,* she said to herself. The puppy snuggled even closer as she reached for the car keys. She didn't have time for a dog, she told herself. She didn't even have time to raise a goldfish. So she'd better just get this over with right now.

Mercifully, the shelter wasn't far from her Glendale home. But her problem, it seemed, was far from over. The two officers in charge were as nice as they could be. They even made a fuss over the darling little creature she was holding. But they were also adamant. They just didn't have a place for another throwaway.

"We'll show you through the ward," one of the attendants offered, when Nora looked shocked.

"And through the adoption section," the second officer said. "You'll see, we're filled to capacity. I'm sorry, we just can't take him."

She couldn't believe it. Desperately, she said, "But he's so cute, someone will *surely* adopt him!"

"You don't want him," the first one explained. "There's no guarantee anyone else will, either."

"But I can't take him!" she insisted.

"Then we'll have to euthanatize him."

She thought she hadn't heard right. "I... What?"

"I'm sorry, it's policy," the second officer said, sympathetic but firm. "You can see, the dog's sick. His eyes are watering, and his breathing is labored—"

She looked down the puppy. True, the dog *had* sneezed twice on the way to the shelter, and she had noticed that he was wheezing a bit. But that didn't mean he should be put to sleep!

"I'm sorry," the first officer was saying. "But we don't have any choice. If people would neuter or spay their animals—dogs *and* cats—we wouldn't have to destroy millions every year. But we can't keep them all, and believe me, we've tried. I've got four dogs and three cats myself."

"And I've got more than I can handle, too," the second officer put in. She held out her arms. "Here, give him to me. We'll make sure he doesn't suffer."

Nora held the puppy closer. "No, thanks. I'll keep him myself before I let him be destroyed."

Both officers beamed. Then they said in unison, "Great. We'll give you the name of a good vet."

NORA HAD BEEN assured that Dr. Greta Carter was one of the best veterinarians in the area. No one had mentioned that she was also one of the most expensive. By the time Nora left the high-tech clinic, her puppy in one arm, an armful of medications in the other, she was in too deep to turn back.

"But he'll be just fine, I guarantee it," the doctor told her. "And he really is a cute little thing," she'd added, holding the puppy up in front of her face with expert, sure hands. She looked at Nora. "What are you going to call him?"

"I don't know," Nora said as Dr. Carter put the puppy down on the examining table. It immediately came to snuggle against her, and as she placed her hand uncertainly on its fuzzy head, she gave a shrug.

"I've never had a dog before, but he doesn't seem to be a Rover or a Spot, does he?"

Dr. Carter laughed. "No, indeed," she agreed. Mysteriously, she added, "I think this dog will surprise you. He's going to need a name worthy of him, I think. Something . . . dignified."

Nora wasn't sure what the doctor meant. But just then the intercom on the wall buzzed, and someone announced that Dr. Carter was wanted in another room. Almost before Nora could say goodbye, certainly before she was ready, the veterinarian was gone.

Left alone, Nora looked down at the dog, who had fallen asleep again in her arms. *A name worthy of this little thing?* she thought. He didn't look bigger than a minute, and she doubted he'd grow much more. Still, since she didn't have any experience with pets, perhaps she should take the doctor's advice.

"Chauncy," she said suddenly, the name popping into her head. She couldn't imagine why she'd thought of it, but she tested it again. "Chauncy."

To her surprise, the dog opened one sleepy eye and looked up at her before sighing contentedly and settling back again. "Well, obviously you agree," she said. "All right, Chauncy it will be."

After making arrangements for a follow-up appointment, Nora said goodbye to the smiling secretary and went out to the car, where she put Chauncy carefully down on the passenger seat. The puppy stretched out without even waking up.

"I don't know," Nora said before getting into the car herself. "I'm willing to bet that by the time you're all grown up, your name is *still* going to be bigger than you are."

BY THE TIME Chauncy was eight months old, he weighed nearly one hundred pounds and stood almost three feet at the shoulder. Dr. Carter was pleased at his progress, cheerfully assuring the despairing Nora that Chauncy hadn't yet reached his full-growth potential, which she estimated at around one hundred and fifty pounds. Long before then, though, the veterinarian had determined that the tiny little creature Nora had rescued could trace its lineage to the bloodlines of the Saint Bernards, with a nod to one of the huge wolfhounds of the Irish, with perhaps a retriever or two thrown in for good luck.

"You'll probably never know for sure," the doctor said blithely. "But aren't you glad you gave him a name that was worthy of him?"

"Oh, yes, glad," Nora said on a sigh. By this time, Chauncy had knocked over, swept off, stepped on, or crushed practically everything in her once-pristine and superbly organized home.

It wasn't that the big mahogany dog was malicious, she thought, stroking his floppy ears while he looked up at her adoringly; it was just that he was so *big* he couldn't help himself. And now that he weighed almost as much as she did, it was getting to the point where he took *her* for a walk, and not the other way around. She'd seen her neighbors smile at the sight of her being pulled along, like a little moon in the orbit of a much bigger planet, and she couldn't blame them for laughing. If someone else had been on the handle end of the leash, she would have been amused, too.

"But at least you're not *lonely*," one of the secretaries at work, Sherrie, had said to her one day, when Nora mentioned yet another item of furniture Chauncy had destroyed over the weekend.

"I wasn't lonely before," Nora said. Then she sighed resignedly. It seemed she was always sighing where Chauncy was concerned, and suddenly it occurred to her that the only other living creature who had this effect on her was her mother.

As though the secretary had divined Nora's thoughts, Sherrie asked, "How's your mother these days? You haven't mentioned her in a while."

Nora sat back. "As far as I know, she's still in Europe somewhere, touring."

"It must be so exciting to have a star for a mother."

"Oh, it's exciting, all right," Nora said dryly. She loved her mother. But even at her most subdued, Theodora DeVere could be exhausting. A renowned stage-and-screen actress, it seemed to Nora that, even asleep, her mother was always performing.

As Sherrie went back to work, Nora reached for a file on her desk. As a rising star at the very conservative firm of Bullard and Sweeney, Nora had her work cut out for her. Her boss Orrin Bullard had recruited her himself from her previous job as a high-level financial planner in New York. Recently she'd been assigned an important client, a recluse named Lester Snook, whose chief aim, besides increasing his wealth, was keeping a low profile. Orrin Bullard had made it clear to Nora that her chances of moving up depended on keeping Snook and her other clients happy.

Today was Monday and after spending a weekend chasing after Chauncy, grabbing things that started to spill off tables as he went by, allowing him to take her for his run in the nearby park and lugging in yet another fifty-pound bag of kibble from the store, she was glad to get back to work. It was so much more... peaceful here, she thought, and was just settling more comfortably into her desk chair when there was a commotion in the outer office.

Hearing raised voices, she glanced up. "What...?" she murmured as her office door burst open.

Theodora DeVere paused dramatically on the threshold, her rainbow-colored dress swirling around her shapely legs. As the gauzy material lost momentum and began to swing gently to a stop, Theodora glanced over her shoulder. Unable to help herself, Nora stood up, stretched up on her tiptoes and looked, too. The two secretaries, Sherrie and Ginger, were standing beside their desks wearing identical expressions of amazement mixed with awe. When she saw them, Nora felt a stirring of panic. Orrin Bullard's office was just down the hall; she could imagine the effect her mother would have on her conservative boss. The thought propelled her forward, and she grabbed Theodora by the arm, pulling her into the office and quickly closing the door.

"Darling girl!" Theodora exclaimed, sweeping Nora into an embrace. "Oh, it's so wonderful to see you again!"

"It's good to see you, too, Mother," Nora said, returning the hug. "But . . . what are you doing here?"

"Oh, you'll never guess!" Theodora exclaimed. "But first, let me look at you. It's been so long—months! I thought I'd *never* finish that stupid show, you know. By the time we got to Berlin, I was ready to lose my mind, and when we reached Vienna, well, I simply told Edgar that I couldn't go on. And you know how I love Vienna. Why, your father and I—"

Theodora stopped. She rarely discussed Nora's father, Patric Carmichael, the actor who had been her second *and* fourth husband. Both marriages had been tumultuous, and not long after their second divorce, Patric had died. Nora had been just six at the time.

"Well, anyway, it doesn't matter, does it?" Theodora said quickly, obviously dismissing the past. "The point is, I finished the tour, and now I'm back where I started. Oh, Hollywood!" she exclaimed, throwing out her arms. Then she laughed and winked at Nora. "Well, it's Studio City, but it's the same thing, really, isn't it? I never thought I would miss it. You know how I've always hated this town. But when Freddie Princeley offered me a juicy role in his new film, I couldn't turn him down. The part is perfect for me, and the actor who's playing opposite me—with name credits *under* mine, naturally, I don't care *how* popular he's supposed to be—"

Nora was still trying to digest what her mother was saying. Theodora was going to do a film. Nora could hardly remember the last movie Theodora had made; when it had opened to mediocre reviews and tepid audience reaction, Theodora had haughtily declared that she would never, under any circumstances, make another.

"Nora, are you listening?" Theodora demanded suddenly. "I said that Lane Kincaid is going to be co-starring. We happened to meet in New York when I came in, and I must say, he's even more handsome than I'd heard. In fact, he almost reminds me of...well, never mind. The point is that I can see why all the girls are mad about him. He has that look, you know, the one that makes fools of women the world over. Why—" Theodora stopped again. "Nora!" she said impatiently. "Have you heard a word I've said?"

"Of course, Mother," Nora said dutifully. But the truth was, she'd stopped listening the instant her mother had mentioned Lane Kincaid. She wasn't interested in Hollywood's latest version of the macho-man, superstar superstud. In fact, a few months ago, during endless promotions for the actor's new film, *Wet Work,* when it seemed that the entire world had been papered with pictures of Kincaid's lean, tanned face, she'd thought she'd go mad if she saw another photo of him, or heard his name mentioned one more time.

She couldn't deny he was handsome, she thought. And she had to admit that there was a certain *look* in his blue-gray eyes. But enough was enough. The man hadn't found a cure for cancer; all he'd done was make one more film—no doubt another of the male-bonding type that glorified violence as the solution to every problem.

Theodora interrupted Nora's thoughts once more. "I know how you feel about the business, darling, but I thought you'd be interested."

Nora saw that her mother was hurt by her lack of enthusiasm, but she couldn't help it. The truth was, she had done her best to distance herself from "the business." Theodora had been married five times—all her husbands had been actors—and if Nora had one word to describe her growing up, it would have been . . . turmoil. With all those clashing egos around the house, quarrels, fights and screaming matches had erupted at the slightest provocation.

Nora hated all the moving around, being hustled from one location to another, depending upon where her parents were currently performing. She knew her mother and father had tried their best to be a family; after all, it would have been so much easier to leave a young child behind. She appreciated their efforts, but throughout her growing up, she'd craved the stability they couldn't provide. She had vowed from an early age that one day, no matter what, she'd find it.

And she had accomplished her goal—or thought she had, she amended wryly, thinking of Chauncy. Still, even considering the dog, she had created a solid, stable world where everything had a place. She liked her life now. Sometimes she thought that her mother drew all her creative energy from chaos, but excess had the opposite effect on her.

Glad that the past was behind her, she smiled. "Of course, I'm interested, Mother. And congratulations. I know you'll be wonderful in the new film. And you're sure to captivate...er...what's-his-name. When does production begin?''

Theodora laughed. "If that's your oblique way of wanting to know if I plan on staying with you, the answer is no. I don't want to hurt your feelings, darling, but you have to admit, you *do* tend to be rather...conventional, while I am...not. We'd drive each other mad in less than a day, so I decided it would be better if I stayed with a friend. Brock Morton has offered me the use of his house, and the place will be just fine for me while I'm here.''

Picturing the Beverly Hills mansion of the noted Hollywood director, Nora had to smile. She'd read that Morton's ''place'' had, among other amenities, twelve bedrooms, a kitchen big enough to serve an army battalion, an indoor swimming pool and a complete serving staff.

"Yes, I think you'll be much more comfortable there than you will in my cramped quarters,'' she said solemnly, but with twinkling eyes. "You were fortunate you caught Brock while he was in town.''

"Oh, he's not here,'' Theodora said with a wave of her hand. "He's in France somewhere, working on another of those dreadfully boring and obscure *films noir*. A pity, though,'' she added, "since he'll miss what I've decided is to be my swan song.''

Theodora paused dramatically, waiting for Nora's reply.

"Mother, you're retiring? I'd sooner believe that California is going to sink unobtrusively into the sea!''

Pleased at her daughter's reaction, Theodora brushed an imaginary speck from her sleeve. "I know you're surprised, darling. But I have been talking about it for years."

"Yes, but I never thought you'd actually *consider* it."

Theodora sighed. "In normal circumstances, I wouldn't have. But even I have to admit that decent parts are fewer and farther between, now that I'm...er...on the cusp of middle age."

Nora hid a smile. She knew how sensitive Theodora was on the subject of age, so she didn't remind her that, at sixty-two, she was a little past middle age.

"And besides," Theodora added, "things have changed."

"Things?" Nora said. "What things?"

"I know you won't believe this, darling, but—" Theodora's voice dropped melodramatically "—I've met a man!"

"Mother, you *always* meet men! You'd meet a man if you and he were the only two people left on earth and you started walking toward each other from opposite poles of the globe!"

Theodora tried to look indignant. "I should have known you would mock me," she scolded. "You always have thought I was...flighty."

"You *are* flighty. You know you are. You take pride in it," Nora said, laughing.

"I certainly do not!"

"Yes, you do," Nora said. "That's just the way you are, and I love you in spite of it. Now, come on. Tell me about the new man you've met."

Theodora sniffed. "He's not just *any* man. His name is Arthur Winslow, and I—"

Nora's eyes widened. "Arthur Winslow! The industrialist?"

"Do you know him?"

Know him? Nora thought. Arthur Winslow was one of the wealthiest men in the country, a workaholic who rarely left his office, much less Los Angeles. She looked at her mother in sheer amazement. "How in the world did you meet him?"

"I have my ways," Theodora said with a sly smile.

"What ways?" Nora demanded. Then she thought of something, and added, "Oh, Mother, what did you do now? You didn't—"

"Seduce him?" Theodora said wickedly. Seeing the shocked expression on Nora's face, she took pity on her daughter. Shaking her head, she said, "No, I didn't do anything like that. It was all rather innocent, in fact. He attended one of my performances in London. When he asked to come backstage to meet me—"

"He came backstage? Oh, Mother, now I know you're teasing. From what I've read about the man, Arthur Winslow doesn't go to meet people! If he wants to see someone, they come to him!"

"Well, he came to *me!*" Theodora laughed. "Of course, at the time I had no idea who he was. I just thought he was another fan."

Nora felt faint. "Only you would think such a thing. Just another fan! Honestly, Mother—"

"Well, how was I to know? So, naturally I refused when he first asked me to supper—"

"You *refused* to go to dinner with him?"

Theodora smiled her famous catlike smile. "At first, darling—yes. After all, he could have been anyone, couldn't he? But then, he was so *persistent* that before I knew it, we were going out to supper every night after the show. At least, until he had to go back to Los Angeles."

"So, Arthur Winslow is the real reason you're here?" Nora narrowed her eyes. "I thought you said it was the film for Princeley."

"Well, it's both," Theodora said, patting her hair. "I know you don't believe me, darling, but I am serious about all this. The new film *is* going to be my swan song, and after that—promise you won't laugh, now— I think I'm going to marry Arthur. It's time for me to settle down."

"Marry Arthur? Settle down?" Nora shook her head. "I'm sorry, Mother, but I... Have you thought about this?"

"Of course I've thought about it. Now, I know what you're going to say, darling, and I couldn't agree more. After all, I was married five times, and I never could get it right. But not *all* of it was my fault, you know. And *this* time it will be different, you'll see. But there. I've taken enough of your time. I know you're busy, and I have a party to plan."

"A party?" Nora was instantly wary.

"Don't look so nervous, darling," Theodora said, patting Nora's cheek. "You know I always give a party when I start a new role. It's tradition."

"Yes, well, it's a tradition I can live without. I still remember some of those wild parties in the past, and I don't want anything to do with—"

Theodora looked dismayed. "But you have to come!"

"Oh, no, I don't. You know how I hate those things."

"But I plan on inviting Lane Kincaid!"

"Be still my heart. Please give him my apologies— not that he'll care in the slightest."

"But—"

"I'm sorry," Nora said firmly. "No parties."

Theodora seemed genuinely distressed. "Nora, please reconsider. It won't be the same without you. Listen, if it will make you happy, I'll just invite a few old friends. I promise it will be a quiet affair."

Nora had to laugh. "I appreciate the offer, Mother, but we both know you've never given a quiet party in your entire life."

"Well, this one will be, I promise! Oh, please. It would mean so much to me." Her mother grasped Nora's hands and pulled her close. "I have missed you, darling. It's been so long since we've seen each other."

Nora tried to move away. She could handle Theodora when she was being melodramatic; it was when Theodora started behaving like a mother that Nora didn't know how to act.

"Please," Theodora said again. "If you come to this party, I promise I won't ask another thing of you the entire time I'm in Los Angeles!"

They knew that wasn't true, and as they looked at each other, they both laughed at the same time. Nora felt herself weakening.

She tried one more time. "Mother, I—"

"Please?"

Nora gave in, but not completely. "All right, I'll come. But—" she held up a hand before her mother took over again "—I'm just going to make an appearance. I won't stay until dawn, which is when your parties usually end."

"Only the boring ones," Theodora said mischievously. "The good ones usually last until brunch."

Nora refused to smile. "I mean it, Mother. I'm only coming for an hour—two at the most."

"Whatever you say, darling, I don't care, just as long as you're there. You won't regret it, I promise!"

And with that, Theodora reached for her voluminous bag, which she had thrown down carelessly on the desk. Turning in a whirl of skirts, she started toward the door, only to pause. "I'll let you know the details when I know them myself, darling. But in the meantime—"

Nora had an idea what was coming, and she braced herself. She knew her mother despaired of her daughter's ultraconservative wardrobe, her minimal makeup, her easy-care hair, but over the years Theodora had come to terms with it.

Except during times like this, when she knew Theodora was aching to say something about the restrained cut of her business suit, or the fact that she wasn't wearing false eyelashes to work.

"Yes, Mother?" she said dutifully.

Theodora looked at her for a long moment. Then she smiled her most brilliant smile. "I was just going to say that I love your new hairstyle. It's so... so... *you.*"

Laughing, Nora kissed her cheek. "Thanks," she said. "I think."

Theodora gave her a fierce, quick hug in return. "I'll call you about the party."

"I can hardly wait," Nora said dryly. But she watched with mixed feelings while Theodora departed in a cloud of gauze and designer perfume before closing the office door. Then with another heartfelt sigh, she got back to work.

CHAPTER TWO

IT HAD BEEN a mistake to come to the party. Nora knew it the instant she pulled up at the end of the circular driveway and heard the loud music drifting out to the street.

"I should have known Mother would never be able to keep a promise about a 'quiet little party,'" she muttered. Right now, as she peered up the driveway, she could see people spilling out the front door and crowding the lawn. When she heard the raucous laughter and shrieks of merriment from inside, she wondered if she should just drive away.

A low whine came from the seat behind her.

Nora glanced over her shoulder at Chauncy. "I agree," she said. "Maybe we should just turn around and go home."

Chauncy whined again, louder this time. His tongue hanging out, his huge jaws open, he thumped his plume of a tail on the seat.

Nora looked at the brightly lighted house again. Then she shook her head. She couldn't drive away; her mother would be hurt if she didn't put in an appearance, so she pulled into a place up the street and stopped the car. She turned to Chauncy.

"You stay here," she said sternly. She knew he hated to stay by himself in the car, but she couldn't help it tonight. She wouldn't have brought him if she hadn't had to pick him up from a late grooming appointment; it had been too far to take him home and come back, and in any event, she'd wanted to get this over with as quickly as possible. Besides, she thought, having the dog with her would give her the perfect excuse to leave early.

She took a huge rawhide bone out of her purse and handed it to the dog. As he took it gently, she gave him another warning.

"Now, I mean it," she said. "No howling, like you usually do. You'll embarrass me. Just chew your bone, and I'll be back before you know it."

As usual the dog seemed to understand her. The treat between his huge paws, Chauncy watched with mournful eyes as she slipped out of the car and quickly closed the door behind her. The night was warm, so she had to leave the windows down for him. As an extra precaution, she had wound the end of his leash around one of the door handles to make sure he'd stay inside. He knew what he was supposed to do; whether he'd do it or not was debatable. When he'd still been small enough for her to handle, she'd taken him to obedience class. True to form even then, he had been such an angel that the instructor had awarded him the best-dog-in-the-class prize. The same instructor would have been horrified, Nora thought now, if he'd seen how the dog behaved at home.

Praying he'd be good tonight, she gave him one last look before heading up the driveway. She planned to find her mother, say hello and then slip out again, but she was just walking by the side of the house when someone stepped out onto the sidewalk, nearly knocking her over.

"I'm sorry!" said a deep voice she thought she recognized. A firm, masculine grip took her elbow and steadied her. "I didn't mean to run into you, little lady."

"It's all right. I—" Having caught her balance, Nora looked up at the person who had bumped into her. Recognizing him, she said, "Zane Whittacker! I don't believe it. It's been years!"

The silver-haired former cowboy star, who in his day had been even more popular than Roy Rogers and Gene Autry put together, peered at her for a moment, then grinned ear to ear.

"Why, bless my soul!" he said delightedly. "Is that little Nora?"

Nora laughed, thinking that if Zane were here, maybe this party wouldn't be so bad, after all. She still had fond memories of Whittacker putting her up on his black horse, Thunder, and leading her around the lot between setups while she waited for her mother on one film or another.

"Not so little anymore, I'm afraid," she said. Her eyes twinkled. "In fact, I think I'm older now than you were when you made *Wild Prairie Fighter*."

"You remember that old oater?" Zane asked. He pretended to be embarrassed, but he still looked pleased.

"That one and all the other films you made with Thunder," she said. She gave his arm an affectionate squeeze. "How are you, Zane?"

"Oh, can't complain. I still work a little, but things are different nowadays. Horses are too slow for these high-tech people now. With all these special effects, I've sort of been put out to pasture."

Her smile faltered. "I'm sorry to hear that."

"Oh, I don't know," he said, patting her hand. "Things weren't the same when old Thunder went. We'd acted together so long I felt like I'd lost my partner. It just took the heart out of things, if you know what I mean."

Last year, Nora could only have guessed how Zane felt. But that was before Chauncy had bumbled into her life. As maddening and exasperating as the dog could be, she knew that she would miss him terribly if something ever happened to him.

"Yes, I think I do know what you mean," she said.

Zane swiped a quick hand across his eyes. "So, Nora, how have you been? Did you ever go to school and get your degree in finance?"

She was touched that he'd remembered. "Yes, I did. I was working for a while in New York, but I recently came out here. In fact, I'm with a firm in Pasadena."

"Doesn't surprise me. We always knew you had gumption."

Blushing at the compliment, she said, "I can't believe you remembered."

"I wouldn't forget something like that, now, would I? We were all rootin' for you back then. Me, and Tip Shugrue—you remember Tip, don't you?"

Nora grinned. "Mr. Wahoo? How could I forget? What's he up to these days?"

"You aren't going to believe it, but darned if he didn't really give up the business and go up to the Tetons, just like he said he would. Last I heard, he bought himself a cattle spread, and he's happy as a hog in...well, he's happy, running those cows around."

"Good for him!"

"And for you," Zane said. "It sounds like you've done just fine, Nora. But like I said, I always knew you would. So did your mother. She was proud of you."

Nora put her hand through his arm. "Thanks, Zane," she said fondly. "But, speaking of our hostess, maybe I should let her know I'm here."

The old cowboy star patted her hand. "Oh, she knows that, all right. She's been looking out the window for five minutes, wondering what we're talking about out here."

Nora turned around. Sure enough, Theodora was just moving away from one of the big front windows. Hiding a smile, she said, "Knowing Mother, she's probably been reading our lips to make sure we're not talking about her."

He chuckled. "Or to make sure we are."

She laughed, and they started inside. When they found Theodora, the actress and the former cowboy star greeted each other like the old friends they were, then Zane winked at Nora and disappeared into the crowd. Left alone with her mother, Nora said, "Nice *little* party, Mom."

"I *tried,* darling, I did," Theodora said. "But you know how it is. As soon as everyone heard I was back in town, well . . ." She spread her hands helplessly.

"It's all right," Nora said. "But now that I've put in my obligatory appearance, I'll just leave the way I came, and—"

"You can't leave now!"

"Yes, I can, Mother. Watch me."

"Darling, don't be so antisocial," Theodora pleaded. "You enjoyed seeing Zane again, didn't you? Well, there are other old friends here tonight. You can't leave without saying hello to them, too."

Nora looked around at the crush. Dryly, she said, "I'd like to say hello, but even if I could find anyone I knew, I don't think we could have a decent conversation. You probably haven't noticed, but the music is a little loud."

"Nora! Is that you?" someone said breathlessly just then, from behind her.

Nora turned and looked into the eyes of the woman who had been known in her day as the Nightingale of Broadway. Miriah Drayton had been retired for years, but her skin was just as luminous as it had been in her heyday and her eyes were the same intense blue that admirers had often sworn could be seen from the balcony.

"Hello, Miss Drayton," Nora said warmly. "How beautiful you look."

Miriah preened. Then she looked archly at Theodora. "You and I might have disagreed about many things in the past, Theo, but I've never denied that your daughter had exquisite manners."

"And she's so clever, too," Theodora said, putting a proprietary arm around Nora. "Do you know she's a high-level executive at a *very* prestigious finance company in Pasadena?"

"It's money management, Mother, not a finance company," Nora said. It might not matter to Theodora, but to those in her profession, there was a vast difference between the two. Still, she didn't feel her usual impatience with her mother about the issue tonight, and as she glanced at Theodora, she realized Zane had been right: her mother *was* proud of her.

"You know, I always saw it, even when you were a little girl, Nora," Miriah said just then, with a sly glance in Theodora's direction. "But it's even more obvious now, I think. The resemblance between you and your mother is remarkable."

Nora laughed. "I wish it were true."

"Why, Nora!" Theodora exclaimed, giving Miriah a haughty glance in return. "How can you say that? I've had several people comment just tonight on how much we look like ... sisters!"

"In your dreams, darling," Miriah drawled to Theodora with a beatific smile. "In your dreams."

Theodora's violet-tinted eyes flashed. Seeing the warning sign, Nora said hastily, "It was lovely seeing you again, Miss Drayton. Look, Mother, isn't that Allie Cheswick? I haven't seen her in ages. Let's go say hello."

To her relief, Miriah didn't follow when Nora grabbed her mother's hand and pulled her away. Theodora came along for a few steps, but then she halted. "You don't have to haul me along like a wagon," she said, giving an annoyed glance over her shoulder. "Raddled old crone," she muttered. "I knew I shouldn't have invited her."

Deciding they were a safe distance away, Nora dropped her grip. "I thought you liked Miriah."

"I do," Theodora said, and sniffed. "But the fact that she has that gorgeous English skin doesn't give her the right to act so damned superior!"

Nora started to laugh, but just then Theodora grabbed her arm. Startled, Nora looked around. "What is it?"

Smiling in a way that instantly made Nora wary, Theodora said, "There's someone I want you to meet, darling."

Nora groaned. "Oh, Mother, haven't I done enough?" The blaring music was giving her a headache and the crush of people was making her feel claustrophobic. She'd done her duty by showing up; now all she wanted to do was go home. But just then, there was a stir at the front door. Nora felt it even before she glanced in that direction, and when she saw who had just come in, she knew why Theodora was smiling.

"Oh, no, you don't," she warned, turning to her mother.

"Now, darling, you have to meet him, you know you do," Theodora said. "He's my new costar, after all."

Nora didn't care if he'd been appointed president of his own country. Stubbornly, she insisted, "I don't want to meet him."

But Theodora's grip was ironclad as she pulled Nora toward the door. The treacherous crowd—through which Nora couldn't have fought her way two minutes before—parted like the Red Sea, and before she knew it, Nora was standing in front of the actor she just knew she was going to despise.

In each poster she'd seen of him, he'd posed in skintight leather jeans with his legs spread suggestively apart. The only other thing he was wearing was a sexy smirk. She thought it made him look as though his pants were too tight.

She couldn't imagine what the public saw in him— or why people stood for hours in every kind of weather to be the first to see one of his films when it opened. To Nora, who had known *real* actors from the time she was small, Lane Kincaid was just another in the long line of studs being promoted by studios hungry for commercial success. She'd been glad her father wasn't alive to see the rise of the beefy-looking macho star, whose acting repertoire and entire gamut of screen emotion seemed to consist entirely of squints, grunts and sneers.

"Darling," Theodora said, her grip still like a vise around Nora's arm, "I'd like you to meet Lane Kincaid." With one of her most brilliant smiles, she looked up at Lane. "Lane, this is my daughter, Nora Carmichael."

Her face stiff, Nora had to force herself to look up at him. Wishing devoutly that she had never agreed to come tonight, she started to say, "Hello—"

And then the world tilted.

The famous gray-blue eyes she'd always thought were mocking a stupid world for being so gullible met hers, and something happened for which she was totally unprepared. Lane's gaze was so intent, so... mesmerizing...that for a moment she couldn't remember her own name.

This isn't happening, she told herself. It couldn't be. She knew all sorts of actors, many like this man, who were shallow and...and totally without any talent whatsoever. None of *them* had *ever* had this effect on her.

Was this what the fans saw? she wondered dizzily. There must have been a hundred or more people in the living room, but it was as though they were completely alone. He hadn't looked away from her and she felt hypnotized by his eyes. To save her life, she couldn't have turned away.

Then he said, in that deep drawl that had thrilled millions of female fans the world over, "I'm pleased to meet you, Nora. But I would have known you anywhere. You look just like your mother."

Abruptly, Nora came back to earth. He was the second person to tell her she resembled her mother tonight and she didn't believe him any more than she had believed Miriah Drayton. She'd heard it from the time she was small, and she had always known it was meaningless, a way some people used to try to impress her famous mother.

Her spine stiffened, and when she looked up at Lane again, she had herself under control—or so she hoped. Her voice cool, she said, "Thank you. It's nice of you to say so."

Those damned eyes of his continued to hold hers. "I wasn't just saying it."

She tensed again. She couldn't understand why he was having such an effect on her, but it was going to stop. She'd known some of the most handsome and charming leading men in the world, and she'd handled them all with the same aplomb. Lane Kincaid was no different. No different at all.

Just then, Theodora laughed. As though Nora had never seen her mother before, she turned and looked blankly at Theodora, who said, "I'd love to stay and chat, but I must see to the hors d'oeuvres." Her eyes met Nora's and she flashed a warning look. "You'll take care of Lane for a few minutes, won't you, darling? I'll be right back."

When Nora realized that her mother intended to leave her alone with Lane, she panicked. She didn't know what to say to this man, with his strange eyes and his intent expression, and as Theodora started off, she reached out.

"Mother..."

Pretending not to hear, Theodora waved and disappeared into the obliging crowd, which swallowed her up before she'd gone three steps. Nora had to will herself not to follow. She could handle this, she told herself as she turned back to Lane. It wasn't difficult. All she had to do was excuse herself graciously and...wander casually away. Then, when she was out of sight, she could run like hell.

"You don't have to stay with me," she said. She tried, but she couldn't meet Lane's eyes. She could smell the after-shave he was wearing; the scent seemed to fill her entire being and she tried to back up a step, only to hit a piece of furniture. Doggedly, she went on, "I'm sure you have a lot of friends here, and I was leaving, anyway."

"So soon?" She hadn't realized he'd be so...so big. Inadvertently or not, he was blocking her path. In fact, she realized uncomfortably, he seemed almost to fill her entire field of vision. Why was he so big? Why was he so undeniably masculine? In his publicity pictures and those awful posters, he'd seemed almost a parody. Why didn't he seem that way in person?

She reminded herself that she could handle this and said, "I told my mother I'd come for a while, but I have to be at work early tomorrow, so I really have to get going. I have appointments all day, and—"

She knew she was babbling, but she couldn't help herself. Desperately, she glanced around. She couldn't understand why, of the seemingly *hundreds* of guests her mother had invited, no one seemed willing to interrupt them. There had to be dozens of people who were dying to talk to Lane, but it was as though a force field had sprung up, separating them from the rest of the room.

He was blocking the way into the living room; a group of people who wanted to come in from the entry looked at him apologetically, and he obligingly moved outside, out of the way. As he did, he took Nora's arm, drawing her with him whether she wanted to go or not.

Nora didn't want to be anywhere near this man. The instant he touched her, she felt something *zing!* between them, and she was so acutely aware of the pressure of his fingers on her arm that her entire body tingled. Wishing all the lights would go out so he couldn't see her flushed face, she tried to appear cool and poised. Then she realized he was staring at her again. His scrutiny made her even more nervous, and before she realized what she was doing, she was demanding, "Why are you looking at me like that?"

Before he could answer, there was another stir—this time from outside. Still trying to get herself under control, Nora thought she heard, in order, a shriek, a cry, a frightened scream, a curse of surprise. Startled, she turned toward the door, wondering what was happening. People were jumping out of the way. She caught a glimpse of something galloping up the walk. When she saw what it was, she gasped.

"Oh, no!"

Dimly, she realized Lane had turned to her. "What . . . ?" he started to ask.

She didn't have time to answer. Just then, trailing a leash with the car door handle still attached, Chauncy heaved into view. Floppy ears flying, tongue lolling, he charged through the door like a giant bear being chased by the devil, scattering the people like leaves. When he saw the crowd fleeing, Chauncy tried to brake. His scrabbling claws couldn't find any purchase on the tiled floor and to Nora's horror, momentum carried him forward. As she watched helplessly, the dog skidded and slid across the tiles like a behemoth out of control.

"Chauncy!" she cried. She wanted to clap her hands over her eyes, but she couldn't move as Chauncy crashed into a statue guarding the entrance to the living room. As the heavy plaster thing started to fall, two women close by began to scream, startling the dog even more. Before Nora could react, Lane had jumped forward to catch the falling statue. As though a savior had suddenly loomed up in front of him, Chauncy changed direction and charged directly at Lane.

"Chauncy!" Nora cried again.

Nora couldn't believe this was happening. She saw the startled Lane turn—in time to catch two huge armfuls of dog. Aghast, she realized that Chauncy was attempting to...to *climb* up. Obviously frightened by all the chaos he had innocently created, the dog was using the actor as a human ladder, trying to get up and out of the way.

In a dreamlike sequence, where everyone and everything looked as though it were moving through molasses, Nora heard Lane's shout of surprise and Chauncy's howl of bewilderment and fright, but even as she lurched forward herself, she knew she was too late. Before her eyes, Lane began to stagger backward with the dog in his arms while Chauncy clung for dear life.

For the next few seconds, Nora and everyone else watched, transfixed, as Lane struggled to catch his balance. His arms went out, windmilling in an effort to stay upright, but with the dog clinging to him like a giant furry limpet, remaining upright was impossible. Locked together, man and dog stumbled back into the buffet table that had been set up behind them. With a sickening crunch, the table started to collapse, and hors d'oeuvres flew into the air like confetti. Cheese-balls pelted down like rain, and when the table began to buckle from the combined weight of Lane and the dog, a giant plate of salmon paté started an inexora-ble slide to the plush-carpeted floor.

Someone had enough presence of mind to grab the paté before it crashed down, but no one could catch the huge silver bowl of champagne punch. Before Nora's horrified eyes, the bowl jumped into the air and upended just as Lane and Chauncy fell heavily to the floor. Punch flooded down, drenching them both.

Nora knew what Chauncy's reaction would be to getting wet.

"No, Chauncy!" she shouted, breaking out of her stupefied trance and rushing forward. She knew there was no way she could get there in time, and she didn't. Lane was still on the floor underneath a hundred-plus pounds of dripping canine when Chauncy dropped his head and gave a mighty shake.

Drops of champagne punch flew out in all direc-tions, showering everyone in sight. Nora took the brunt of it, and as she put her hands up to protect her face, she wondered if it were possible to die of sheer embarrassment. All the noise had died down by this time; the entire place...the *world*...was silent. The first deluge had barely abated when Nora lunged for-ward. Reaching down, she grabbed Chauncy's collar and was almost jerked off her feet when the dog hunched his shoulders in preparation for a second good shake.

"Chauncy!" she cried.

Panting, the dog looked up at her. As though he didn't know what else to do, he sat down, just like an obedient dog should—right on Nora's foot.

Wishing he'd just sent her through the floor, Nora risked a quick glance in Lane's direction. By this time, the superstar who had made his reputation vanquishing *armies* single-handedly on screen, had scrambled out from under the buffet table. When Nora saw how he looked, she closed her eyes. Still dripping, with a cheeseball peeking out of the pocket of his drenched silk sports shirt, and a piece of pasta perched jauntily over one shoulder, a sodden Lane got to his feet. The entire room was quiet, waiting for...no one knew what.

Nora couldn't have spoken if her life depended on it, not even when Lane looked down at the huge dog by her feet. His floppy ears trickling champagne, Chauncy wagged his tail tentatively. Then, because no one else was saying anything, the dog looked up at Lane and barked.

CHAPTER THREE

"GOOD HEAVENS!" Theodora exclaimed into the ringing silence that followed. "Does anyone know to
whom this... this *creature* belongs?"

If Nora could have, she would have turned around
and run. The only thing preventing her from doing it
was the fact that Chauncy was still sitting on her foot;
she felt as though her shoe had been nailed to the
floor. Since escape or disappearance into thin air
seemed unlikely, there was nothing to do but confess.
Swallowing, she said, "He's... mine, Mother."

As Theodora turned disbelievingly in her direction,
Nora forced herself to look at Lane Kincaid. "I'm so
sorry, Mr. Kincaid," she said. "I... he's never done
anything like this before. Please, accept my apologies."

Before Lane could do more than pick the pasta off
his shoulder, Theodora exclaimed, "Nora, this dog is
yours?"

Nora nodded faintly. "I had to bring him with me,
but I thought I made sure he'd stay in the car. I'm
sorry. I didn't mean for this to happen, believe me."

Finally shorn of hors d'oeuvres, Lane bent over and
picked up the end of the leash. Nora's car door handle still dangled from it. In her embarrassment, Nora

couldn't be sure, but was there a twinkle in his eyes as he glanced at her before turning to Theodora? "I believe her," he said solemnly. "In fact, I think we're lucky the dog didn't bring the rest of the car in here with him, don't you?"

It was obvious what Theodora thought. She started to reply, but then she saw Nora's face and apparently changed her mind. Summoning her considerable stage presence, she laughed gaily and said, "And here I thought *I* knew how to make an entrance!"

Nora just wanted to get away. "I really am sorry, Mother," she said, her voice low. "I didn't mean to ruin your party."

Smiling tightly at a guest who was edging nervously by, Theodora said, "Don't be silly, darling. I've already forgotten this ever happened."

Nora wished she could do the same. The party had moved to the opposite end of the room, where a second buffet table had escaped her one-dog demolition team. Deciding this was a good time to make her escape, she looked around quickly for Lane, but he was nowhere in sight.

"Mother, where's Lane Kincaid?" she asked.

Theodora glanced around, too. "He must have gone upstairs to clean up. I'll send someone to—"

"No, don't do that," she said hastily. She suddenly realized she didn't want to see him again. "When you see him, just tell him again how sorry I am. I'll send him a note tomorrow, but for now, I think I'd better get Chauncy out of here before he does something else."

"I agree," Theodora said. Quickly, she gave Nora a kiss. "I do thank you for coming, darling," she added. Her eyes began to sparkle. "You certainly know how to liven up a party."

"Oh, Mother!"

"I'm just teasing, sweetheart. Go on, now—scoot."

Nora left by a side door, her hand firmly on Chauncy's collar. The dog seemed to know he was in trouble; instead of bouncing around and pulling her along as he usually did, he paced sedately by her side as they went down the walk. Aware of those sad eyes watching her, Nora forgave him before they got to the car. She even managed, as she opened the undamaged back door, to give his still-wet head a resigned pat.

"It's okay, it wasn't your fault," she said. "I shouldn't have made you stay in the car by yourself."

As though remorseful over what he'd done, Chauncy gave her a forlorn look and climbed inside. Taking up most of the back seat, he lay down, his nose on his paws.

Nora got in herself and started the car, but before she drove off, she took one last look at the brightly lighted mansion at the head of the curved driveway. She would have liked a chance to apologize to Lane.

Was that what she'd really wanted? Her cheeks began to burn again. What was going on here? She'd never been so strongly and instantly attracted to a man in her life. Even more bizarre was the fact that the man was an actor. She didn't even *like* actors, and she had vowed long ago that—her mother aside—she wouldn't have anything to do with them. She didn't want to deal with the egos and the temperaments and tantrums that people in her mother's profession took for granted, and seemed to thrive on.

Not that there was any problem where Lane Kincaid was concerned, she thought hastily. After what had happened tonight, she doubted he'd ever want to see her or speak to her again—and that was fine with her, just fine. Now that she thought about it, in fact, she was glad it had worked out this way. Tomorrow she'd send him a formal note of apology, along with a request for his cleaning bill, or perhaps an offer to buy him a new shirt. But she was going to do that only because it was the polite thing to do, *not* because she wanted to see him again.

Pleased that she had resolved this and put it behind her, she pulled into her driveway at last. Then she went inside to wash the champagne off Chauncy.

THE INSTANT she arrived at work the next morning, she knew something was wrong. For one thing, Sherrie and Ginger, who were usually standing around the coffee machine at this hour, were both at their desks typing furiously away. For another, there was no sign of Rodney Jones, her nemesis and chief competition for promotion. Normally, Rodney would have been hanging around, boasting of yet another brilliant scheme he'd devised to make someone a lot of money. Wondering what was going on, Nora said a cautious good morning. Reluctantly, Sherrie looked up from her keyboard.

"Uh . . . Nora," Sherrie said. "Mr. Bullard wanted to see you in his office as soon as you came in."

This wasn't an unusual request; Orrin Bullard often asked for personal progress reports from his employees. But something in Sherrie's voice made Nora ask, "What's wrong?"

Ginger looked up. "I take it you haven't seen the morning paper," she said.

"The paper?" Nora shook her head. "No. Should I have?" They both looked so glum that she tried a little joke. "Don't tell me the stock market crashed again."

"Worse," Sherrie said. She handed Nora a newspaper. "Here, maybe you'd better read it before you face the boss."

Nora took the paper. It had been folded to the entertainment section, and when she saw the photo, she gasped. "Oh, no!"

"Oh, yes," Sherrie said. Then she and Ginger both leaned forward. "Did that *really* happen last night, Nora? Did you meet Lane Kincaid, and did your dog attack him?"

Nora didn't answer; she was transfixed by the unflattering picture of her, Lane and Chauncy. The photographer had caught her with her mouth open and a horrified expression on her face as she lunged for a huge, bedraggled apparition that was her dog, but which looked like the creature from the Black Lagoon. To complete the picture, Chauncy was straddled over the recumbent Lane, who had never looked less like a superstar. Pinned on the floor under her dripping canine, Lane wore an expression that in any other circumstances would have been comical. As it was, it just underscored how awful the entire incident had been.

Nora looked at Sherrie. She didn't have to read the short article that accompanied the picture; she had a good idea what it contained. "Tell me Mr. Bullard hasn't seen this."

"Oh, he sure has," Ginger said. "Rodney made certain of that as soon as he came in this morning."

Nora should have known. She and Rodney had started at Bullard and Sweeney at about the same time, and had been at odds since then. Their relationship had become even more strained when they realized they were contending for the same promotion. Of medium height, pale and thin, with light blue eyes and slicked-back brown hair, the man would have been difficult for her to like under the best of circumstances. She knew he was good in his field, but he was also a whiner...and a telltale. And it seemed that this morning he'd been doing what he did best: carrying tales.

"And that's not all," Sherrie said unhappily, bringing Nora out of her thoughts.

"What else?"

The secretaries glanced at each other, then Sherrie said, "Lester Snook called this morning. Apparently, he's seen this, too." After a pause, she added, "I don't think Mr. Bullard was too happy after he took the call."

Nora didn't have to ask why. She'd noticed the caption under the picture clearly identifying her as a member of this firm.

"What are you going to say?" Sherrie asked.

"I don't know yet," she answered with more bravado than she felt. "I'll think of something."

"Did you *really* meet . . . *him?*" Sherrie breathed.

"Him?"

Blushing, Sherrie said, "You know who I mean—
Lane Kincaid! Oh, Nora, what was he like?"

"He was just fine until my dog knocked him into
the punch bowl. After that, I lost track of him in the
confusion. Listen, I'd love to discuss it, but I'd better
go see Mr. Bullard."

"Good luck," Sherrie said.

She'd need more than that, Nora thought as she
started off down the hall. She knew how dedicated
Orrin Bullard was to pleasing his "old money" clients—all of whom regarded any kind of promotion or
publicity worse than they'd view the plague. Well, it
didn't matter now; the damage was done. She took a
deep breath, knocked at Bullard's door and went in.

Rodney Jones was sitting opposite her boss. She
should have known he'd want to see her grovel; it was
just like him to gloat. This morning he was wearing a
black suit with a white-on-white shirt and a black-and-
blue rep tie, and looked, she thought uncharitably, just
like an undertaker. Without a word, she nodded coolly
at him, and then directed her attention solely to her
boss.

"Good morning, Mr. Bullard," she said. "You
wanted to see me?"

Orrin Bullard was a big man who looked more like
a retired lumberjack than the head of one of Pasadena's oldest and most respected money management
firms. Barrel-chested and bald, with a florid face and

brown eyes behind glasses, Bullard invariably wore dark blue suits and plain blue ties. "Yes, I did," he said. He glanced at Rodney, who was obviously eager to stay, and added pointedly, "That will be all for now, Rodney."

Reluctantly, Rodney left. But as he passed Nora, he said under his breath, "I'm not surprised that you're late this morning, Nora. Obviously, you had a busy night."

"Not as busy as your morning, apparently," she said in return. She knew it was petty, but the man was so damned sanctimonious!

The boss waited until the door closed behind him before he said, "Sit down, Nora. I'm sure you know that I had a call this morning from Lester Snook."

"Yes, I heard he called," she said, plunging right in. "I imagine it's about that...unfortunate picture in the paper. I'm sorry, Mr. Bullard. I know how much Mr. Snook dislikes publicity. I'll call him immediately."

He looked at her for a moment, then he sat back, tenting his hands in front of his face and tapping his lips with his fingertips. Nora knew from experience it was a bad sign, and she tensed even more. But she wasn't going to beg his forgiveness. What had happened, had happened, she told herself. She was sorry, but she couldn't change it.

"If you don't mind," Bullard said finally, "I'd like an explanation, myself."

"There's nothing to explain, Mr. Bullard. My mother came back to the States after months abroad, and she asked me to come to a party she was giving. I had no idea a photographer would be there. In fact, I was shocked when I saw the picture."

"I see," he said. She couldn't tell what he was really thinking, and she felt an ache begin to radiate from her taut shoulder blades.

"And the dog?" Bullard asked.

"The dog?" she repeated. Then she took a deep breath. "The dog is mine, Mr. Bullard," she said, looking at him directly. "I left him outside, but he doesn't like to stay in the car by himself. I knew that. It was my fault. I never expected him to get loose. When he did, he came looking for me, and..." She paused, faltering despite herself when she saw his expression, then continued. "Well, you can see what happened. He didn't mean to cause trouble. He just panicked."

"Panicked," Bullard repeated. "I see." He looked at her from under his eyebrows. "All right, Miss Carmichael, because your work thus far has been exemplary, I'll accept your explanation, *this* time. But if there's another incident—"

She could hardly believe her good fortune. Restraining herself from leaping out of the chair, she stood up calmly, and said, "There won't be."

He gave her a severe look that boded ill for any future indiscretions, no matter how minor. "See that there aren't."

Nora managed to wait until she reached her own office before heaving a huge sigh of relief. Miraculously, she thought, she'd escaped unscathed—this time. She decided not to question her reprieve as she collapsed into her chair. Just then the intercom buzzed.

"Nora, your mother's on line two," Sherrie said. She hesitated before adding, "Is everything all right?"

If she'd had the strength, she would have danced around the room. "Everything's fine," she said fervently. "I'm still here."

Sherrie giggled. "I think I'll just mention that in passing to Rodney."

Smiling herself, Nora keyed off and punched the line-two button. "Mother?"

"Is this a bad time, darling?" Theodora asked. "I know how busy you are, but I wanted to call before I started getting ready for lunch."

Nora glanced at the clock. Although it felt like a lifetime had passed, she saw that it was barely ten o'clock. "Lunch? Don't you mean breakfast?"

"Now, darling, don't start in on me, please. You know I'm not at my best at the crack of dawn, and with Arthur insisting that we dine at twelve, well, I'm hardly going to be able to get myself together as it is."

"You're having lunch with Arthur?"

"Yes, dear. On his boat. The only reason I agreed to the ungodly hour is that he so rarely takes time away from the office. So when he offered to take me to lunch at the marina while his pilot drives us around on the water, I could hardly refuse, could I?"

"No, of course not," Nora agreed dryly. She sat back. "Mother, we haven't had much time to talk about Arthur. I think we should have a chat sometime soon. I can't remember your getting out of bed before noon for any man, including my father."

Theodora was wounded. "How can you say that? You know how many years I've gotten up in the pitch-*black* for early makeup calls! The rest of the world would be sound asleep—including you, I might add—and there I was, stumbling down the freeway because some silly director wanted my hair done before five o'clock!"

Nora's eyes twinkled. "It's a hard life, Mother, I agree."

"Yes, it is. You just don't know."

Nora knew she never would. "You had a reason for calling?"

"Yes, I did," Theodora said. "Now, Nora, I don't want you to be upset about this—"

"Upset?" Nora said, alerted. "About what?"

"Oh, dear, I knew you'd be angry."

She sat up. "I'm not angry—at least, not yet. What are we talking about?"

"I didn't mean to, darling, really, I didn't," Theodora said in a rush. "But there was all that business with the dog last night, and Lane was so good about it, and when we were talking later and he asked about you, well, naturally, I told him you were an important financier—"

"I'm not a *financier*, Mother!"

"Well, a money manager, it's the same thing, isn't it?" Theodora said, with her usual blithe disregard for the distinction. "The *point* is that when Lane said his accountant has been on at him for some time to get someone reputable to advise him about investments, well, of course I said you'd be happy to—"

"To *what*?"

"To advise him, of course. Oh, I knew you'd be upset. But Nora, really, you do owe him something, don't you? After all, it *was* your dog—"

Nora gripped the phone. "Yes, it was my dog, but Mother, why can't a simple note of apology do? I told you I'd pay for any cleaning bills—"

"He doesn't need someone to take care of his cleaning, darling. He needs someone to plan for his future!"

Nora could feel herself backpedaling emotionally as fast as she could. She didn't want anything more to do with Lane Kincaid, and she wasn't going to allow her mother to manipulate her. "There must be hundreds of people eager to advise someone like him," she said. "All he has to do is call—"

"But he knows you."

"He doesn't know me!" Hearing the shrillness in her voice, she tried to calm down. "For heaven's sake, Mother, we just met once."

"Yes, but he *likes* you!"

"Well, that's just not—" she started to say, and paused. "He likes me?"

"Well, of course he does. You're a beautiful, charming, intelligent, professional woman, darling! He'd be a fool not to like you. And I assure you, Lane Kincaid is no fool."

She couldn't help herself. Hotly, she asked, "Then why has he built this reputation as a beefcake superstar? From what I've heard, the characters he portrays in his films would probably keel over with shock if they ever had an intelligent thought!"

"I'm surprised at you, Nora," Theodora scolded. "You, of all people, know that the roles we actors take on have nothing to do with the way we are in our personal lives."

Properly chastised, she sat back. "I'm sorry. You're right, and I shouldn't have said that." Then she sat up again. "But damn it, that's not the point, anyway. Even if I had time, I couldn't accept Mr. Kincaid as a client."

"Why not?"

Nora glanced around her office, with the beige carpet and the beige paint and the conservative still-life on the opposite wall. The most radical thing she'd done when she came was to bring in the ficus plant that stood in the corner, and sometimes she wasn't sure Mr. Bullard approved of that. Thinking of the close call she'd had just this morning, she knew she had to make her mother understand the situation.

"For one thing, Mother, I just don't have time for him, and for another—" How could she say that filmdom's superstud superstar just wasn't the right image for Bullard and Sweeney? It sounded awful even to her, so she said instead, "For another, our clients are . . . older. *Much* older. And much more conservative. I don't think he'd be happy with us at all. Not at all."

Theodora was silent a moment. Then she said, "That's too bad."

"Yes, it is," Nora said. "But—" She stopped, then asked suspiciously, "What do you mean by that?"

"Oh, nothing . . ."

"Mother!"

"Well, all right, if you must know, I'm afraid you're going to have to explain all this to him yourself."

"What? Why? What do you mean? Why can't you tell him?"

"Because I gave him your number at Bullard and Sweeney, darling. He's going to call soon—"

"Oh, Mother!"

"Darling, I'd really like to chat, but I've got to get going," Theodora said quickly. "Now, do wish me luck with Arthur today. You know how much I hate boats."

Theodora was gone before Nora could reply. Oh, this was too much! Nora thought as she hung up. Her mother was always promising things someone else was supposed to deliver. Well, it was just too bad. She couldn't help Lane even if she wanted to—and she *didn't* want to. Her boss had let her off lightly this morning, and she wasn't going to jeopardize her position even by talking to Lane Kincaid. Besides, she wasn't the only money manager in town. A man—a *star*—like Lane wouldn't have any trouble at all finding someone to handle his investments.

That decided, she reached for some stationery. She didn't want to get involved—any more than she already was—but she did owe Lane an apology. Quickly, she wrote out a note. Then, for good measure, along with her offer to pay for his cleaning bill, she included the names of some financial advisers and consultants she knew would be able to help him. Signing her name with a flourish, she addressed the envelope in care of Lane's studio, then sent it by courier.

Finally, she put the maddening man out of her mind and sat down to get some work done.

CHAPTER FOUR

PANTING WITH exertion, Lane Kincaid headed for the steps up to his beachfront home. It was early, not seven o'clock yet, and he'd gone down to the beach for his morning exercise. He didn't expect fans to be watching for him at this hour; the bikini-clad girls surprised him by jumping up from behind a pile of driftwood as he ran by.

When he saw the publicity shots two of the girls were carrying, he winced. He'd never liked that picture of himself, with his blond hair sun-streaked and carefully tousled by the studio hairdresser, and his gray-blue eyes touched up, he was sure, to make them seem more blue than gray. Whenever he saw that photo, he wondered who that guy was, staring out at the world like some damned cock-of-the-walk.

"Lane! Lane Kincaid! Could we please have your autograph? Oh, please, please, please!"

As always, he stopped to oblige. He'd met other actors who wouldn't give their fans the time of day, but he'd never been like that. Fans had put him where he was now, and the way he figured it, they'd keep him there until he disappointed them in some way. Signing a few bits of paper—or even, as he had been required to do on occasion, body parts for the more

fervent of his admirers—was a small price for success.

"Sure, I'll be glad to," he said in the deep drawl that
made women swoon. As two of the girls shrieked in
delight, he gestured toward his jogging attire and
grinned the famous grin. "You'll have to help me out
with a pen, though. Anyone got one?"

They all produced something, one of the girls
handing him a laundry-marking pen and begging him
to sign a breast. "How about a shoulder, instead?" he
suggested, scrawling his signature while silently asking the girl's mother to forgive him for permanently
marking her daughter. Not to be outdone, another girl
pushed forward, displaying her thigh, which he obligingly signed with a flourish.

"Oh, Lane, I just *love* your pictures!" one of the
girls gushed. "I've seen every one—fifteen times!"

Lane judged her to be about fifteen, herself. Although, he thought, these days, you never knew. With
twelve-year-olds looking twice their years as they
posed for magazine covers, it paid to be cautious
about deciding a woman's age. Still, he said, "I appreciate the support, honey, but I hope you're not neglecting school in favor of the movies."

She looked surprised. "Well...er...no, I guess not,"
she said. Then she leaned forward, asking breathlessly, "Did you go to school, too?"

An image of a school hallway flashed through his
mind, graffiti on the walls and lockers, surly kids
strolling the halls looking for trouble. The school he'd
gone to had been in a tough section of the city, where
sometimes the graduation prize was getting out alive.

But he didn't want to think about that part of his life, and he sure as hell didn't want to spoil the image for these girls. "Sure did," he said easily. "But not as long as I should have, sweetie. So take it from me— you get that diploma and make it count for something. You never know what's going to happen."

The girls were agog at this unexpected lecture on the merits of education; it was clearly the last thing they expected from the macho superstar whose last movie had grossed over a hundred million.

Ah, well, Lane thought, as he waved goodbye, and who was he to complain? If he wanted to protest something, it should be this exercise. He hated jogging, especially in the sand, but it was good for the legs and the calves—and the "cute little buns" his female fans claimed he had.

Fortunately for his fast-depleting stamina, the steps that led from the beach up to his Pacific Palisades house were right ahead. At the top, he pressed the hidden button to open the heavy iron gate, and when he was safely out of sight, he immediately bent over, gasping. Thirty-nine wasn't supposed to be old, but damn, he thought, today he felt ancient.

Although the morning wasn't close to being hot, sweat was running down his face, and he decided to cool off with a swim. The pool and pool house were some distance ahead, and as he walked in that direction, he looked over his huge, Spanish-style home with undisguised pride. Who would have thought the kid from the wrong side of the city would ever live in a place like this? Even now, there were times he wondered if he were dreaming.

He'd waited to buy the house until he was reasonably sure his success wasn't just a fluke. His first film had smashed box-office records; his second had topped it, and then his third had topped that. Suddenly, far from being just another obscure, struggling actor, he couldn't go anywhere without being recognized. Those had been the days, he thought with a nostalgic smile: he'd been young, and virile, and things hadn't been so dangerous then. He could put in eighteen-hour workdays and party afterward; he could drink and dance and have a new girl every night of the week if he wanted and still show up at the studio the next day. It was all so exciting then. His smile faded. These days, fame felt more like a burden than a blessing, and the notoriety that had delighted him before chafed him. He didn't mind stopping for autographs or to chat with fans; it was the *expectation* that was getting to him, the uneasy feeling that all those people out there who loved him now would be disappointed if he dared try something different.

And what about the women? a little voice asked, since he was on the subject.

He sighed. Women could be wonderful. But he was so tired of females who only wanted to meet him so they could be seen with him—or because they wanted an introduction to a director or a chance to read for a part. What he wouldn't give for a woman who didn't give a damn about his stardom.

A pair of green eyes flashed into his mind just then, and he stopped. Nora Carmichael hadn't seemed to care about his fame, he remembered, thinking of the party. He grinned again. But then, they hadn't had much time to get acquainted, had they? Before he knew what was going on, he was being manhandled by her brute of a dog, and after that, Nora had disappeared.

Wondering why he was even *thinking* about Nora, he shook his head and started toward the pool again. When he'd first bought the house, he thought it was ridiculous to have a pool when the entire Pacific Ocean was only a stone's throw away, but now he was glad of it. He might be fair game down on the beach, but in his own backyard, he didn't have to worry about being ambushed. He was too well protected by Cosmo, his caretaker, and by Esperanza, Cosmo's wife, who was also the cook and housekeeper here. He doubted even the most persistent fan could get past the giant six-foot-five Cosmo, but if someone was unfortunate enough to succeed and get into the house, he or she would be faced with Cosmo's diminutive but equally formidable wife. From the beginning, the couple had guarded Lane's privacy fiercely, and he was grateful. God knew, he had little enough of it.

His good humor restored by the thought of his protectors, he stepped onto the hot coping around the pool. This was one of his favorite places on the entire estate, for in addition to the teardrop-shaped swimming pool with the waterfall at one end, there were deck chairs and chaises, two tables with umbrellas, an adjoining spa and a cabana-style exercise room off to one side. The lush shrubbery that had been planted all around added to a jungle-like atmosphere. At the end of the vast expanse of carefully tended lawn, beyond the high bluff upon which the house had been built, the Pacific sparkled in the sun. It looked peaceful and inviting until he spotted the man who was waiting for him. It was his agent, Wyatt Parmalee, and when Lane saw Wyatt's expression, he groaned. He knew that look: it meant Wyatt had something serious to discuss, and that Lane wasn't going to like it.

"Morning," he said warily as he came up to the table where Wyatt was sitting. "You're up early. Join me for a swim?"

Wyatt Parmalee was a few years older than Lane. A buttoned-up kind of man, he had brown hair, light brown eyes and, it seemed to Lane, a calculator for a mind. Even though it was early, he was already dressed in suit and tie. Sitting there, under the warm Southern California sun, the agent should have appeared uncomfortable and overdressed. Instead, except for his frown, he seemed perfectly at ease. As he gazed at Wyatt, Lane wondered irreverently if the man had been *born* with a tie around his neck.

As he'd expected, Wyatt politely declined his invitation. "No, thank you, I don't have time," he said. Esperanza had already brought out coffee and croissants; the agent lifted his cup, took a sip, then put it down again. "I thought we might talk."

Lane didn't want to talk. He had a good idea what Wyatt was going to say. "Do we have to?" he asked. "It's such a nice day."

"Lane—"

"All right, all right. I know what you want to talk about," he said, "and to save us both time, the answer is no."

Wyatt sighed. "Have you even read the script?"

The script Wyatt was referring to was for a new film called *Nobody Home*. Lane had been scornful even of the title—until he'd thumbed through it. He hadn't expected to be interested at all in the story, but he'd become so involved he couldn't put it down. He'd read it again and again. When he found himself wondering if he could actually play a character like the angst-ridden Tyler Dane, who spent nearly three-fourths of the film denying the events in his past that had shaped him into the twisted man he had become, Lane had put the script aside and hadn't looked at it again.

"No," he lied. "I haven't read it. Why should I? From what you told me, it just isn't my style."

"I think it could be."

Lane had already told himself he wouldn't— *couldn't*—consider it, so he said, "Think again, then. I've spent my career playing superhero, macho-men types who make the Rambos and the Terminators of filmdom look like wimps. You can't be suggesting that I reverse course at this late date and expect my fans to take me *seriously,* for a change. I'll be laughed out of the business. I'll never make another film again."

"I don't think so, Lane."

"Well, I do. And that settles it, doesn't it?"

"Not for me, it doesn't. Don't forget, Lane, among other things, you're paying me to guide your career. I think it's time for a . . . stretch."

"A stretch!" Lane laughed. "This part is a little more than that and you know it."

"How do you know?" Wyatt asked slyly. "I thought you hadn't read the script."

Too late, Lane saw his mistake. To save face, he took a huge swallow of orange juice, then banged the glass down on the table. Defiantly, he said, "I haven't. Not the whole thing, anyway. I just glanced through it."

"And you don't think you can do it."

"I didn't say that. I said it wasn't right for me."

"So, you *could* do it, if you wanted to."

"I didn't say that, either! What's the matter with you today? Why are you twisting everything I say?"

"Because I want you to think about this. Because no matter what you say, I know you can do it. It's time, Lane. I want you to get beyond these shoot-em-up, crash-every-car-in-sight, take-six-bullets-in-the-chest-and-still-keep-going parts you've been so comfortable with. I want you to do some *acting* for a change."

"Do some acting!" Lane didn't have to pretend outrage. "Do you know how hard it is to—" Abruptly, he stopped. Even he couldn't defend what he was doing as an emotive challenge. "You've got some nerve," he muttered as he fell back against the chair. "As I remember, *you're* the one who wanted me to sign when the studio offered me that last three-picture deal."

"Because it was right at the time," Wyatt said quietly. "Now, it's not. Will you at least think about it?"

"No," Lane said, but when Wyatt smiled, he knew he hadn't sounded as forceful as he intended. He scowled.

"Good," Wyatt said, getting to his feet. "I'll talk to you soon. Don't get up. I know the way out."

"Yeah, well, don't come back if all you're going to talk about is that damned film!" Lane shouted after him. "I mean it, Wyatt! It's not for me. I won't do it, and you can go to the bank on it!"

Wyatt didn't reply. Without looking back, he raised his hand in farewell and disappeared through the open french doors that led into the house. Lane was still looking fierce when Esperanza appeared a few minutes later, carrying the phone.

"Telephone call, *señor*," she said, setting the instrument on the table.

Lane sighed. No matter how many times he'd told her, asked her, pleaded with her not to call him that, she'd just look at him serenely and do it again the next time. Finally, he'd given up.

"Who is it?" he asked.

"Martin Raab, *señor*," Esperanza answered. She gave the name a slight Spanish inflection, making it sound like 'Marteen.'

By whatever name, the last person Lane wanted to talk to right now was his accountant. As he had with Wyatt, he had a good idea what Martin was going to say.

"Tell him I'm not home," he said.

Esperanza looked reproachfully at him. "You want me to lie?"

"It wouldn't be a *lie*," Lane said, and sighed when he saw her expression. "Never mind," he said, exasperated. "I'll take the thing. But tell me, why do you have to be so damned truthful all the time?"

"I do not know, *señor*. But do you not agree that things are so much simpler this way?"

"No, I don't," he said. But as his housekeeper headed back to the house, he reached for the phone and said, "Hello, Martin. What can I do for you?"

As always, the accountant got right to the point. His voice gravelly in Lane's ear, Raab said, "Well, for one thing, you can stop spending money faster than you make it."

Lane sighed again. It seemed that was all he was doing this morning. "I take it you just got the bill for the boat."

"The cabin cruiser? Oh, yes, I got that. Along with several other incomprehensible statements."

Lane sat back. "Which ones do you mean?"

"Well, this one for a house at north Lake Tahoe, for instance. I didn't know you were thinking of establishing a residence in Nevada. You should have discussed it with me. It makes a difference with tax bills, you know."

"Oh, that's not for me," he said flippantly. "I bought it for a friend of mine."

There was a tiny pause. "I see. May I assume that the three cars you recently purchased were gifts for friends, too?"

"Now, Martin, everyone needs a car in L.A."

"Yes, of course," the accountant said dryly. "Brand-new, too."

Lane smiled. "Anything else?"

"No, not really. I suppose there's no point in asking about the ten cruise tickets to Alaska—"

"Some friends had never been," Lane said.

"And I suppose the same logic also applies to the charter flight for twelve to Epcot Center in Florida."

"Everybody should see Disneyland, don't you think?"

"I've never thought about it. May I ask, have you ever been there?"

"I plan to go someday."

"I see." There was another small pause. Then, "Lane, I know it's none of my business, but this is only the tip of the iceberg, so to speak. You've also been putting quite a lot into that place downtown—"

He wasn't going to argue about that. "I know I'm overspending, and I know you warned me," he said. "I wish I could tell you what's going on, but I don't know myself. Maybe—the Center aside—I'm just bored."

"How can you be bored, spending all this money?" the accountant retorted. "Just thinking of all these extravagances takes time and energy, not to mention going out and buying things like boats and condominiums and charter flights while supporting a neighborhood—"

"I can afford it, can't I?"

He'd expected Martin to make a sharp reply, but when there was silence at the other end of the phone, he felt guilty. Martin had been warning him for months now about the state of his finances—ever since he had fired his business manager after a heated argument. The accountant had been urging him for some time to look into hiring an investment counselor.

"Look, Lane," Martin said finally. "It's your money. I don't care how you spend it. Well, that's not quite true. I do have a certain responsibility here, after all. If you want to spend every last dime on your friends, or buy a flotilla of boats you don't use, or a fleet of cars you don't drive, it's your concern. But like I've told you before, you have to start thinking of investments, not just consumables."

Lane didn't want to think of investments; he and Martin had a different idea about just what those were. He couldn't deny that he was spending money like water, but so what? He had it to spend. And if the time came when he didn't, he'd . . .

What?

He didn't want to think about that, either, so he said, "You're right, as always. I'll tell you what. You find a couple of investments, and I'll invest in them. Would that make you happy?"

Raab wouldn't bite. "What would make me happy is if you found someone knowledgeable to sit down with you and map out some kind of financial future. In my capacity, I can only advise you so much. Now, I know you don't like to think of such things—"

"You're right, I don't," Lane said. "That's why I want you to do it. You're the accountant. Why can't you manage my money, too?"

This time it was Martin who sighed. "Because it's not what I do and you know it, Lane."

"But you obviously know more about money than I do."

"It's not a matter of money so much as it is a question of planning," Martin stated. "You have to start thinking of the future. After all, you're going to be forty this year—"

Grimacing fiercely, Lane said, "Don't remind me. I'm planning on throwing myself a death's-head ball." He paused. "If I can afford it, that is."

"You laugh, but the point is—"

"I know what the point is, Martin. And I promise, I'll give some thought to what you said."

The accountant sounded hopeful. "No more condos?"

"Not unless they're for me," Lane replied cheerfully.

"Will you really think about being a little more . . . sensible?"

"I'll be as circumspect as a monk, I swear," Lane said virtuously, thinking that Martin had no idea how true it already was. He couldn't remember when he'd last actually had a date the studio hadn't arranged, and as for . . .

Lane shook his head and forced himself to listen to Martin's lecture.

After a few moments, he raised his eyes heavenward. "Don't worry so much, Martin. I'll do better, I promise. Trust me."

With relief, he broke the connection and put down the phone. He liked Martin, but the man had no sense of humor. What fun was it to make the kind of money Lane did, if he couldn't spend it the way he wanted?

But then, even as he tried to defend his extravagant ways, he had to admit Martin had a point. That remark about turning forty this year had struck home, and he knew he had to get a handle on things before this ephemeral thing called success dried up and blew away. He didn't want to be like some of the entertainers, the actors, he knew: on top one day, wondering where it had all gone the next. Despite the warm day, he shuddered. He hadn't come this far to end up back where he'd started. His jaw tightened as he dived into the pool to begin his fifty laps.

HALF AN HOUR LATER, Lane awoke to the ringing of the telephone beside his deck chair.

"Mr. Kincaid?" said a voice he didn't recognize. "This is Jane Merit, at the studio. I hope I'm not bothering you."

Now he remembered. Jane was a production assistant on *Time and a Half,* the film he was doing for Freddie Princeley. "No, it's okay," he said. "What's up?"

"Well, I know you aren't supposed to come in until this afternoon, but you just got a letter by courier delivered here, and I wondered if you wanted me to hold it until you came in, or if I should send it out to the house."

A letter by courier? Curious, he asked, "Who's it from?"

"Uh...hang on a second, and I'll check." There was a rustling sound as Jane tore something open, then she said, "It's an envelope from a firm called Bullard and Sweeney, in Pasadena."

He frowned. "It must be a mistake—" he started to say, then he remembered the conversation he and Theodora had had last night after Nora left. Hadn't she told him that's where her daughter worked? His curiosity really aroused now, he said, "Open it, Jane. Read me what it says."

"Oh, I don't think... What if it's personal?"

Remembering how Nora had acted toward him last night at the party when they were introduced, Lane grinned. "I don't think it's personal, Jane," he said. "Go on, read it to me."

"Well, if you're sure..."

There was another rustling sound as Jane took out the letter. "'Dear Mr. Kincaid,'" she read. "'I'm writing to apologize again for what happened last night—'" She stopped. "Are you sure you want me to read this?" she asked.

Looking smug, Lane crossed his feet up on the table. How had he ever doubted she'd come around? he asked himself with a smirk. They always did, didn't they?

"Go ahead," he said, propping the telephone against his shoulder so he could put his arms behind his head. He was going to enjoy this.

"Well, all right," Jane sounded doubtful as she continued to read aloud. "'—to apologize again for what happened last night, and to offer to pay for any dry-cleaning bills that resulted, or to buy you a new shirt, if you prefer. Also, my mother mentioned to me this morning that she recommended this firm for financial consulting. I'm sorry to inform you that she spoke out of turn. We are not accepting new clients at this time, but if you need advice or assistance about financial matters, following is a list of very competent people I am authorized to recommend—'"

Jane stopped again. "There's a list of firms here, Lane. Do you want me to read them to you?"

Lane couldn't believe it. He was so shocked by the obvious brush-off that he jerked his feet off the table. In the process, one foot caught the handle of the orange-juice carafe, and as it started to fall, he made a grab for it.

"Damn it!" he shouted as orange juice spilled down his front.

"I'm sorry, Lane, what did you say?" Jane asked.

Slamming the now-empty container down onto the table, he tried to get himself back on track. This was the second time in twenty-four hours that he'd gotten drenched because of Nora Carmichael, and he was getting tired of it.

"Never mind," he growled, feeling sticky and stupid and irritated as hell. What did she *mean,* telling him that her firm didn't accept new clients? Wasn't his money good enough for her? Didn't she know who he was?

Then he realized that she knew very well who he was—and wasn't impressed by it at all. With a mother like Theodora DeVere, she'd probably grown up with famous actors dropping by day and night. She probably knew more stars than he did. He scowled, but despite his irritation, the irony didn't escape him. Not five minutes ago he'd assured himself that he'd give anything to meet a woman who wasn't overwhelmed by his stardom. Now, it seemed he had met one, and what was his reaction? All he could think about was why she wasn't awed because he was a star.

"Lane?"

He'd forgotten all about poor Jane. "What?" he grunted, his mind still on Nora Carmichael.

"I . . . er . . . what do you want me to do with this?"
Jane asked.

As far as he was concerned, she could throw it on
the fire. *Not taking new clients!* he thought. *She was
authorized to recommend . . .*

Well, he'd see about that, he thought. Martin had
been after him to do something about his finances:
here was his chance. He wasn't sure right now just how
he was going to go about it, but before he was finished, Miss Nora Carmichael was going to accept him
as a client whether she wanted to or not.

"Keep it," he said. "No, on second thought, toss it
out." It had been a long time since he'd been this interested in a woman, he realized, the light of battle
beginning to glow in his eyes. Eager for the challenge,
he added confidently, "I won't need it. I'll deal with
the lady myself."

CHAPTER FIVE

NORA WAS EXHAUSTED when she got home that night. All she wanted to do was take a long, hot bath, and fall into bed. Unfortunately for her, Chauncy had other ideas. He bayed a greeting the instant he heard her car drive up, and he was waiting for her by the sliding doors to the patio when she came in. When she saw how eager he was, she sighed.

"Sorry, Chaunce," she said as she let him in. "I just don't have the energy to—"

She didn't get a chance to finish. Although Chauncy had finally learned not to jump up on her, he could still nearly knock her over with mighty sweeps of his tail. Tonight, as usual, after he'd welcomed her home to his satisfaction, he went to the pegboard where she kept his leash and took it down. Holding it delicately in his massive jaws, he came back to where she was standing and sat down in front of her. His tail thumped the floor.

"Oh, Chauncy," she said. She couldn't refuse him when he was looking at her like that and he knew it. Resigned, she took the leash from him and put it on the counter. "All right, we'll go, but I have to change first," she said. "Can you wait that long, at least?"

Obviously satisfied that he'd made his point, Chauncy followed her upstairs and waited while she changed out of work clothes and into a blouse and jeans. Ten minutes later, they were out the door, the big dog leading as always.

As soon as she was on her way, Nora forgot how tired she was and began to enjoy the walk. She didn't even have to exert much energy, for as they headed down the sidewalk, Chauncy pulled her along at the end of the leash like a boat towing a duck. There was a special section in the park where dogs could be let off the leash to run, and when they arrived, she unsnapped the lead. Chauncy immediately took off, lumbering along with his nose on the ground while she sat down on one of the benches and watched.

Usually the park was crowded with owners and their dogs, but tonight she had the place to herself. There weren't even any traffic noises nearby; it was peaceful and quiet, and as she sat there, she felt the tension leaving her body. Without Chauncy she would never have experienced something like this, and she looked fondly at the dog who was playing with a branch he'd found, throwing it up in the air and catching it on the way down—most of the time. He was clumsy despite his efforts, and the sight made her smile. Now that she felt so much better, she might even have the energy to look at some of the work she'd brought home. Of Lane Kincaid, she wasn't even going to think at all.

Now, where had that thought come from? she wondered, annoyed. After sending her note this morning, she'd assured herself she'd forgotten all about him. Now he'd intruded into this quiet moment, and she resented it. Suddenly, the park didn't seem quite so peaceful as it had moments ago, and she stood, calling to her dog. It was time to go home.

It was almost dark by the time they reached the walkway to her house, so at first she didn't see that someone was waiting on her porch. But Chauncy did. With a happy bark, he bounded forward so suddenly that she was almost pulled off her feet. The leash slipped from her hands, and he took off up the walk.

"Chauncy!" she cried. "What . . . ?"

"Hey!" she heard a man exclaim.

She froze. Did she recognize that voice? No, she had to be mistaken. *It couldn't be,* she thought, throwing herself after her dog.

By the time she reached the porch, the damage was done—again. Horrified, she saw Lane Kincaid sprawled on the porch steps, covered with daisies and carnations and roses, but triumphantly holding aloft a bottle of wine. Nora stopped dead in her tracks. She couldn't believe it. What was *he* doing here? Even worse, what had Chauncy done to him? Embarrassed and off-balance, she whirled around to her dog.

"Oh, Chauncy, what have you done? You bad dog!"

"Now, now, don't blame him," Lane said. "And look, this time I was prepared." He brandished the bottle again with a grin. "He got the flowers, but I saved the wine."

Nora didn't know what this was all about, but she didn't want to find out. "Chauncy, heel!" she commanded. The dog just sat there, looking adoringly at Lane.

"Chauncy!"

Still grinning, Lane looked at the dog. "I think your mistress is calling you, buddy," he said. "Go on, now."

To Nora's amazement—and chagrin—Chauncy obediently got up and came to her side. Scowling, she looked first at her insubordinate canine, and then at Lane. Chauncy was *her* dog. Why did he ignore her and obey this maddening man?

Annoyed, irritated and flustered all over again, she decided to take the offensive. It seemed the only course where Lane Kincaid was concerned. Arms akimbo, she demanded, "What are you doing here?"

He finally got up, flowers raining down around him in a shower of blossoms. Brushing off the last of the baby's breath, he said, "You know, between the two of you, I think I prefer Chauncy's greeting. He's a lot more friendly."

Nora could feel her face turning fiery red. "Well, that's too bad," she said rudely. "But what did you expect? You show up here unannounced—"

"Didn't you get my message on the answering machine?"

"No," she declared ungraciously. At this point, she wasn't about to admit that she hadn't even looked at the phone when she'd come in. She'd been too tired . . . and it was all because of *him. He* was the reason she'd had such a bad day at work. Suddenly, she thought of something. "If you *did* call, how did you get my home number?" she asked suspiciously. "It's unlisted, and—" Another thought occurred to her, and she exploded a sigh. "My mother gave it to you, didn't she?"

"Don't blame Theodora," Lane said with that devastating smile. "She didn't want to, but I bribed her with a case of Dom Pérignon."

She looked at him in disbelief. "You gave my mother a case of champagne so she would give you my phone number?"

"Cheap at the price," he said with a shrug. "But useless after all, if you didn't get my message about coming over tonight."

She lifted her chin. She wasn't going to be taken in by his good looks, or the twinkle in his eyes. "Obviously, then," she said, "you didn't get my note."

"Oh, yes, I got it," he admitted easily. "That's what I wanted to talk to you about, in fact."

Nora didn't want to talk to him about anything. Her pulse was racing despite her vow not to be affected by him, and she didn't like the breathless feeling that had started the instant she'd heard his voice. "You could have called the office," she observed. "You didn't have to come all the way out here."

"Well, I'm here now," he said reasonably. "So maybe we could go inside? But first, I think I'll pick up these flowers. Would you mind holding the wine?"

Before she could reply, he thrust the bottle at her and squatted to gather the scattered bouquet. She watched him for a moment, then she bent down to help. Increasingly annoyed—with him, with herself and with this uncomfortable situation—she asked impatiently, "Why did you bring flowers and wine? What do you really want, Mr. Kincaid?"

Even in the dark, she saw his eyes crinkle with amusement. "Please call me Lane," he said. "And why are you so suspicious?"

"I'm not suspicious!" she said, standing up.

Lane retrieved the last rose and stood with her. She knew he was waiting for her to invite him in, and if she didn't, the situation would be even more awkward than it already was. *Damn him!* she thought furiously. It had been clever to bring flowers and wine. Now she had to hear him out or appear even more gauche than he was. Irritated anew that he'd so adroitly boxed her in, she said, "Well, since you've gone to all this trouble, I guess I'd better put the flowers in water. Whatever you've got to say, you can say it then."

He was not in the least deterred. With a maddening smile, he glanced down at Chauncy and said, "What do you think, old man? Should I accept such a gracious invitation?"

Nora already knew how Chauncy felt about Lane Kincaid. Before her dog could betray her again, she took her keys out of her jeans pocket and unlocked the front door. She switched on the lights, went in and called over her shoulder, "When you're through bonding, you can come in. I'm going to find a vase."

They followed her into the kitchen. When she set the wine bottle on the counter and started rummaging through the cupboards, Lane said, "I'm really sorry about this."

Sure, she thought. She found a vase, held it under
the tap, and dared a covert look at him as she ran the
water. He was wearing jeans, and a blue sports shirt
made his famous eyes look more blue than gray. He
looked so handsome leaning against her kitchen
counter that her breath caught despite herself, and she
turned back to what she was doing just as the water
started gushing over her hand. She turned off the tap
quickly.

"I know I shouldn't have come without making sure
it was okay with you first," he said. "I'm sorry."

As long as I don't look at him, I'll be all right. Attending to the flower arrangement with more attention than a surgeon to an operation, she managed a
shrug. "You're lucky I came home."

"I know. You could have been out . . . on a date."

Was this his way of trying to find out if she was
seeing someone? she wondered. Then she scoffed at
the thought. This was a man who could have any
woman he wanted. He was only here because she
hadn't fallen to his feet the other night in instant ad-
oration. Or maybe he really *did* want financial advice. At any rate, he wasn't interested in her...and she
certainly wasn't interested in him.

To prove it, she said, "How do you know I'm not
married?"

He grinned that grin. "Your mother would have
told me."

Oh, yes, her mother, she thought grimly. That was
another thing. Tomorrow morning, she and Theodora were going to have a little talk about giving out

private phone numbers and interfering in daughters' lives. "My mother talks too much," she said.

"Oh, I don't know. She's very proud of you, you know. And she did say that you were very good at what you did. She suggested that maybe you could help me out."

Nora couldn't fuss with the flowers anymore; the stems were practically drooping from all her attention. She set the vase on the kitchen table, brushed her hands together and looked at him.

"I gave you a list of names to call," she said. "Don't tell me they were all too busy to see you."

"I don't know if they were or not. I didn't call them."

"Mr. Kincaid—"

"Didn't we agree that you'd call me Lane?"

"No, we didn't. And I thought I'd made myself clear. I work for a very conservative firm with an established client list. I'm afraid I just can't help you."

He pushed himself away from the counter he was leaning against and took a step in her direction. Before she could stop herself, she took one back. He looked surprised and halted.

"Nora—may I call you Nora?"

She didn't care what he called her, as long as he stayed where he was. Stiffly, she nodded.

He took another step toward her; she took another back. Now the edge of the counter was pressing into her spine, and she didn't have anywhere to go. Reaching behind her, she grabbed the counter with both hands and held on tight. She knew she was being ridiculous, but she couldn't help it. Why couldn't she just hear him out, refuse whatever he wanted and show him to the door?

"Look," he said, seemingly unaware of her inner turmoil, "I know this is an imposition, but I wouldn't ask for your help if I didn't need it. You, of all people, know how things are in the business. I've gone through six managers the past five years. Every one of them cheated me. I need someone I can trust to manage my money."

He was so close she could smell the after-shave that had had such an effect on her at the party. Trying not to inhale, she said, "You can trust any of the people I recommended, Mr. Kincaid—"

"Lane," he reminded her.

She made the mistake of looking up at him. He was staring down at her, and when she saw the force behind those dazzling eyes, she remembered thinking in the past that his intensity had somehow been a result of clever lighting or photography. After all, she knew the tricks of the trade almost as well as the people involved, didn't she? She'd grown up listening to her mother talk about filters and gauzes and which lights played to her best side.

Boy, had she been mistaken. Even without artificial enhancements, Lane Kincaid had that certain *something* that the camera loved. The look in his eyes, the way he held his head, the curve of his mouth... He was a natural.

No wonder he drives women crazy, she thought—and quickly brought herself up short. She wasn't one of his fans. She knew all about men like Lane Kincaid. She was immune.

At the thought, she said stiffly, "I'm sorry, but I just can't help you. I'd like to, but I can't. If you don't like the names I gave you, I'll give you some others. Please try to understand."

He looked at her a moment longer, then he finally stepped back and put his hands in his pockets. With the motion, something taut seemed to collapse inside her, and suddenly she could breathe freely again.

"I understand," he said. "Your mother told me you were busy and might not be able to take me on. It's all right. I'll find someone else."

He was manipulating her, she told herself, but the maddening part was that she could feel herself weakening. "Look, Lane—"

"No, it's all right, really. I shouldn't have pressed you. After all, you don't know me. For all you know, I could be just another Hollywood flake, right?"

She wanted to agree with him and be done with it, but she couldn't make herself say the words. Somehow she sensed that behind his good looks was another man entirely, and she hated herself for being intrigued. But before she could stop herself, she reached out and put her hand on his arm.

It was a big mistake.

As she touched him, she felt a jolt. It flashed through her mind that if he suddenly took her in his arms and kissed her, she wouldn't resist. What was going on here? What was the matter with her?

She didn't know. It didn't matter. The point, she told herself fiercely, was to get this…whatever it was, under control. Quickly, she snatched her hand back. Appalled by her reaction to her own simple gesture, she glanced wildly around and spotted the bottle he'd brought. She had to put some emotional distance between herself and this man. "Would you like some wine?" she blurted desperately.

He looked confused at the quick change in her. "Wine?" he said, as though he'd never heard of the stuff. He glanced at the bottle she was pointing at. "Oh...sure. I'd like that."

She took a shaky breath. This was better. Now that they were about to partake in such a familiar ritual as having a simple glass of wine, she was sure she had control of the situation—and herself. She even remembered Chauncy, who was sitting patiently by his dinner bowl, waiting for her to notice he hadn't been fed. She took a corkscrew out of a drawer and found two wineglasses, all of which she put on the counter, saying, "Would you mind? I have to feed Chauncy, and then we can go out to the backyard."

Chauncy's dog bowl was almost as big as a tire; when she had filled it and the dog was chomping away happily, she risked a quick look at Lane. He was occupied with pouring the wine, and at the sight, she caught her breath again. Was it her imagination that he seemed to belong in her kitchen? Telling herself she was being ridiculous, she glanced away before he caught her staring. She had cheese and crackers on hand, and to give herself something else to do, she took them out, along with a plate. To her dismay, Lane came over with the two glasses in hand to watch.

"It looks like you've done that before," he said.

It was an effort to concentrate when he was standing so close. She caught another whiff of his after-

shave and closed her eyes. Trying to keep her mind on
what she was doing, she forced a laugh as they went
outside, saying, "When you have a mother who gives
parties at the drop of a hat, you learn these things
from the cradle on."

"Theodora does like to entertain, doesn't she?"

She didn't want to talk about the party. "Maybe it's
in the genes," she said lightly. "Don't all actors like to
show off?"

He smiled. "I guess they do."

"I'm sorry, I didn't mean—"

"Yes, you did," he said easily. "But you're right.
Actors *do* like to show off. It's a prerequisite."

"Did you always want to be an actor?"

"No, it was the last thing on my mind."

"Then how did you get into the business?"

"Do you want the truth or the publicity stuff?"

"Which one's more interesting?"

He appeared to consider, then shrugged. "Neither,
both, I guess. The truth is that I was working at a gas
station when a talent agent saw me. This was in the
'old days,' when some stations still gave service, remember? Well, I was filling up the tank of his
Mercedes and washing the windows, when he gave me
his card. What he saw I don't know. But I didn't have
anything better to do the next day, so I called him. The
rest, as they say, is history."

Now that they were outside, in the open, with the
night breeze cooling her flushed face, she was able to
relax a little. "Sounds like a new version of the Lana
Turner story."

"Well, she was discovered sitting on a stool at Schwab's, wasn't she?" he said with that self-mockery she already found much too attractive. "I think that's a little classier than being tapped while working as a grease monkey."

"I guess it depends on where the gas station was located."

He laughed. "It wasn't in Beverly Hills, believe me. It was just some dinky little place in Los Angeles."

She was about to ask him if he could be a little more specific, when she saw a shadow pass swiftly across his features. Instinct told her not to push him. She lifted her glass.

"Here's to success."

"Financial and otherwise," he said, clinking his glass with hers. He took a sip and then asked, "So, what about you?"

"Me?"

"Why aren't you, as they say, in pictures?"

She shook her head. "I was never interested. After living with actors all my life, the *last* thing I wanted was to follow them into the business."

He looked a little surprised by her vehemence. "Really? I would have thought that'd be your first choice. After all, you had so much experience to draw on."

"The experience I remember is a lot of *emoting*." She made a face. "Usually at the top of my parents' lungs."

"I can imagine, where Theodora is concerned," he said with another smile. "I haven't worked with her yet, but I can see that she's a corker, all right."

"Don't kid yourself," she said dryly. "In his day, my father gave as good as he got."

"Your father?"

"Yes, my father was Patric Carmichael."

"*The* Patric Carmichael?"

She laughed. "He would have loved the look on your face just now. And naturally, he would have accepted it as his due. Yes, my father was *the* Patric Carmichael—whatever that means."

"I don't believe it! I've seen every one of his films— ten times, at least!"

"You have?" She looked at him in real surprise. "But my father was a classical actor. I wouldn't have thought you'd be—" She stopped, flushing as she apologized once more. "I'm sorry, Lane. I didn't mean—"

He wasn't offended. "It's okay. It's nothing I haven't heard before. And, after all, my career so far hasn't exactly been of a Shakespearean order, has it?"

"If you feel that way, why don't you do something about it?"

"Something about what?"

Was he never serious? She knew she was overstepping her bounds, but she persisted. "Well, are you happy doing the films you do?"

"Happy? I can't complain, I guess," he said nonchalantly.

"But at this point in your career, you're surely able to pick and choose."

"That's why I pick the big moneymakers. All those greenbacks just keep rolling in."

"But there's more to life than money!"

He gazed at her over the rim of his glass. "Now, that's a strange thing for a financial consultant to say, don't you think?"

"But don't you want to try something different?"

"What, and kill the golden goose? No thanks, I'm having too good a time."

Exasperated, she asked, "Is that what it's all about—having a good time?"

"What do you think?"

She told herself not to tell him what she thought, but she did it anyway. "I think there are more important things."

"What? Power? Status?"

She stared him down. "Satisfaction. Contentment. Pride in a job well done."

"Is that what you feel with your work?"

"Yes, of course it is. Why do you think I do it?"

"I don't know. From what you've told me tonight, maybe you chose a profession that was as far removed from what your parents did as you could think of."

"That's ridiculous," she said indignantly. "I was interested in finance from the time I was a small girl!"

At her fierce expression, Lane put his hands in the air in an attitude of surrender. "Okay, okay, don't get excited," he said. Then he added with a grin, "Like mother, like daughter. I can see you and Theodora are just alike."

"I'm nothing like my mother!"

He laughed. "You can't mean that."

"Indeed, I do!"

He looked at her in disbelief, then he shook his head. "All right, then, maybe you're just like your father."

"I'm not like him, either!"

He looked at her curiously. "Why are you so upset?"

"I'm not upset!"

But she was. Chauncy, who'd been lying under the table, sensed her distress and lumbered to his feet. He sat down beside her with a whine, and placed his head on her lap. "Now see what you've done," she said accusingly to Lane. "You've upset my dog."

"Boy, I don't want to do that," he said. "As I've already experienced twice, he can flatten me without thinking about it. I'd hate to see what he can do when he's really upset."

"So, you take it back."

"What's that?"

"That ugly remark about me being like my parents."

He looked amused again. "Only if you take back what you said about me playing Shakespeare."

"I never mentioned him. *You* did."

They stared at each other for a moment. Then, Lane winked and despite herself, Nora smiled. As soon as she did, she relaxed, Lane sat back and Chauncy plopped down again.

"Friends?" Lane asked.

When he looked at her like that, she forgot that she didn't want to have anything to do with actors. In fact, she forgot her even more specific resolve not to have anything to do with Lane Kincaid.

"Friends," she agreed.

Satisfied, he finished his wine. "Now that that's settled, I think I'd better go."

She didn't ask him to stay. The sooner this little visit was over, the sooner she could get back to feeling normal again. Remembering his stated reason for coming, she said as they started to go inside, "I'll get you those other names before you go."

Setting the wineglasses in the sink, he gave her an injured look that would have done Chauncy proud. "But I thought *you* were going to be my financial adviser."

She put her hands on her hips. "Now, Lane, we talked about that. Just because you plied me with flowers and wine doesn't mean—"

"Can't you just look over my situation and give me some advice? That's all I ask." But his eyes twinkled again when he added, "Of course, if you want to do more than that—"

"I told you, I can't even do that much!"

"Please?" he said, ignoring her stubborn expression. "It doesn't have to be a formal thing. Just give me a little shove in the right direction. That won't hurt so much, will it?" He paused. "I'll give you tickets to my next premiere."

It was so ridiculous she had to laugh. "I'll bet you say that to all the women," she declared with a toss of her head. "All right, I'll look over your situation. But that's all," she quickly warned when he started to smile. "I'll make a few recommendations—investing in transportation stock or utilities may suit you—and then give you some more names so you can choose a new manager yourself. Agreed?''

"I can't ask for more than that."

But she was sure she saw his eyes twinkle again when they said good-night, and as she watched him walking jauntily down the walk to his car, she had the feeling that he had already asked her for more than she wanted to give—much more.

CHAPTER SIX

LANE COULDN'T remember the last time he'd over-slept, but the next morning he was dead to the world when Esperanza came knocking at the master bed-room door. From a distance, he thought he heard, *"Señor!* Señor Kincaid! Are you going to get up, or do I have to send Cosmo in there to drag you out of bed? You have to be on the set at eight-thirty, and it's al-most eight now. *Señor!* Do you hear me?"

The shouting and the pounding got through to him at last. Groaning, he cranked open an eye and peered at his bedside clock. When he saw what time it was, he bolted upright. He couldn't believe it. He hadn't slept this late in years.

Was he sick? Disoriented, he put a hand to his forehead. No, cool as could be. Had he had too much to drink last night? He swallowed. No, one glass of wine at Nora Carmichael's could hardly qualify as a bash.

"Señor!"

"I hear you!" he shouted back before Esperanza could make good the threat to send Cosmo in. He knew from the old days that the man had no pity. Cosmo would come in, jerk him out of bed and throw him in a cold shower—just as he used to do years ago.

During that first flush of success when he couldn't seem to get control of anything, he couldn't count the times he'd needed Cosmo's help in the morning after he'd celebrated too much at some party the night before. But that hadn't happened in longer than he could remember.

"Señor!"

"I'm up, I'm up!" he shouted, swinging his legs over the side of the bed. Bracing his elbows on his knees, he shook his head to get the cobwebs out. He felt as though he'd been run over by a herd of buffalo.

Nora was responsible for his state, he thought irritably. Before he'd met her, things had been so simple. Now she'd raised all sorts of questions in his mind; she'd forced him to think about things he didn't want to think about, and it was exhausting. He might have been in bed early, but he hadn't fallen asleep until after three, and then he wasn't sure he'd really slept. He was getting too old for this kind of turmoil.

"Señor!"

Groaning again, he rubbed his hands through his hair and staggered into the shower before Esperanza forgot about calling Cosmo and came in herself. Ten minutes later, dressed in jeans and a clean sports shirt, he ran into the kitchen to snag some juice before he took off for the studio. He hadn't taken time to shave, and he knew he'd catch a reproving glance from Esperanza. He did. She took one look at him and said pointedly, "If I'd known you wanted to be awakened this morning, I would have set the alarm myself."

Normally he was tolerant of her mothering, but today he wasn't in the mood for it. He grabbed the carafe of orange juice and drained it in one long swallow—again to her sniff of disapproval—and said, "No breakfast this morning, Esperanza. I've got to get going."

"But you have to eat!"

"I'll take a rain check," he said, waving goodbye. He snatched his keys and he hurried out to the car. If the fates were willing and traffic cooperated, he'd get there before Theodora—he hoped. He'd heard she was always notoriously late for everything, but today he had the feeling that because *he* was tardy, she'd be there on the dot. Freddie had scheduled their first rehearsal this morning, and he'd wanted to make a good impression. Now, he was not only going to be late, he'd arrive unshaven, to boot. Damn it, why had he chosen this day of all days to oversleep?

Because he'd been preoccupied with Theodora's daughter last night, that's why, he thought. He'd never met anyone like Nora, and it was driving him crazy. He hadn't been interested, really interested, in a woman in a long time, and it wasn't fair that the one time he *wanted* someone to be interested back, she'd practically yawned in his face. What was wrong? Was it because she'd been around actors all her life and just wasn't awed by one more, not even the reigning box-office star? He had a sudden thought, but then shook his head. It couldn't be that she just hadn't been impressed by *him*.

Oh yes, it could. He might as well face facts. Nora Carmichael's dog was more star-struck than she could ever be. It was a bad blow to his ego, but there it was. "Just accept it, fella," he muttered, "and forget it."

Why was it so damn important, anyway? he asked himself. Her reaction last night should have been enough. After stopping by her house—

Stopping *by?* Even to himself, he couldn't get away with that. He'd gone sixty miles out of his way so he could pretend to be "in the neighborhood" last night—and what had happened?

He scowled. What had he wanted to happen? For her to fall into his arms as other women did? For her to look at him adoringly and gush that he was the handsomest man she'd ever met?

At the thought, he stopped a moment, and grinned. That would have been nice, he thought...and then shook his head again. He didn't really want that. Hadn't he had enough of the same these past few years?

So what *did* he want?

Well, he could have done without the criticism about his career choices for starters, he decided. He was doing just fine; he certainly didn't need Nora Carmichael to tell him that he was taking the easy way out.

Drumming his fingers impatiently against the wheel, he remembered that Nora had hinted as much last night. In fact, he thought, she might as well have come right out and told him he was wasting his life playing action heros whose chest measurements were bigger than their I.Q.'s. After what she'd said, he was sure that if she happened to read the script for *Nobody Home,* she'd be right there along with Wyatt, telling

him he'd be a fool not to take the lead part of Tyler
Dane. His hand clenched. Well, what neither of them
understood, he thought, was that whoever accepted
the role would have to reach down much too deep inside himself. It had taken Lane too many years to
block out the emotions and pain that had nearly devastated him as a child. No way was he going to risk
releasing all that grief.

A sudden *honk!* from a car pulling abreast on his
left brought Lane abruptly out of his reverie. "Hey,
Lane Kincaid, is that you? Are you really the man?
Hey, guys, it's him! I told you it was! Great car,
Lane."

Lane glanced over at the carful of teenagers who
had pulled up beside him. They were laughing and
waving, obviously thrilled, excited...*impressed*. He
gave them one of his best grins and a casual wave as he
turned off the exit highway.

"Good morning, Mr. Kincaid," the guard said
when he pulled up at the studio gate a few minutes
later. The man's name was Charlie, and he pushed
back his peaked cap, giving Lane's gleaming red
Porsche an envious look. "Man, that's some fine car
you got."

Lane didn't have the heart to tell him that the car
had been a present from the studio, so he said wryly,
"That's what some kids thought just now on the freeway. Sometimes I don't know if they're waving to me
or acknowledging the car, instead."

"Oh, it's the car, I'm sure," Charlie said, grinning.
"You have to admit, it's one fine machine."

"You got that right," Lane agreed. "Has Miss DeVere come in yet?"

"About ten minutes ago—in a champagne-colored Lincoln about a block long," Charlie said approvingly. "Now, there's a lady who knows how to be a star."

As he headed to the sound stage, Lane hoped Theodora wouldn't be displaying her famous "star" temperament. Everyone was on the set when he came in, and, like a queen holding court, Theodora was the center of attention. Even Freddie Princeley, a director notorious for his own tantrums, was hovering. Lane's hope that he could just slip in vanished when Theodora looked up and said, "Well, Lane, darling, how nice that you finally joined us. Perhaps now we can get started? Oh, and Freddie, you will ask the writers to make those changes, won't you? I can't say those lines until they make sense. You understand, I'm sure."

Lane didn't know what changes Theodora was talking about, but he knew how Freddie protected his scripts. He expected an explosion, but was astounded instead when the director simply nodded and said, "I'll take care of it immediately, Miss DeVere."

As Freddie turned to give the production assistant new instructions, he said to Lane, "We're doing a run-through of scene seventy-six, where your character and Theodora as Vicky first meet. Remember, Vicky's been around, she knows the score—"

"In other words, she's a tough old broad who won't take any baloney from a police detective who's still wet behind the ears," Theodora drawled. She smiled benignly at Princeley. "You don't have to walk on eggs, dear. I've been around, too."

Theodora was standing in a mock-up of a bar in what was supposed to be a seedy part of town. In her role as Vicky Renfro, a torch singer long past her prime, she would wear tight, sequined gowns—her favorite kind, she had confided with a laugh to Lane when they first met. For rehearsal today, she was wearing an informal suit of some soft material in shades of purple and teal. Thinking that she resembled a tough old broad about as much as he did, Lane grinned when she winked at him. Even on the sleazy bar set, she looked, he thought, regal.

Already looking forward to this, he dodged some cables that snaked over the floor, stepped around a couple of cameras and came onto the lighted oasis of the set. "I'm sorry I'm late, Theodora," he said. "It won't happen again."

She smiled and reached up to pat his check. "It's all right, dear," she said. "And I'm sure it won't. Are you ready to begin, or do you need some time to get into character?"

His role of Nick Archer was so similar to all the others he'd played that he felt he could have done it in his sleep. "I'm ready to go if you are."

She nodded. Then before his eyes, she . . . changed. One minute she was Theodora DeVere, sophisticated, charming, absolutely in control of herself, the set, and everyone else; the next, she *was* Vicky Renfro, a worn-out, boozy lounge singer who had seen much better days.

Lane was fascinated. He'd worked with many actresses, but none, he realized, as good as this. When Theodora transformed herself right in front of him, he could almost believe they *were* in that bar in a bad part of town, and that, as Nick, he *was* talking to a lounge singer who'd been around. He was so impressed that on the first try he completely forgot his first few lines; on the next, he overshot his mark. He did better on the third attempt, and by the fourth, he'd mercifully hit his stride. As long as he forgot who Theodora was and thought of her as Vicky, he was okay. The instant he allowed his awed admiration for her to intrude, he fell on his face.

Sometime around noon, they took a break, and Lane was more than ready. The trailer he'd been assigned was parked just behind the sound stage. Along with everyone else, he'd been working on the project for weeks, but Theodora hadn't been needed until now. As he came out the back door, he saw that another, bigger trailer had been brought in and parked right in front of his. The royal-purple-and-gold color scheme had to belong to her, and at the sight, he laughed. It was appropriate, he thought. After what he'd seen this morning, she deserved the number-one spot. He was just passing by when Theodora herself opened the door and put her head out.

"Do you want some time by yourself, or would you like to join me for lunch?" she asked.

A sandwich while he studied lines for the afternoon couldn't compare to having lunch with Theodora DeVere. Suddenly, his weariness vanished and he smiled in return. But just to tease her, he said, "I don't know. What're you having?"

Her eyes twinkled. "*I'm* having a salad and mineral water. But I think I can probably find something more appropriate for you, if you'd like."

"Don't go to any trouble on my account."

"Oh, it's no trouble," she said, holding the door open for him. "Chan is a wizard. He always cooks for me when I'm working." She laughed as though it were the most amusing thing in the world. "I never cook. As my daughter says—pointedly, and as often as she can—I find it difficult to make a cup of tea by myself."

Wishing she hadn't mentioned Nora, whom he'd actually managed to put out of his mind these past few hours, he said, "You have other qualities, Theodora, as I've just seen. In fact, you really are amazing. I've learned more from you this morning than I would have in six years of acting lessons."

"Flattery will get you chocolate cake for dessert," she said, gesturing to the table where a slightly built man—obviously Chan—was already setting another place, with china and linen napkins. "Please, have a seat."

First he held her chair. As he sat down opposite her, he said, "You know how to live."

Accepting the compliment with another silvery laugh, she said, "Well, life can be so difficult at times that we might as well pamper ourselves when we can. Don't you think so?"

He suppressed a flash of himself as a young boy, eating soup out of a can because it was the only thing he could find in a cold, dirty kitchen and said lightly, "I think we can try."

Chan began serving—the promised salad for Theodora, and an open-faced roast beef sandwich for him. When he saw what was being put before him, Lane said to Theodora, "I think you've mastered the pampering technique much better than I." Then he looked up at Chan. "This looks great. Thanks."

Chan just smiled and moved to another section of the trailer, close enough so that he could wait on them, but far enough away so that he wouldn't appear to be listening to the conversation. Still marveling at the efficiencies in Theodora's life, Lane dug in. How could he have thought he wasn't hungry?

"So," Theodora said, picking at her salad, "I think the morning went well, don't you?"

"Thanks to you. I meant it when I said you were wonderful, Theodora. I don't think anyone else could bring so much to the part of Vicky."

She smiled. "It's all a matter of knowing your character, Lane. As you seem to know Nick Archer."

"Only because I've played him before," he said.

"I didn't know Archer is a recurring character."

"He's not. I meant that I usually play characters similar to him." He smiled self-consciously. "It's sort of my stock-in-trade. You know, what the public expects."

She looked at him lazily. "And do you always give the public what you think it expects?"

He silently cursed himself for bringing up such an uncomfortable subject. "I've seen what's happened to other actors who gained fame from playing a certain kind of role and then tried to step out of it. They paid the price," he said.

"Not all of them."

"Well, no, not all," he agreed. He didn't know why he was telling her any of this, especially since he had never told anyone else. "But enough did, so that I decided long ago not to rock the boat."

"I see."

He didn't know how she could; Theodora DeVere had won two Tonys and an Oscar and lord knew how many other awards. But his curiosity got the best of him. "Can I ask you a personal question?"

She slanted her eyes at him. "You may ask."

"Why did you take the role of Vicky? It doesn't seem like something you'd be interested in."

She shrugged delicately. "Perhaps I wanted the challenge."

"When you've played Blanche, in *Streetcar?* Or Desdemona? Or Lilith?"

Playfully, she shook her finger at him. "You've been reading my bio."

He wasn't going to deny it. "Yes, I have. You've had quite a career, Theodora."

"And so will you," she said enigmatically. Then she smiled. "But your question deserves a proper answer, which is—I wanted to take the role of Vicky because she does something in the end that I've been thinking of doing myself."

"But Vicky gives up singing—" He stopped suddenly, and looked at her intently. "You're not thinking of giving up your career!"

An emotion he couldn't identify flashed across her expressive face. But she wasn't an award-winning actress for nothing, and she said casually, "I have been contemplating it, yes."

He couldn't believe it. "I'm sorry, but...why?"

"Why not?"

He didn't have an answer. When she saw his expression, she patted his arm. "I don't know why it should be such a surprise. After all, I've put in my years. Don't I deserve my retirement?"

"But you're still—"

"Young?" Theodora shook her head. "No, I might pretend to be—" She looked at him sternly. "If you ever repeat this conversation, I'll haunt you, I swear it."

He made a production of crossing his heart. "I'll go to the grave with the secret."

"You'd better," she stated. Suddenly, she got up from the table. Without looking at him, she said, "All right, then the truth is, there just aren't that many good roles for women of my...age."

He started to deny it, but she turned to look at him, holding up a hand. Her violet-tinted eyes flashed, and this time he was sure he saw a look of pain cross her beautiful face. "No, we both know it's true." She drew herself up haughtily, looking every inch a queen. "And so, I've decided to leave while I still can—on *my* terms!"

He didn't know what to say. "But—"

She wasn't finished. "Besides," she added dramatically, "there's something else."

"Something...else?"

She raised a commanding, graceful finger, stifling him as effectively as if she'd clamped a hand over his mouth. "Yes," she whispered in a voice that raised the hairs at the back of his neck. "I'm going to...settle down!"

He stared at her in complete astonishment. Unable, it seemed, to stop repeating everything she said, he did it again. "Settle down?"

She laughed. "Don't look as though you've never heard the term, darling," she said. "I realize that you're still filled with—" she sighed melodramatically "—*joie de vivre*, so the concept of settling down is an alien one. But for me, it does have a certain intrigue."

His eyes twinkled. "I suppose you've selected the man?"

She laughed again, genuinely amused. "Well put, love! And of course I have. I'm just not ready to tell you yet!"

"What does Nora think of this?"

"Ah...Nora." Several emotions crossed her face: tenderness, faint exasperation...love. She looked at Lane. "When I first told her, she was as surprised as you seem to be, but I think she's adjusting to the idea." She glanced down and calmly adjusted the folds of the caftan she'd changed into. "After all, I've been an embarrassment to her for years now—"

"You!"

"Oh, yes, me," she said with another heartfelt sigh, unable to resist playing him. She looked at him from under her long lashes. "Still, it's the truth. I had to come to terms with it a long time ago, you know."

"I don't think—"

"Oh, it's all right," she said sadly. "I didn't have any choice. I had to live my life, just as Nora has to live hers. I never wanted her to go into the business, anyway. Neither did her father. We did everything we could to discourage her, and sometimes I think we succeeded a little too well."

"You may be right," he said glumly. "Present company excepted, she does seem to have an aversion to actors. At least, she does to me. I'd like to believe it's my profession and not my personality, but at this point I think it's fifty-fifty."

She laughed. "Nora likes you."

He made a face. "You could have fooled me."

"You'll see when she advises you about those financial matters you told me about."

"I'm not so sure that's going to happen. I asked her—"

"And?"

"And . . . nothing. She said she couldn't take me as a client. All she'd do was agree to give me a few suggestions—and some names to call."

Theodora sat back thoughtfully. "You know, Nora is my daughter, and I love her more than anything in the world, but sometimes she is a little stuffy."

He looked wry. "A little?"

She smiled. "I admit she can try the patience of a saint, but don't give up. She really is very good at what she does—" She stopped suddenly, giving him a meaningful stare. "Or is what she *does* the thing you're really interested in?"

He reddened. "I don't know what you mean."

"Oh, pish. You know very well what I mean. Are you interested in my daughter?"

"Me? I hardly know her."

"Ah . . . but you want to, don't you?"

"Well, I—" He stopped midsentence. Then he decided he might as well just lay his cards on the table. "Would you mind if I said yes?"

"I? Not at all." She gave him another sly look. "Would it matter if I did?"

"Of course it would—"

She laughed again. "You know, you remind me of Patric, in a way. He was just as impulsive, just as determined and just as good-looking." She sat back, shaking her head. "Oh, dear, I just hope Nora knows what she's getting into."

"Nora?" he said plaintively. "What about me?"

She gave him a pitying look. "You don't know it yet, love, but you're already lost. I recognize that look on your face." Her expression became almost dreamy. "You see," she added, "my Patric had it, too." She looked at him suddenly, impaling him with her eyes. "Now, what do you think of that?"

He didn't know what to think. Fortunately, just then there was a knock at the trailer door. "Five minutes, Miss DeVere," a voice said.

Theodora looked at him again. "Well," she murmured. "Is that good timing, or what?"

IT WAS LATE when Lane finally started home that night. Theodora had gone home hours before, but Freddie had kept him and his stuntman on, mapping out some of the action scenes that still had to be shot.

By the time he drove out, he was dead-tired, hardly able to keep his eyes open. He was so weary, in fact, that he missed the entrance ramp to the freeway and was halfway down the next block before he realized it. He was about to turn around and go back when he saw two teenage girls standing on the street corner having an animated conversation—as only teenage girls can do—until a gang of four boys swaggered up.

He smiled at the sight. They weren't doing anything he hadn't done at the same age. He looked away, searching for a spot to turn the car around. Then he heard a scream. One of the boys was scuffling with one of the girls. She screamed again. Lane came to a screeching halt beside the group. The sound of his tires caught their attention, and they all looked over at the red Porsche.

"Hi, guys," Lane said easily, getting out of the car. "Is there a problem here?"

They recognized him. To murmurs of: "Isn't that Lane Kincaid?" and "Yes, you idiot, it's him." and "Oh, he's such a hunk!" to "What's he doing here?" he got out of the car, shoved his hands into his pockets and ambled over to the group. The boy who had grabbed the girl's arm was still holding it. Lane pointedly glanced at the kid's hand and the boy muttered something and released her. She gave the boy a dirty look and quickly stepped away from him.

"So," Lane said. "What are you guys doing out so late?"

"Are you kidding, man!" one of the boys said aggressively. "It's not even ten o'clock!"

Casually, Lane nodded. "That's true. But then, I suppose you're not worried because you've done all your homework, right?"

"Gimme a break!" Another of the boys spat on the ground to show his disdain. "Who does homework?"

"I do," one of the girls said. Her eyes shone as she looked at Lane. She had an armful of books, and with a defiant glance at the boys, she added, "We were just coming home from the library, when these...these *geeks* started bothering us."

"Geeks! I'll show you—"

Predictable outrage erupted on the boys' part, but with Lane standing right there, they couldn't do more than posture. He let them bluster for a few moments, then he took his hands out of his pockets and said, "I think it's time for everybody to go home, don't you?" He grinned the famous grin. "As far as I know, it's a school day tomorrow, and I'm sure you're all going to be there, bright and early and...prepared, right?"

A second boy, the one who had grabbed the girl's arm, stepped forward. "I bet you didn't go to school," he challenged.

Lane looked directly at him. "Indeed, I did. I graduated, too. It was the best thing I've ever done for myself."

"Yeah, sure," the boy sneered. "Even better than making a bazillion dollars doin' all those great movies, huh? What did you need *school* for, with all that money?"

"Well, I needed it so I could read my lines, for one thing. And I needed it so I could understand the contracts I was signing." Lane grinned again. "And if I hadn't had math, how would I have been able to calculate if the percentages they offered to pay me were good enough?"

There was an uneasy shuffling from the boys, while the girls seized the opportunity to look superior. Deciding he had given them something to think about, Lane said good-night and started off. He hadn't gone two steps before they surrounded him again to ask for his autograph.

"Sure. Has anyone got a pen and paper?"

Naturally, both girls did. With condescending smirks at the boys, who had nothing in their pockets but their hands, they tore two pages out of their notebooks and gave them to Lane.

"Hey, I'd like one, too!" one of the boys said.

The girl who had been grabbed turned to look coolly at him. Tossing her head, she said, "Too bad you don't have any paper."

He glowered at her. "I'll give you a dollar for one piece of damn paper," he growled.

She lifted her chin haughtily. "I'm sorry, this notebook is very valuable. I'll have to charge you five dollars, at least."

"That's robbery!" another boy cried, outraged.

"That's the free enterprise system," Lane said, trying not to laugh. "It's a concept you study in history or economics or sociology classes." He winked at the girls. "Along with the law of supply and demand, right, girls?"

"Right!" they both chorused, then looked pleased and happy as the four boys handed over their five dollars apiece.

After Lane signed one for everyone, he watched them go their separate ways, the girls down one block, the boys down another. He waited a moment to make sure the boys weren't going to double back, but when he saw them start to punch each other and poke and jab as teenagers do when they're just messing around, he was satisfied they wouldn't give the girls any more grief—at least tonight. Smiling, he started the car and drove home.

CHAPTER SEVEN

NORA WAS at the office when Lane called. As soon as
Sherrie buzzed through with the news that *Lane Kincaid* was on the phone, Nora slammed down the file
she'd been reading. Was the man oblivious, or what?
She'd *told* him she'd get back to him; why was he
calling her...*bothering* her here? She didn't have time
for this. In addition to everything else, she had to give
a lecture tonight about money management. Once a
month, Bullard and Sweeney offered a free seminar to
interested investors, and it was her turn to give the
talk. She'd been so busy today she hadn't had time to
prepare.

"Tell him I'm gone," she said to the secretary.

"Gone!" Sherrie was horrified. "But...but it's
Lane Kincaid!"

"I don't care if it's the president of the United
States. I can't talk to him now."

"But—"

Nora closed her eyes and counted to five. She, of all
people, knew how persistent he could be, and she
doubted he'd give up just because she gave an excuse.
The next thing she knew, he'd probably show up at the
office, and since she could imagine how her boss
would react to *that,* she said in exasperation, "Never

mind, Sherrie, I'll take the call." Waiting ten seconds, she punched down the button on the blinking line one. "Nora Carmichael."

She should have known he'd be amused at her stiff tone. "Good afternoon, Nora Carmichael," he said while she tightened her lips. "This is Lane Kincaid. Am I calling at a bad time?"

Nora looked at the pile of reports on her desk, at the correspondence she had to answer before she left, at her scribbles for the lecture tonight, and said ungraciously, "As a matter of fact, you are. But now that you're on the line, what can I do for you?"

"Well, first off, I wanted to thank you for your hospitality the other night. I enjoyed the evening."

So had she, far too much. "I don't know how you could have, not after Chauncy knocked you down again," she said.

He chuckled. "Well, I admit, if we're going to keep on seeing each other, we'll have to do something about those excessive greetings of his."

"Seeing each other?" She sat up. "I thought we had an understanding—"

"Oh, we do, we do," he said. "But you did agree that you'd look things over for me and make a recommendation or two, didn't you? We have to see each other for that much at least, don't you think?"

"No," she said flatly. "Now that I've thought about it, I think we can do this over the phone."

"Is that how you usually deal with your clients?"

"You're not a client. I told you already—"

"Nora, I'm sure you're many things—all of them wonderful. But not even you can be omniscient. How

can you give me any advice until you see my portfolio?"

"Fax it to me."

There was the tiniest of hesitations, then he said, "I
think it would be better if we did this in person."

That was the last thing she wanted. "Now,
Lane—"

"Oh, I get it," he said. "You want me to come over
to your house again, right? Or... I know! You could
come to my place. With my shooting schedule, that
would be easier, but I'll leave it up to you. What would
you like?"

What she'd *like,* she thought, was never to have met
this man. She didn't want to see Lane Kincaid again
anywhere, under any circumstances whatsoever. It was
humiliating to admit, but she was being rude and ob-
structive because she couldn't trust herself where he
was concerned. Just hearing his voice did something
to her that she didn't like, and when she imagined
seeing him again—

But she had promised to advise him. It didn't mean
that she was committing herself to anything. After all,
no one said she had to be *involved* to give him the
benefit of her professional opinion.

"You're right," she said abruptly. She'd do this
thing, but she was *not* going to have him out at the
house. Whatever business they had, they'd take care
of here—at the office. "I think we should meet here,
after all. The problem is that I don't have any time this
week or next."

"Oh, that's not a problem," he said easily, making
her grit her teeth. "I don't have any time during the

day for the next couple of weeks myself. You know the business. Princeley has decided to make up for lost time, so we have a hectic shooting schedule. I don't know about Theodora, but I'm going to be tied up from dawn to dusk."

Nora felt light-headed with relief. This was her reprieve. "That's too bad," she said, with mock regret. "It looks like we'll have to put off meeting indefinitely, doesn't it?"

"No, I think it means we'll just have to get together after work," he countered. "Look, why don't we stick with the original plan—"

She stiffened. "Wait a minute. We don't *have* an original plan!"

"Yes, we do. It's the one where I come to your house tonight. I'll bring all the pertinent financial records. And maybe a pizza, or something. We can—"

"No, we can't."

"What's the matter? Doesn't Chauncy like pizza?"

"Chauncy likes anything that doesn't move, but that's not the point. I told you we have to meet at the office. Investing money is serious business—"

"It is?"

"Yes, it is," she said tartly. "In fact, your attitude is probably the reason you're having problems in the first place."

"You see how much I need you? So, what's a good time? About seven? Eight?"

"I *told* you, tonight's not a good time. As incredible as it must sound, I'm *busy*. I'm giving a lecture at the local library."

"A lecture?"

"Yes, you've heard about those, haven't you?" she asked sarcastically. "It's where there's a speaker and an audience, and an exchange of information."

He was unperturbed. "And what information are you going to impart?"

Annoyed, she answered, "I'm going to talk to potential investors about what we do here."

"Really? Maybe I should come."

She just barely prevented herself from shouting, *Don't you dare!* and managed a calm "No, I don't think that's a good idea."

There was a short silence. Then he said, "Nora, let's not make a big thing out of this, all right? I sense that I'm making you uncomfortable, and that's the last thing I want to do. I know you're busy. I am, too. But I really need advice. My accountant's having fits because I spend too much money, and I'm not so pleased about the state of my finances myself."

She couldn't help herself. "Maybe all you need is a little self-control."

To her intense annoyance, he laughed. "I can't deny it. I'm good at what I do, but I don't think I can be playing macho superheroes when I'm in my dotage—which, according to my accountant, is how old I'll be before I get these debts paid off."

"I can't believe it's that bad."

"I don't know, you'll have to tell me."

She gave up. Just wanting to get it over with, she said, "All right. You can come to the house—but tomorrow night. And no dinner. This will be strictly business, understand?"

"Perfectly. And Nora, thanks."

"Don't thank me yet," she warned. "I'm good at what I do, Lane. You might not like what I say."

"I'll be strong, I promise. See you tomorrow night."

He'd manipulated her again, and she liked it even less than she had the first time. Vowing not to get distracted by this... this *business* appointment until tomorrow night, she was just reaching for her notes again when Sherrie poked her head in.

"Can I talk to you for a minute, Nora?"

"Yes, but only that. I've got a lot of work to do before I leave today and I still have to plan my lecture. What is it?" she said.

Slipping into the office, Sherrie leaned against the door. "Was that really *him?*"

Sherrie had drawn the word out adoringly, and when Nora saw the fatuous smile on the secretary's face she said, "By *him,* I assume you mean Lane Kincaid?"

Sherrie pushed away from the door. "Oh, Nora, you know that's who I mean. Tell me it really was him, and not just someone playing a joke!"

"No, it was Lane. Why?"

Her eyes wide, Sherrie came over to the desk. "I know this is a personal question, but I just can't help myself. You don't have to tell me if you don't want to, but... are you *dating* him, Nora? Oh, if you are, I'll just die!"

"No, I'm not dating him! He just called to ask for some financial advice. It's no big deal."

"No big deal?" Sherrie looked at her as though she'd sprouted another head. "The biggest star in movies today calls to ask your opinion about something, and you say it doesn't *matter?"*

Wanting to end this conversation, Nora said, "Don't forget that I grew up around actors. My father was one, and my mother's still in the business."

"Oh, yes, I know. I've told you before how much I envy you."

"Well, you wouldn't if you'd seen what I have. Besides, they're not gods, you know," she added sternly. "Far from it, in fact. They're people, like you and me."

"Oh, Nora, they're not like you and me, and you know it," Sherrie said reproachfully. "Especially not someone like Lane Kincaid! Oh, how do you stand it? I wouldn't even know what to say to someone like him. I practically stammered just answering the phone!"

"Sherrie, I really have to get some work done."

"Oh, yes, you're right, I'm sorry, I shouldn't have interrupted. But I had to know!" At the door again, Sherrie turned and looked longingly over her shoulder. "I'd give anything to be in your shoes, just for a little while!"

I'd give anything to let you wear my shoes, at least for tomorrow night, Nora thought as she pulled her notes toward her again. She had to plan her talk; if she didn't, she'd look like an idiot up at the podium tonight.

A few minutes later, she threw her pen down in disgust. It was no use; she couldn't concentrate. Restlessly, she got up to peer out the window, but she wasn't really seeing the street outside. She was seeing Lane, instead—at her place, covered with flowers when she found him on the porch; then later, sitting opposite her on the patio, toying with his wineglass. She couldn't deny that he was one of the most attractive, magnetic men she'd ever met—

Impatiently, she shook her head. He was *supposed* to be attractive and magnetic, wasn't he? she told herself scathingly. It was what he *did*. What *she* had to do was plan her lecture for tonight, so she'd better get busy and do it.

"WHAT ARE *you* doing here?"

"What do you think?" Lane answered Nora with that damned grin. "I came to hear you speak, of course."

"This isn't funny—" she started to say, but just then she was interrupted by a middle-aged woman who was following the crowd into the conference room where Nora was to speak.

"I don't believe it!" the woman squealed. "Are you...no, you can't be! But are you Lane *Kincaid?*"

When her voice rose on his name, Lane glanced quickly at Nora. Seeing the murderous look on her face, he bent down and whispered to the woman, "Let's keep it to ourselves, okay? I'm researching a role and I want to keep a low profile. Can you help me?"

"I won't breathe a word, but—can I have your autograph? My daughter will be *thrilled!*" the fan whispered.

As Lane obligingly took out a pen, Nora barely prevented herself from impatiently tapping her foot. Aware that she was about to explode, Lane signed his name and handed the paper to the woman.

"Oh, thank you, thank you, Mr. Kincaid!"

Holding the page lovingly to her chest, the fan gave him an adoring look before she turned and went inside. The instant she was gone, Nora said, "Lane—"

"Er...Ms. Carmichael?" It was Hobart Manning, the librarian who was chairing the meeting. "It's a little after seven, and we do only have this room for an hour," he reminded her.

Trying to conceal her irritation, she nodded. "I'll be right there," she said, and turned again to Lane. "I'll talk to you later."

"I'll be waiting," he said, while she clenched her jaw. Smiling as though there weren't a thing wrong in the entire world, he followed her inside. He took a chair at the back, and sat down while she continued to the lectern in front of the room.

At first, Nora had been nervous about public speaking, but after giving several of these talks, she now felt comfortable in front of an audience. At least, she thought, she had, before tonight. After Manning introduced her and she took her place, she realized that her palms were clammy because Lane was in the audience, sitting right there at the back, *staring* at her with that *smile* on his face. Deciding she wasn't going to look at him again, she began to speak.

"Tonight I'm here to talk to you about managing your money," she began. "Now, money managers are called financial planners, advisers, consultants, whatever you like. But, contrary to what you might have heard, we're not soothsayers." She smiled. "Although I have to admit, being able to forecast the future with real accuracy, especially in these changing times, would certainly come in handy."

There was appreciative laughter at that. Satisfied that she had relaxed her audience as well as herself, she continued. "So, the question is—what do money managers do? Well, simply put, we take care of our clients' assets by investing in the best possible way, and by providing personalized counseling on issues ranging from tax-exempt investments to trusts and estates..."

She went on to talk for almost an hour about the business of investing, then she called for questions. Naturally, the first one came from Lane. The instant he raised his hand, she tensed.

"Yes?" she said stiffly.

"How do money managers differ from, say, stockbrokers?" he asked.

She hated to admit it, but it was a good question. "In a way, we're not dissimilar in our overall approach. One difference, of course—and an important one to clients, I might add—is in the fee structure. A stockbroker takes a commission for each transaction, but a money manager handles an entire portfolio for a single fee."

"How much is the fee?" someone else asked.

"Usually half a percent to two percent of the total assets."

"Are there any other differences between money managers and stockbrokers?" someone at the front asked.

"Well, depending on the transaction, of course, managers can usually get their clients better deals than someone affiliated with a brokerage house," Nora said.

At the back of the room, Lane stood up. As much as she wanted to, Nora could hardly ignore him and nodded curtly in his direction. "If you could advise us to invest in one thing, what would it be?" he asked.

She should have known he'd put her on the spot like that, she thought crossly. "It's not that simple," she said. "Different cases require different approaches—"

"I understand that," he said. "But let's say you had to recommend one type of investment—just one. What would it be?"

She didn't appreciate being pinned down like this. "There are many types of investments—"

"I know. But name one. In fact, I'll make it easy for you. Something in . . . stocks. How about that?"

People were turning around to look at him, recognizing him, starting to murmur among themselves. "Transportation or utility stocks are generally a good bet. But again, it depends on the market and the economic climate. Does that answer your question?" she said through her teeth.

Apparently, it did. That, or he'd decided he'd pushed her enough. Still smiling, he finally sat down, and out of the sea of hands that shot up, she selected the first one she saw.

"I don't want to seem rude," a woman said, "but if we're unfamiliar with money managers, how can we find a good one?"

This was one question she could answer safely. Deliberately shooting a quick glance in Lane's direction, she said, "*You're* not being rude. That's something you should ask if you're thinking about getting someone to handle your money. And, since money managers generally require one to three percent of assets under management, it can be a substantial sum. So first, I'd advise you to find out what the firm's track record is. Then tell them what you want, and listen to what they have to offer." She smiled briefly. "If anyone tells you they can double your money in six months, run—don't walk—to the nearest exit."

The meeting broke up soon after that, and as several people came up to ask questions, Nora was aware that Lane had gathered his own crowd of admirers at the back of the room. She forced herself to heed her own audience, and by the time Hobart Manning thanked her for coming and praised her for her lecture, the crowd had thinned considerably. Covertly, she glanced around. Telling herself she wasn't disappointed that Lane had already left, she said good-night and started out to her car. Lane was leaning casually against the door, his hands in his pockets.

"I thought you'd gone," she said, gripping her keys so tightly they cut into her palm.

"I couldn't leave without telling you that I enjoyed your talk," he said. "So did everyone else, it seems. You had quite a crowd surrounding you after your lecture."

She couldn't help herself. "So did you."

He grinned. "Oh, you noticed that?"

"I could hardly help it," she said frostily. "But I suppose that's just business as usual for you. Don't people surround you wherever you go?"

"It's my charm."

"Aren't you ever serious?"

"Not if I can help it," he said. "Here, let me take that. It looks heavy."

Before she realized what he was about to do, he took her briefcase from her hand. His fingers grazed hers when he did, and at the contact, it was all she could do not to jump back.

"You didn't have to do that," she said, trying to recover her composure. She still had the keys in her hand, and she looked down at them quickly. "I'm leaving right now."

"Don't you even have time for a cup of coffee?"

"No, I don't. It's late, and—" Just in time, she realized she was about to say she hadn't yet had dinner. Hastily, she amended, "It's been a long day."

"You're angry with me again."

"No, I'm not. I'm tired and I want to go home." Her lips tight, she tried to brush by him. He moved at the same time, and before she knew it, his arms were around her and he was pulling her close.

"What are you—"

"I can't help myself," he said, looking down at her. His eyes never leaving her face, he said quietly, "I've been wanting to kiss you from the first moment I saw you."

"Well, I haven't—"

"Yes, you have," he said softly. Then he bent down and kissed her.

For the first few seconds, she didn't move. She couldn't; she was paralyzed by the whirling kaleidoscope of sensation that swept over her. She'd never felt like this, she thought in a panic—never. Then the pressure of his lips increased on hers, and when she felt his arms tremble, she reacted. She couldn't stop her arms from lifting; she couldn't keep her fingers from winding themselves in his thick, blond hair. When she caught a whiff of his after-shave, along with a muskier scent that was so...so male, so completely Lane, she shuddered and pressed her body closer to his.

She knew she should pull back, step away, do... something. But all she could do was move her lips under his, enjoying his body against her, feeling his chest under her hand, his flat belly, his...

Gasping, she finally pulled back. *What was she doing?* They were in a public place, under a streetlight, totally exposed to the entire world. If someone had seen them; if anyone knew who she was—

She almost laughed aloud. Why would anyone know who *she* was? Any passerby would only be interested in Lane. *He* was the star, wasn't he?

"Nora?" he said. He tried to put his hand under her chin to make her look at him, but she jerked away. "Nora?" he said again, sounding as confused as she felt, herself.

She drew in a shaky breath, and backed off. As unbelievable as it was, she wanted him more than ever. Even though they were no longer in contact, she could still feel the pressure of his lips on hers; she could still remember the way his arms had trembled when he held her, and how his body had reacted. She knew what he did to her; the wonder of it, she thought dazedly, was what she'd done to him.

How was this possible? she wondered. She didn't even like him. She didn't approve of him—not of his profession, his career, of anything he was or anything he had done.

"I don't know why that happened," she said, her voice shaking in spite of herself. "But it's not going to happen again."

"Nora, I—"

"No," she said. "I'm not going to make a bigger thing of it than it was."

"And what was it?"

His eyes glowed. She couldn't bear it. He looked as though he wanted to kiss her again, to take her in his arms and—

Or was that just the way *she* felt? "Don't look at me like that," she said.

"How am I looking at you, Nora?" he asked softly. "As though I find you a desirable woman? But I do. What happened right now when I kissed you—"

"Didn't I say we should forget it? Why are you pressing me like this? Why are you making such a big deal out of it?"

He took her arm. "Because it *was* a big deal," he said quietly, looking down at her. "You know it, and so do I."

She shook her head vehemently. "No. Nothing happened. It was just a ... a kiss that shouldn't have taken place. Now, let me go. I told you, it's been a long day and I want to go home.''

Mercifully, he took her at her word this time. But just as she was about to start the car, he leaned down and asked, ''Are we still going to see each other tomorrow night?''

She closed her eyes. After what had happened here tonight, the last thing she wanted was to meet in her home alone. ''I don't think that's a good idea.''

''If you're worried about—''

''I'm not worried about anything,'' she interrupted fiercely. ''I just don't think it's a good idea that we see each other again.''

''But what about—''

''I'm sorry, Lane.'' She couldn't stay here any longer. Starting the car with a roar, she put it in gear and drove away.

CHAPTER EIGHT

"OH, that was just great," Lane muttered to himself on the way home. He'd really handled *that* well. Nora had been so overwhelmed that she drove off and left him standing like a prize idiot right in the street.

What *was* it about that woman? he asked himself. Why didn't he just leave her alone—as she so obviously wanted him to do?

Because he couldn't, that's why. Nora Carmichael was unique; because she was so different from anyone else, maybe, with her, he could be himself.

Himself? Now there was a thought. He'd spent the past ten years—no, longer than that—denying the real Lane Kincaid existed. Was he really so tired of the subterfuge that he longed to expose the man under the facade, even to just one other person in his life?

The truth was he didn't know what he felt. All he could think of now was how Nora's slender body had felt in his arms, and how soft her lips had been under his.

He really didn't want to go home to his empty beach house, so he decided to head in another direction. As the Porsche purred under him, he wondered if he knew what he was doing. It was getting late, and he still had lines to study. Freddie had given everybody the night

off because he'd had to meet with some bigwigs up-
town, but that meant that they'd all be doing double-
time from now on. The project was in danger of going over budget, and word from on high was that if
Princeley insisted on spending so much money, the
least he could do was bring the enterprise in on time.

"Forget it, man, just go home," he muttered. But
he still found himself turning off the freeway some
time later into a rundown part of town.

Now he did slow down. Even though it was almost
ten, the main drag was crowded with kids—some in
cars driving aimlessly around, others hanging out in
groups on the sidewalks. Many of the stores were
empty; some had For Rent signs plastered across dirty
windows while other were simply boarded up. The
only businesses still open were the liquor stores, the
fast-food restaurants and the quick-check-cashing
places. Everything else that operated during the day
was locked up tighter than a drum. Lane couldn't help
thinking that there were more bars here than there
were in some prisons.

What have we come to? he wondered, feeling de-
pression settle on him like a weight, as it always did
when he came down to this area.

The street he wanted was just ahead. He never liked
coming here, but the kids drew him. He identified with
them. Once, he'd been just like they were, roaming the
streets at all hours, cutting school, driving aimlessly up
and down. It was a miracle, he knew, that he hadn't
gotten into more trouble than he had.

He recalled one incident that had happened during
those early years. He hadn't thought about it in a long

time, but in a strange way, it had been his salvation. What was that line people used? *Scared straight.* That had applied to him, all right.

Even now, he could remember how it had felt when the cop hauled him to his feet; he could still hear the awful slam of the patrol-car door when they'd locked him in the back seat. He'd been about fourteen at the time, recently dumped—for the last time, it turned out—by his mother to live with his grandmother. He hadn't wanted to be there, and because he was feeling so sorry for himself, it was easy for him to fall in with the wrong crowd.

The boys had all been older than he was—but not that much. How they'd gotten the liquor that particular night, he didn't know. He hadn't asked, he recalled: the night they'd taken him to their clubhouse, he'd been too eager to join the gang, too proud and awed to question anything.

He'd also been too scared to ask how the pint bottles had suddenly sprouted in their hands. Wanting desperately to belong to *something,* he'd gotten drunk like the rest of them. By the time the patrol car cruised by, he'd been so plastered he couldn't move. The other boys had scattered like leaves in a light wind, leaving *him* behind to explain to the cops—a sort of initiation rite, it seemed. If he survived it, he was in.

Remembering the incident, he smiled faintly. The problem, as he recalled, hadn't been explaining things to the cops, so much as it had been convincing his furious grandmother that he deserved a second chance. Like a ship in full sail, she had come steaming into the station house telling everyone who would listen that she didn't care if they locked him up and threw away the key. Scared, sick and sure that she meant what she said, he had promised never to be bad again.

He'd realized a long time ago that it had been an act to frighten him—and it had succeeded. From that day on, he had been a model citizen, or at least, as model as anyone could be, down here. But he'd worked hard, kept up his grades and finally graduated. The proudest moment of his life was when he had received his diploma. His grandmother had died before then, but he was sure that she'd been watching from somewhere, proud of him, too.

Still swamped with memories, he stopped the car outside a small building a block away from the main drag. Illuminated by a spotlight, a hand-painted sign hung over the entrance to the building. It read, simply, Teen Club. He remembered the day he'd hung that sign, and smiled again.

"You're not going to put up a sign that just says 'Boys' Club,' are you?" came a voice at him out of the past. It belonged to a girl who'd been leading a group of indignant teenage females. Her arms akimbo, she'd glared at him as he held the original sign. *"What about us?"*

"What would you like it to be?" he'd asked.

The paint was still wet. *"Teen* Club," she'd said, handing him a brush.

And so, with a few strokes of paint, the club belonged to both males and females. He was smiling at the memory as he started up the walk. On the way, he noted approvingly that the tiny patch of grass in front had recently been mowed. Everyone involved with the project knew that he didn't mind paying for what they needed, as long as they all made the effort to take care of it. As he reached for the door, he noted this was probably the only public building within twenty miles with no gang graffiti on it. Even better, he thought, the windows were not only unbroken, but actually clean, with real curtains hanging inside.

The club room itself was huge, with tables and chairs scattered around and on the far wall, a soft-drink machine with a counter and sink beside it. Bookshelves stuffed with everything from horror novels to microbiology texts were attached to another wall; opposite that was a hobby-craft workshop area, with built-in cupboards and strips of electrical outlets. A sign hung above the worktable listed two rules: *Put back what you take;* and *Leave someone else's business alone.*

"Lane! Hey, Lane, my *man!*" someone shouted over the thunder of rock music blaring from the stereo. There was a small television set on the table beside it, but it was switched off. A good thing, Lane thought. The rule was no television on school nights. The music was bad enough.

A group of kids were standing by one of the two pool tables at the end of the room. They all lifted their hands when they saw him, and he waved back. Normal conversation from this distance was impossible with all the noise, so he started in that direction. When he reached the table, he said teasingly to the boy who had greeted him, "What are you doing here, Hector? Aren't you supposed to be home studying?"

Hector grinned. "Aw, man, studyin's for sissies, you know? What use am I gonna have for calculus and chemistry and all those things you *gavachos* study?"

Lane grinned with him. He knew Hector was his family's pride and joy, a straight-*A* student who would be the first Saldano to attend college—on a scholarship, yet. Before meeting Lane, Hector had held down two jobs in addition to attending high school classes. Now he managed the club from after school until ten, with two stipulations: he had to do all his studying while he was here, and he couldn't take on another job until he graduated. Only a few people knew that Lane supplemented Hector's income. It was worth it, he thought. The pride in the boy's eyes proved it.

"And what about you, Anita?" he asked, turning to a tiny teenage girl wearing a short leather skirt and T-shirt that left little to the imagination.

Anita Rivera grinned at him, impudent as always. The big gold circles swinging from her ears were almost as big as she was, but he was aware that appearances were deceiving where Anita was concerned, too. He knew how difficult it had been for her parents to approach him a few years ago; the Riveras had been almost in tears because their daughter wanted a piano and they couldn't afford one. For Anita's sake, they had swallowed their pride and asked if he could buy one secondhand for the club. They'd do anything to pay him back, they'd said: cook his meals, clean his house, run all the errands he required. But Anita had to have a piano so she could practice.

"Can she play?" he'd asked.

Could she play? Another of the club's success stories, Anita had just been accepted to Juilliard, all expenses waived. The scholarship committee had been euphoric. Anita Rivera was a prodigy.

"I'm giving a recital here for everyone soon, Kincaid," Anita said sassily. "Sort of a going-away present before I leave for New York, you know? Do you think you can take time from your movie-making to come and hear it?"

"Just tell me when, and I'll be here," he said. Then he added with mock severity, "And don't give me a hard time about the movies, do you hear? Not all of us are musical geniuses, you know. Some of us have to work."

Anita tossed her head. "You call what you do work?"

"Well, I realize that playing pool for money is a little harder," he said, making a reference to Anita's habit of hustling newcomers.

Another girl moved forward, this one named LeeAnn. She was a tall, leggy blonde whose science project, something to do with kinetics, had won second prize in a prestigious state competition. She'd done it for fun, she'd told Lane. Her real interest was high fashion.

"So, Lane, whatcha doin' here so late at night?" she drawled with a grin. "Checkin' up on us, to make sure we're bein' good little boys and girls?"

"Well, someone has to keep track," he drawled back.

"Well, you know what I think?" She turned to her friends. "I think he's met a woman, and she's driving him crazy. That's why he's out so late, driving all the way down to the barrio from the beach." She turned back to him. "Am I right?"

"No, you're not right," he said. "And what makes you think that?"

Anita giggled. "Are you kidding, man? One look at you, and it's not hard to guess."

"Yeah, well, you ladies are wrong, I'm telling you. I'm always meeting women, it's no big deal."

With a knowing shrug, LeeAnn said, "Whatever you say, boss. But I've got a feeling that there's something different about this woman, whoever she is." Lazily taking her arm off his shoulders, she jerked her head in the direction of her friends. "Come on, we might as well go, now that Cinderella has arrived to ruin the ball."

Anita followed LeeAnn out, waggling her fingers at him before she left. "See you later, man," she said, her eyes bright. "I'll let you know about the recital."

"I'll hold you to it," Lane said.

"Oh, man, *girls,*" Hector muttered when they had gone. Shaking his head, he had just started toward the office to get the keys when there was a noise at the door. Lane thought the girls had come back to tease him, but when he glanced in that direction, what he saw was a tough-looking teenager dressed in jeans and leather jacket lounging against the door frame. Beside him, Hector tensed.

"Who's that?" Lane asked.

Hector's expression had turned hard. Out of the corner of his mouth, he said, "He calls himself Lobo, for Lone Wolf, but his real name is Jesse Hicks. He's been hanging around here a couple of days, looking for a chance to start trouble.''

His eyes still on the newcomer, Lane asked, "Any problems until now?''

Hector gave a brief shake of his head. "Maybe he thought I'd be alone tonight, who knows? Whatever it is, he's bad news. I'd be careful if I were you, man. Word is, he could be packing.''

"Packing" could mean carrying a knife or a gun. Lane had faced down hundreds of villains in his time, by outshooting, outfighting, outthinking and out-smarting even the most vicious Uzi-wielding gunman. But that was in films. This was real life, where there was no script, no marks to hit, no chances to do it over if you made a mistake with your lines.

Jesse looked about seventeen—young and hard. His long hair was half-hidden under a black baseball cap turned backward; the aggressive, looking-for-trouble expression in his dark eyes wasn't promising. Lane decided that the best defense was a hey-we-got-no-problems-here offense, and strolled over to the kid. Behind him, he sensed that Hector was ready to sprint for the telephone.

"Hi," Lane said easily. "We're getting ready to close up for the night. What can we do for you?''

Jesse's eyes flickered. Lane wondered whether the teenager recognized him. Or maybe Lane's size made the boy hesitate. In spite of his tough stance, Jesse stood only about five foot six. Straightening from his loutish position against the door, he said sullenly, "Nothin', man. I jus' came in to see what was hangin', you know?''

"I haven't seen you around before," Lane said. Casually, he moved a step or two forward. "You from this neighborhood?"

It was clear that Jesse wanted to back up to give himself breathing room, but since the door was behind him, his only alternative was to step through it and lose face. Caught, he glowered belligerently. His hand moved in his pocket, and, seeing it, Lane tensed.

"What's it to you, man?" Jesse asked.

Lane shrugged. "It's nothing to me, I just wondered. This is a neighborhood club, so if you're not from around here, I'm afraid you can't join."

Jesse's lip curled. "Join? I'd sooner burn the place down."

"Was that what you had in mind?"

"What if it was?"

Lane took another step closer. Every sense was tuned in to that hand in the leather jacket pocket.

"If it was," he said easily, "I wouldn't like it."

"Yeah?" Jesse sneered. "Well, man, I know who you are. You're the big movie star who comes slummin' now and then. The guy who kills everybody in the movies. Well, you know what? I came to see just how tough you really are."

Before Lane could move, Jesse pulled a switchblade. The deadly *snick* the blade made as it extended sounded like a firecracker in the taut silence. Behind him, Lane thought he heard Hector draw in a breath, but he didn't take his eyes off the kid with the knife.

"Put it away, Jesse," he said quietly.

But instead of retracting the lethal blade, Jesse lunged toward Lane with it. If Lane's reactions hadn't been as quick as they were, he would have been cut. As it was, the knife missed his face by a millimeter. Jesse was just swinging it around again for another attack when Lane grabbed the boy's wrist. His grip was so powerful that Jesse cried out.

"Let go! Let go, man!"

Lane had no intention of letting Jesse go—at least not until he had the weapon. He tightened his grip, effectively paralyzing the kid's hand; when Jesse's knees started to buckle, Lane reached up with his other hand and took the knife from him.

"Give that back!" Jesse cried, despite the obvious pain in his arm. "It's mine! You got no right!"

"No right?" Lane repeated, staring him down. "You pulled this on me. You tried to cut me with it. I'd say that gives me a right." For emphasis, he gave the kid's arm a shake, and Jesse's face whitened with new pain. He began to look scared.

"I wasn't goin' to do anything, I swear it. I was just tryin' to scare you!"

Lane didn't change expression. "Yeah, well, you succeeded. And now I'm going to pay you back."

"Pay me... What are you goin' to do?"

He still had a hold of the kid's wrist. Jesse tried to free himself with his other hand, but his fingers just scrabbled ineffectively against Lane's superior strength. Real fear leaped into his eyes as he looked up at the man; sweat shone on his face.

"I didn't mean anything, honest," he said, almost in tears. There was no trace of the bravado he'd swaggered in on before. "Come on, mister...please. You're hurtin' me."

"Like you would have hurt me with that knife?"

"I *told* you, I was just tryin' to scare you! I promise, I'll never do it again!"

Lane wasn't ready to let him off the hook. "To anyone? Do I have your word on that?"

"I swear!" The boy was now so frightened that he actually crossed his chest. "Never again."

"Good," Lane said. "Because we don't allow stuff like that at the club. No weapons, no smoking, no drinking, no dope. You got that?"

Wincing, Jesse tried to struggle against Lane's vise-like fingers. "Who said I wanted to belong to this stupid club? I told you, I just came around to—"

"To what? To scare the kids here? To threaten them? Maybe you got a little business going on the side, and you wanted to recruit, was that it?" He tightened his grasp on the kid's wrist again. Jesse looked like he was about to fall into a faint; the only thing that kept him upright was the fact that Lane was holding him there.

"No, man, I swear! It was nothin' like that! I just wanted to see what was goin' down, you know? What's wrong with that?"

Lane had grown up on these streets. He knew when someone was lying, and when they weren't. Jesse was scared enough now to be telling him the truth. For a long, tense moment, Lane looked him in the eye.

"All right," he said at last. "But I'm going to hold you to that promise. If I ever hear that you've threatened anyone, or tried this on again..."

There was a dart board across the room. In one swift move, almost too fast to see, Lane turned and threw the knife. It flew through the air, landing with a resounding *thud,* point first, almost in the center of the bull's-eye. It was still vibrating when he turned back to Jesse. Behind him, Hector's eyes were out on stalks.

His eyes wide as he stared at the quivering knife, Jesse forgot all about the pain in his wrist. "Man," he whispered, "I never saw *anyone* do that!"

"Yeah, well, don't forget it," Lane said. "You can come around, but if I ever catch you carrying anything more dangerous than a toothpick, *you'll* be the one hanging from that dart board, got it?"

"I got it," Jesse said meekly.

"Good. Now, get going. It's time for us to close up."

Lane didn't realize just how tense he was until Jesse had gone. Hector was still standing in the middle of the big room staring at the dart board. When Lane saw the teenager's expression, he grinned.

"I couldn't do that again in a million years," he said. "So don't ask."

Awed, Hector shook his head. "Seeing it once was worth it. I didn't think *anyone* could do that with a switchblade."

Lane decided not to tell Hector about the knife-throwing expert who had spent three weeks with him one time on location, teaching him to throw a knife so that it landed where he aimed it. At the time, he'd cursed both his clumsiness and the blisters that blossomed on his hands. He'd never thought he'd have to use that particular skill again. How he'd dredged it up again after all this time he didn't know, but he wasn't going to ask questions now.

"Yeah, well, I don't think that kid will give you any more trouble, but if he does, let me know, will you?"

"The minute it happens," Hector said, glancing at the knife. "Thanks, Lane."

"Just glad to help, pilgrim, just glad to help," Lane said, in a parody of John Wayne. He patted the boy's shoulder. "Time to lock up and head for home."

HE WAS ALMOST home when an idea struck him. It came because of his joking around with the cowboy talk. He'd been thinking of Nora again when he came up with something so brilliant that he just knew it had to work. Nora had suggested he invest in transportation stock, hadn't she? Well, tomorrow he was going to do just that. Delighted with his cleverness, he drove the rest of the way home feeling fine. She was going to be so surprised, he thought. He could hardly wait to see her face.

CHAPTER NINE

NORA WAS HEADING out to work when the phone rang. She stopped, wondering if she should answer. The answering machine would pick up, she thought...and then realized she'd forgotten to switch it on. What was wrong with her lately? She never forgot things like that.

When the phone rang a second time, she knew that if she didn't answer, she'd never know who called. It could be someone from the office, Mr. Bullard, maybe, or one of the secretaries. It could even be...

Now *why* would she think it might be Lane? she asked herself irritably. That was absurd. She couldn't have been more clear about her feelings than she had been the other night.

The phone rang again. Sighing, she put her briefcase and car keys down and reached for the receiver.

"Hello?"

"Darling!" Theodora exclaimed. "Oh, I'm glad I caught you. I know you leave early, so I took a chance and called at the crack of dawn."

"Eight-thirty is hardly the crack of dawn. Even so, what are you doing up? It's so rare that you see the sun before noon."

"Mock all you like, my girl, but I'll have you know that Freddie has had us all hard at work since early this morning. I tried to protest the beastly schedule, but he just muttered something about the light at that hour. *What* light, I'd like to know. It was still black as ink when my driver came to get me, so what was the point?"

"I'd like to ask you the same thing, Mother," Nora said, her eye on the clock. She'd already put Chauncy out in the backyard, and usually she left for work immediately after that. Now, obviously sensing that the routine had been interrupted, the dog had come to peer in through the sliding-glass patio doors. Turning her back on his sad eyes, she asked, "Did you call for a reason?"

"Of course, I did. Would I have bothered you otherwise?"

"Well, not at this hour, anyway," Nora said dryly. Then she thought of something and asked quickly, "Is anything wrong? You're not sick, or in the hospital, are you?"

"Now, darling, you know I promised never to do that again, didn't I?"

Theodora was referring to an incident some years before, when she had been hospitalized in London with pneumonia. Nora had found out like everyone else had—through an item in the celebrity section of the newspaper. Frightened—and angry that she hadn't been notified—she'd called every hospital in that city until she'd located her mother. But when she'd finally gotten through, Theodora's reaction was typical. She felt fine. The hospitalization was just a precaution insisted upon by an overzealous producer. She hadn't wanted to worry anyone, especially her daughter.

"*Worry* me next time," Nora had ordered. "Promise!"

Theodora had promised. She'd kept it until now, at least as far as Nora knew.

"I'm just fine," Theodora said this morning. "The reason I'm calling is that Arthur would like to meet you. And I'd like you to meet him, of course. After all, you're the two most important people in my life."

"I won't ask in which order. I'm flattered, anyway. I'd like to meet him, too. What did you have in mind?"

"Well, he is giving a dinner party soon—"

"Oh, Mother, you know how I hate those things!"

"Don't worry. Even *I* wouldn't subject you to something like that. Arthur's guests are business acquaintances, so while I usually adore parties, I can imagine that—despite my considerable talents at entertaining—it's going to be something of a drag."

Nora had to smile. "I can't imagine you allowing that to happen at any party you attend."

"Why, thank you, darling," Theodora said warmly. Then she teased, "But it seems to run in the family, doesn't it? As I recall, you made quite a splash the last time you attended one."

Nora didn't want to talk about that. "Since the party's out," she said pointedly, "what do you suggest?"

"Well, I thought the three of us could have dinner. Did I tell you I persuaded Chan to come to California with me? I really hate to eat out—there are always so many interruptions—but we could have our own little do here. What do you think of that idea?''

"I'm not sure. As you so subtly pointed out, I don't know if that house is safe where I'm concerned.''

She'd been joking, but Theodora immediately said in alarm, "You're not going to bring that *dog,* are you?''

She laughed. "No, I think this time it would be better if I left Chauncy at home. All right, Mother, what night shall I come?''

"I thought... Wednesday? But if that's not convenient, you choose the time. I'll have Arthur there if I have to hog-tie him.''

Nora smiled. "He's that eager to meet me, then?''

"Oh, he is, believe me. But sometimes even *I* have to make an appointment to see him. I'm sure I've told you what a workaholic he is. In fact, despite my somewhat vehement protests on occasion, he's never without one of those silly beepers, in case any of his people have to get hold of him.''

"Are you sure he has time for me?'' Nora asked dryly. "Maybe we should forget dinner, and I'll make an appointment to meet him in his office.''

"No, we're having dinner, and that's all there is to it,'' Theodora insisted. "So, shall we say Wednesday? I know you both have to work the next day, and heaven knows what kind of schedule my sadistic director is going to have us on. We'll make it an unfashionably early evening. How about... seven?''

"Seven's just fine,'' Nora said. Reminded of the time, she glanced at the clock again and started to say, "I'll see you—''

"Wait! I had something else to ask you."

Trying not to sound impatient, she asked, "What?"

"Well, it's about the dinner party Arthur is giving."

"What about it?" Nora asked. Could it be that she'd heard an anxious note in her mother's voice? It was hard to believe. Theodora had nerves of steel and a constitution to match. She had performed before royalty without a qualm; she'd had a private audience with the Pope. She'd even been presented to the Queen of England. Surely, she couldn't be nervous about a simple little dinner party.

"Arthur has asked me to be his hostess," Theodora said. "And would you believe it, I'm actually feeling a little nervous about it!" She laughed shortly. "Isn't that ridiculous? But I do so want things to go well, and I'm not sure they will."

"Why do you think that?"

"Well, as I said, Arthur's guests are all business-people, and you know how I feel about that. And . . . oh, Nora, you have to help me. You must attend affairs like this all the time. How *do* women dress for business dinners these days?"

"You mean, what do we ordinary females wear for such occasions?" Nora asked.

"Darling, please!"

"Oh, all right, if you're serious, just think of this. When in doubt, wear a simple black dress."

"Black?" Theodora repeated doubtfully. "But you know I've always detested black. It does terrible things for my skin, and besides, I've always believed it's for people with no imagination at all!"

"Well, thanks!"

"Oh, you know I didn't mean it like that. It's just that the party is looming, and after going through my closet, I realized I don't have anything to wear."

Nora smiled. Her mother traveled with a minimum of six trunks, plus a variety of suitcases and dress bags—and that was just for a weekend. At home, Theodora also had a closet the size of a small house, but since she was only here for a short while, Nora suspected that her wardrobe had probably been squashed into only *one* of the bedrooms at Brock's Beverly Hills mansion.

"Now, Mother, I know you," she said. "But if you really don't have anything suitable, why don't you ask the costume department? They've supplied you before, too many times to count."

"Not this time. Oh, what am I going to do? You know, it's all Freddie's fault. He's working us night and day. None of us have time for a *life,* much less a spare minute or two to go shopping!"

"Yes, Lane told me—" she stopped abruptly, biting her lip. She hadn't meant to mention Lane Kincaid. Like a retriever sighting a bird, Theodora came to a point.

"Lane, did you say?" Theodora asked innocently. "You didn't mention that you were seeing him."

"*Seeing* him? I hardly know him. We had a business discussion—once. And the other night he came to a lecture I gave."

"Oh, dear, how *very* romantic."

"Exactly the point."

"That's not what I meant, darling. Besides, don't you think Lane is—"

"If you say good-looking, I'm going to hang up. Besides, I don't care *how* attractive he is."

"Ah, so you do think he's attractive. That's a beginning, at least."

"Mother, I don't know where you're going with this, but you can stop right now. You know how I feel about actors—"

"Oh, yes, you've made your feelings very clear over the years. It's just that I thought—"

She paused, and before Nora could stop herself, she asked, "You thought what?"

"I thought this time might be different, that's all."

"And why would you think that?"

Theodora laughed gently. "Well, darling, if you could hear yourself—"

"Well, I can't," Nora said peevishly. "And as much as I would love to continue this conversation, I'm afraid I have to cut it short. I have to leave for work—"

"I understand," Theodora said blithely. "We won't talk about it anymore, if you wish."

"I do."

"You aren't angry with me, are you?"

"No, I'm not angry. I'm just in a hurry."

"Are you sure that's all it is? I know how you get when you sound so prickly."

"I'm not prickly!"

"Whatever you say," Theodora said meekly. "But may I say one thing?"

"Only if you make it fast."

"I had lunch with Lane the other day, and I really think there's more to him than meets the eye."

"Oh, really? Well, you could have fooled me."

"Why, Nora, what a thing to say!"

"Well, it's true." Before she knew it, she was going on in a rush, "If he's so special, why hasn't he done anything to prove himself? Why keep doing the same thing over and over? You don't do that, you never did. You constantly challenge yourself. And so did Dad—" She stopped. "I'm sorry," she said. "I didn't mean to bring up Dad. It's just that Lane is like so many of the other actors I've known."

"Oh, you mean self-centered and egotistical and needing always to be in the limelight?"

Nora flushed at the implied rebuke. "You know you're the exception. As for Lane—I think all he cares about is his image. It was clear the other night when he came to the lecture. He draws a crowd everywhere he goes, and he loves it. He's always showing off, and he's glib and flippant. I don't think he's ever had a serious moment in his entire life."

"It might seem that way to you because you don't know him," Theodora said calmly. "I still think that one day he's going to surprise you."

"Oh, no, he won't."

"Why not?"

"Because I'm not going to give him the chance, that's why. Now, I really have to get off the phone, Mother. I'm late, and I've got a full day."

THEODORA MIGHT BE a professional at work, but she was a star in every other sense. On Wednesday night, before she arrived, Nora had bet herself that her mother wouldn't be ready. She won, hands down.

"I knew you'd be late," she said accusingly, when one of the maids had let her in and she went upstairs to find Theodora still sitting at the dressing table.

Blithely ignoring her daughter's words, Theodora waved to a nearby chaise. "I'm almost ready. Freddie didn't let us out until the last minute. And besides, Arthur isn't here yet, so we have plenty of time." She paused in the act of applying more mascara, peering at Nora through the mirror. "You didn't bring that dog with you, did you?"

Nora couldn't help teasing her a little. "His name is Chauncy, Mother, and he's down in the car. Do you mind if I bring him in? He promised he'd be good. No destroying statues, or attacking guests."

"A pity then, that Lane can't be here," Theodora said calmly. Capping the mascara, she looked at Nora innocently.

"Oh, Mother, you didn't—"

Theodora laughed. "No, darling, I didn't. Although I admit, I was tempted. *I* happen to think Lane is a wonderful man. I can't imagine why—"

"Then, don't," Nora said testily. "Why are we talking about him, anyway? I thought we agreed—"

"We did, darling," Theodora said. She got up from the dressing table, and gave Nora a quick kiss before she went to the walk-in closet. As she disappeared into its vast interior, she added, "I still don't understand why you don't like him. But I respect your wishes. I knew you'd be angry if I invited him—"

"That's an understatement," Nora muttered.

"What's that?"

"Never mind," Nora said. Just then, she heard the doorbell chime, and she raised her voice. "Unless you've invited someone else I don't want to know about, I think Arthur's here."

Theodora came back to the closet doorway and stuck her head out. "Would you go down and entertain him for me, darling?"

"Me? But I don't even know the man!"

"Oh, but I've told you both so much about each other, I'm sure you won't have any problems at all," Theodora said before vanishing inside the closet again. Her voice slightly muffled, she added, "Do go on down, Nora. I'll be ready in two minutes, I promise."

"I've heard that before," Nora said. But it seemed she didn't have any other choice, so she went downstairs.

A man was waiting in the living room when she entered, his back to her as he studied a painting over the fireplace.

"Hello," Nora said. "I'm Nora Carmichael. And you—"

He turned with a smile. "Arthur Winslow," he said, grasping her outstretched hand. "I'm pleased to meet you at last, Nora. Your mother has told me so much about you."

Nora had seen Arthur Winslow's picture on countless magazine covers; she'd read numerous articles about him and his industrial empire. But when they sat on one of the couches to get acquainted, she realized that nothing she'd seen or read had prepared her for the actual man. His publicity photos invariably depicted him as patrician, stately, almost austere; in person, he seemed anything but. His smile was warm and his blue eyes twinkled. When he laughed at something she said about her mother's tardiness, she realized that he either deliberately fostered a cold image for business purposes, or she'd gotten a completely wrong impression of him. Probably both, she thought.

"Your mother tells me you work for Bullard and Sweeney, in Pasadena," he said, when they were seated.

"Yes, I'm an investment consultant for the firm," she said, deliberately downplaying her role. She knew that Arthur Winslow had people after him all the time and she didn't want him to think she was going to be one of them. "I came to them last year."

"You're being too modest, my dear," he said. "The way I heard it, you were recruited from the Allfred Trust in New York."

She smiled. "My mother talks too much."

"Your mother has an understandable pride in her daughter's accomplishments," he corrected with a smile of his own. "But I must be honest here. Theodora didn't tell me about your former position with the Trust. I admit, I was curious and did a little checking. It's a bad habit of mine, I'm afraid. I hope you aren't offended."

"Offended?" How could she be offended that a man of his stature and position had taken the time to find out more about her? "Actually, I'm flattered."

"Thank you," he said, pleased. Then he looked at her curiously. "I also hear that you've got the biggest dog in canine history. What's his name? Don't tell me—Chaucer? No, Chauncy.''

Her lips twitched. "You *are* well informed."

"Love dogs myself," he said. "I used to have a pack of 'em when I was younger. Beagles. Now, there's a busy little dog for you. And my mother raised Afghan hounds. Beautiful creatures, but hard to keep penned in. I still remember them floating over the fences at the house in Connecticut, all that long hair drifting out behind them." He paused a moment, his expression faraway. Then he shook his head. "Hadn't thought about those dogs for a long time. Now that I think about it, I miss them."

"You don't have a dog now?"

"Don't have time, I'm afraid. Dogs need attention, you know, or what's the use of having them?" He looked at her again. "You pay attention to Chauncy, don't you?"

"Oh, indeed, I do," she said, her eyes twinkling. "If I don't, he reminds me loud and clear that I'm neglecting him. Besides, when a dog as big as Chauncy wants something, you give it to him!"

They were laughing together when Theodora came into the room. "Well, well!" she exclaimed, pausing dramatically on the threshold, her rainbow-colored caftan swirling around her. "Shall I be pleased or piqued that you two seem to have forgotten all about me?"

"Oh, definitely pleased, Mother," Nora said. "I've enjoyed meeting Arthur."

"As have I enjoyed meeting Nora," Arthur said, rising. "I knew she would be, Theodora, but your daughter is absolutely charming."

"Oh, I'm so glad you like each other!" Theodora exclaimed.

As though he'd been waiting for her entrance, Chan appeared in the doorway behind her. Bowing slightly, he said, "If all are ready, dinner is served."

Smiling brilliantly, Theodora held out her hands, one to Arthur, the other to Nora. "Shall we, my dears?" she said.

NORA DIDN'T get home until almost one in the morning. The "early evening" she and her mother had planned had extended effortlessly until they were all amazed to see that it was nearly midnight.

Nora was just letting Chauncy in, and giving him a rawhide bone as a reward for successfully guarding the house when the phone rang. She knew who it was even before she answered, and she picked up the receiver with a smile.

"Hello, Mother," she said.

"How did you know it was I?"

"Who else is going to call me at one in the morning?"

"Well, I wanted to catch you before you went to bed. So, what did you think? Isn't Arthur a darling?"

"He is," Nora agreed.

"You don't think he's a . . . well, a touch too somber?"

Nora felt mellow enough to poke a little fun at herself. "You're asking me, the one who sometimes thinks the chairman of the fed is too frivolous?"

"The chairman of the fed?"

"Never mind. It was a little financial community humor. But to answer your question, I think Arthur is perfect for you."

"Then perhaps the question is, am I right for him?"

Surprised, she asked, "Why do you say that?"

"Oh, because...well, Nora, you know how I am—"

"All too well, I'm afraid," she said dryly. "But apparently, so does Arthur. And it's obvious that he's in love with you, so *he* must think you're right for him, and isn't that what matters?"

"Oh, darling," Theodora said. "How did you get to be so wise, at your young age?"

Before Nora could reply, an image of Lane's face flashed through her mind. When she remembered how she had acted the last time they'd met, she frowned. That hadn't been wise, had it?

"I'm not wise," she said, not realizing how forlorn she suddenly sounded. "I think it's easy to have perspective when you're not involved yourself."

Theodora was silent a moment. Then she said, "Yes, I think you're right. Well, thank you, darling. I do so appreciate your coming tonight, and Arthur was absolutely delighted to meet you. You made quite a hit, you know."

"Did I? Well, he did with me, too. Oh, and good luck with your upcoming dinner party." Wickedly, she added, "Have you decided what to wear yet?"

"Not yet," Theodora answered. "But I'll have to come up with something, won't I? Good night, darling. Sleep well."

"You, too. Let me know what happens."

"You'll be the first one I call."

CHAPTER TEN

WHEN NORA ARRIVED at the office, she was immediately irritated by the sight of Rodney Jones, who had cornered the new temporary typist in the lunchroom. Due to a recent influx of clients, Ginger and Sherrie couldn't keep up with all the work, so Stephanie Meadows had been hired on an interim basis. Nora liked Stephanie, whose typing was machine-gun quick, but she had seen right from the beginning that the girl was going to be susceptible to the smooth-talking Rodney. She knew it was none of her business, but since they were standing in the room when she went to get a cup of coffee, she couldn't ignore them.

Stephanie smiled at her when Nora entered, but Rodney could barely conceal his annoyance at the interruption. "Good morning," he said, pointedly glancing at his watch. "Running a little late, are we?"

Seeing Nora's expression darken, Stephanie said hurriedly, "Rodney's just started to tell me about insider trading. It's the most interesting thing!"

"Is it?" Nora reached for a coffee cup. She and Rodney had had discussions about the subject before; to say they were in disagreement was putting it mildly.

"Oh, yes," Stephanie said. "In fact, Rodney was just mentioning the Stamford company. Have you heard of them, Nora?"

Nora put the coffee carafe back on the hot plate. "Do you mean the investment bankers?"

"They call themselves investment bankers," Rodney said patronizingly. "But what they really do is specialize in IPO's."

"IPO's?" Stephanie asked.

"Initial public offerings," Nora said, reaching for the sugar substitute. She knew it would irritate Rodney if she stole his thunder, but she didn't care. "When a company wants to offer stock for the first time, it's called an initial public offering. Stamford is one of the firms that underwrites such offerings."

Rodney glared impatiently at her before he turned to Stephanie. "That means they put up the money."

"Well, it's a little more complicated than that," Nora said. "The normal function of investment bankers is to put capital into a young company to help it grow. Then, at a later date, when the company is more solid, they take it public to make their money back. Stamford does it differently."

Rodney knew what Nora was going to say. "It's an entirely legal way of doing business!"

She looked at Stephanie again. "What Rodney is trying *not* to say is that Stamford is an example of insider trading. Instead of taking the risk themselves, they let investors do most of the financing by convincing them to buy into a company that doesn't even exist yet."

As though she were at a tennis match, Stephanie's head was swiveling back and forth between Nora and Rodney. "I don't get it," she said. "Why would someone invest in something that doesn't exist?"

"Because they think they're going to get rich, that's why," Rodney said. Figuratively elbowing Nora aside, he explained. "Look, here's how it goes. Let's say you're working in a garage somewhere and you come up with a new way to do something. It's a great idea, but it's going to cost a lot of money that you don't have. You need financing, so where do you go? To someone like the investment bankers at Stamford, who will invest in your project."

Nora wasn't going to let him gloss over it. "Yes, but what the inventor doesn't know is that Stamford has their own deal going."

Rodney glowered at her. "They put up some of the money."

"Only because they have to," Nora retorted. "Most of the capital isn't theirs, and even before they offer stock, they make their own deal with the inventor— usually for around sixty percent."

"Well, so what?" Rodney demanded. "If someone is willing to give them that much, what's the harm?"

"The harm," Nora said, "is that Stamford not only uses other people's money to finance a new company, they end up owning more than half of that same company."

"Only if it's successful," Rodney stated, as if that justified it.

Disgusted, Nora retorted, "But if the new company goes under, they haven't lost anything, either. After all, it's someone else's money, not theirs."

Apparently even Stephanie felt the temperature rising. "I'd better get back to work," she said, edging toward the door. "Thanks for the...er...discussion. I really learned a lot."

Nora was about to follow Stephanie out the door when Rodney put a hand on her arm. Surprised, she looked at him. He was so close that she caught a whiff of his strong after-shave, and her nostrils contracted. But whether it was from the cologne or dislike, she couldn't tell.

"You wanted something?" she asked pointedly. She looked from his hand on her arm, back to his face. Lately he'd adopted the affectation of wearing the little round wire-rimmed glasses that young men favored these days. He obviously thought it made him look sophisticated; Nora thought it made him look silly.

He leaned toward her. She hadn't noticed before, but in addition to the cologne and the glasses, he was wearing some kind of gel on his hair. It made him seem even more slick.

"Don't think I don't know what you're up to, Nora," he said, his voice low and menacing. "If that little display just now was meant to show me up, you failed."

"Did I?" She didn't want to argue further with him, but she was curious. "And what makes you think I want to show you up?"

"You know why," he said nastily. "You want that promotion as much as I do. Well, you're not going to get it. I am."

Unimpressed by his bluster, she said, "Is that so? And what makes you so certain?"

"I can read between the lines. You might be good at your job—damn good, in fact, I have to admit it. But you could be the absolute best and you'd never get that promotion—or the partnership I also know you want."

Nora was doing her best to hold on to her temper. "Well, we'll see, won't we?" she said. "In the meantime, I think—"

"Don't you want to know why you won't succeed?" he asked, his eyes glinting maliciously behind his glasses. Before she could tell him she didn't care about his opinion, he told her. "You see, I *know* people like Orrin Bullard—I grew up around them, I know what they're like. They might *say* they're open-minded, they might even believe they are. But when it comes right down to it, they go with their own. And the truth is, with your background, you just won't make the cut."

Nora was so angry she could have struck him. Her lips stiff, she said, "Perhaps you'd better explain that remark. What do you mean by my 'background'?"

"Oh, come on, Nora, don't be dense. You know exactly what I mean." His lip actually curled. "It's the show-business element, of course. People of, shall we say, more *liberal* bent love to rub elbows with those in entertainment, but I guarantee you that Mr. Bullard doesn't. It's just not the right image for the firm. Oh, he doesn't mind having you on the team—as I said, you're damn good at what you do and he knows it. But as for being promoted to a more *visible* position? Never." He sneered again. "I'm surprised you haven't figured that out for yourself."

"Thank you so much for the input," Nora said frostily. "But as interesting a theory as it is, I believe that Mr. Bullard will make the decision, not you. Until then, we can only do what we can do. But let me tell you one thing—"

His eyes glinted again. "What?"

"If you don't get your hand off my arm, I'm going to break it."

EVEN BEFORE she slammed the door to the office, she was sorry she'd threatened Rodney. She knew she should have simply walked out, dignity intact, but once again, the temper that she thought she'd learned to control had betrayed her.

Angrily, she banged her fist down. She'd always known that Rodney couldn't stoop low enough to get what he wanted—and what he wanted was the same promotion she did. They were both aware that whoever got it would eventually be in line for partner, for even though Brent Sweeney's name was still on the door, he had retired some years before. Bullard had managed without him until now, but in the future, he'd need someone to help carry the load. That was one of the main reasons Nora had moved back to California. The possibility of rapid advancement had been an irresistible lure.

It was still a goal to be pursued. Until this morning, the competition between her and Rodney had been tacitly understood; they hadn't made any secret of the fact that they didn't like each other, but they had managed to be civil. Now things had changed. The fact that he was trying to intimidate her must mean that he felt threatened, too. Well, good, she thought fiercely. She *wanted* him to be off-balance. She might not be able to do anything about his remarks just now, but no one could deny performance. She'd work so hard and put in so many hours and clinched so many good deals for her clients that Orrin Bullard would *have* to reward her. On that thought, she reached grimly for her briefcase.

Three hours flew by. Determined to make her anger work for her instead of against her, she was concentrating so deeply that she didn't even realize it was lunchtime until she heard a commotion in the outer office. Alerted by the buzz, she glanced toward the door. That wasn't the usual noon-hour flurry of secretaries leaving, she thought; it sounded like...

She stood with a rush. Her mother had caused that exact reaction when she'd first dropped by the office, and at the thought, she groaned. The last thing she needed right now was for her mother to sail in, causing an uproar. Dropping everything, she ran to the door, jerked it open and dashed into the hall.

"Mother—"

It wasn't Theodora. When she saw who was standing out by Sherrie's desk, amiably signing autographs, she froze in midstep. Oh, no! she thought. What was *he* doing here?

"Lane!" she cried.

As though he hadn't a care in the world, he turned toward her with a smile. "Hi, Nora," he said. "I'll be with you in a minute. I just want to sign these."

Fuming, she had to watch while Sherrie and Ginger acted as though they'd reverted to teenagers. Nora could have shaken them both.

She waited until Lane began to walk down the hall with the nonchalant long-strided walk that had helped to make him famous. "What are you doing here?" she demanded. "In case you hadn't noticed," she added as she hustled him into her office and slammed the door, "this is a place of business. Why didn't you make an appointment?"

"Would you have seen me if I had?"

He had her there, so she didn't answer. Moving away from him, she went to her desk and sat down. Trying to hide the mortifying fact that her heart had begun to pound the moment she'd seen him, she said curtly, "I'm very busy, Lane. What do you want?"

"You're always busy," he said, perching casually on the edge of the desk with an amused expression. "That's why I came, to rescue you from yourself."

She glared at him. "I don't need rescuing. Especially by you."

She hadn't wanted to, but she'd noticed that his slacks and blue-on-blue sports shirt did great things for his tan and his eyes. In fact, the contrast between Lane and the other men in the office—particularly Rodney—was so great that she couldn't blame Sherrie and Ginger for swooning. She could almost swoon, herself. How was she supposed to resist him when he looked like this?

She had to; that's all there was to it. "What do you want, Lane?" she said again. "As I said, I'm—"

"I know—busy. Well, that's okay, I'll understand if you don't have time to come with me. I just thought you might like to see the investment you recommended."

Aggravated that she couldn't seem to get herself under control, she said, "What do you mean, *see* what I recommended? I don't know what you're talking about!"

"Don't you remember?" he asked. "You told me to invest in transportation stock, and I did."

Just for an instant, curiosity got the best of her, but she squashed it ruthlessly. She didn't trust him, she reminded herself; she trusted herself even less. She wouldn't be drawn into...whatever this was. All she had to do was keep her mind on business.

"Fine, then," she said, holding out her hand. "Show me the certificates."

"The certificates?"

"Yes, Lane, the stock certificates," she snapped. As long as she remained angry or impatient with him, she wouldn't think about the way he looked...or how his body had felt against hers the other night.

And why was she thinking about that right now? she wondered in exasperation. Really annoyed with herself, she said, "Well, I'm glad you listened to me about something. And if you're finally acting sensibly at last about your finances, I congratulate you. Now, if you don't mind—"

"I really would like you to see this, Nora. It won't take long. I'll have you back in an hour or two, no longer than that, I promise."

She didn't want to go anywhere with him. Even in the relative safety of her office she could feel a...a *pull* toward him. She couldn't take the chance of something more happening if they went out, so she shook her head. "I told you, I can't. I have meetings, appointments—"

"I'm not leaving unless you come with me."

She looked at him sharply. "That's ridiculous. This is a workday. I can't just take off!"

"Of course you can. Tell your boss that you have a meeting with a client." His eyes twinkled. "An important client. Or—wait. If you like, I'll go tell him. Where's his office?"

"Wait!" she cried when he got up from the desk. "You can't talk to Mr. Bullard!"

He turned back to her with a smile. "Does this mean you've changed your mind?"

"No, I haven't! Now, Lane, you have to stop this. We both know you're not serious—"

"Oh, yes, I am," he said. His smile vanished, and he started around the desk toward her. As he came closer, she backed up until the file cabinet stopped her. He was so close now that if she took a step forward, she'd walk right into his arms.

"Why are you doing this?" she asked, her voice shrill.

He started to say something, but then seemed to change his mind. "Because I think we got off on the wrong foot. And because I know what a bad opinion you have of actors. I wanted to show you we weren't all irresponsible, Nora. Will you give me the chance?"

She knew she should say no. She knew she should tell him to turn around and leave and never bother her again. She couldn't make herself do it.

I'll see what he has to show me today, she thought. *It's only fair. But after that, I'll never see him again. Never.*

"So, are you coming with me?" he asked, his eyes on her face.

"Okay. But only for an hour. That's all the time I have, and I shouldn't even take that."

"We'll call it your lunch hour, if you insist. You *do* get one of those, don't you?"

Her lips tightened. "Tell me where we're going."

His eyes twinkled again. "You'll see."

"WHAT ARE WE doing here?" she asked as they pulled into a special section of the vast parking lot in front of one of horse racing's landmarks, Santa Anita Race-track, in nearby Arcadia.

He ignored her question, which irritated her. He was whistling as he got out and came around to open her door. She ignored his proffered hand, and climbed out by herself. "Why are you so cheerful all the time?" she asked crossly.

"Well, it's a beautiful day, and I'm with a beautiful woman, and we're about to do something I've been looking forward to ever since I arranged it. Why shouldn't I be cheerful?"

Making a pretense of smoothing her skirt, she didn't answer. She felt overdressed in her heels and severe business suit—especially when, over in the main parking lot, race-goers in jeans and shorts and sneakers were heading toward the main gates. Nora had never been to the track, so the sign indicating that the lot in which Lane had parked was reserved for trainers and owners didn't mean anything to her.

"What are we doing here?" she repeated her question. "I thought you said you bought transportation stock. Is this some kind of joke?"

"Lord, woman, you are so suspicious," he said with a sigh. "Come on, let's go before someone sees me. No, wait. I forgot my disguise. It won't be as much fun if I'm recognized."

With that, he took a pair of wraparound sunglasses from his pocket, then reached back into the car for a baseball cap, and pulled it so low over his ears that it hid half his face. Nora burst into laughter despite herself.

"You look ridiculous in that getup!"

"Hey, it works—sometimes," he said, and then put his hand over his heart in mock shock. "Wait a minute. Was that an actual laugh I heard? I don't believe it. Maybe I should take a picture—"

"No pictures," she said quickly, remembering what had happened the last time she'd been careless about that. "Just tell me what all this is about."

"You'll see," he said. "Come on. If we don't hurry, we'll miss the first race."

"The first . . . Lane, I can't go to the *races!*"

He'd started off. Turning to look at her, he asked, "Why not?"

"Because . . . because . . ." Because, as Orrin Bullard had so recently pointed out, she was a member of a very conservative investment firm; she had certain

standards to uphold, a reputation to guard and protect. She couldn't just run off, willy-nilly, to the races.
It wasn't . . . proper.

"Well?" he asked.

She looked at him, intending to tell him just that.
But suddenly, a little devil seemed to spring to life inside her, whispering evil thoughts, convincing her that
she deserved this. Wasn't it too beautiful a day to be a
slave to some dull standards of behavior when, just
beyond those gates, excitement awaited? Why
shouldn't she take a break? She'd been working so
hard, toeing the line for far too long. What harm
would it do? Who would it hurt?

"You're right," she said, impulse carrying her away.

"I am?" Lane said, surprised.

"You are," she said firmly. "Come on. If we don't
hurry, we're going to be late."

Now that she'd committed herself, Nora became
caught up in the excitement as she and Lane followed
the crowd. It was all new to her. Barkers hawked
computed racing odds for a dollar; track employees
were everywhere selling racing programs and newspapers and copies of *The Daily Racing Form.* The
smells of hamburgers and hot dogs and french fries
vied with those of popcorn and orangeade and beer;
everywhere she looked was a confusion of color and
noise and activity. Nora started toward the fence separating the racetrack from the grandstand to see if the
horses were out yet. Laughing, Lane held her back.

"What is it?" she asked.

He pointed. They had to go through a special section to reach a box he'd reserved, and as they hurried

up, guards made way. When they finally reached their seats, Nora sat down with a gasp.

"Whew, I'm glad we made it," Lane said.

"Oh, so am I!" she exclaimed. Below them, people wandered to and fro on the concrete apron in front of the grandstand, while out on the grass beyond the track the tote board flashed numbers every few seconds.

"Lane—" she started to say.

But just then, the sound of music interrupted her. Startled by the noise, she looked down and saw a man dressed in red coat, top hat, breeches and black boots standing out on the track. He was playing a melodious tune that seemed to excite the crowd.

"What's that?" she asked, grabbing Lane's arm. "What's he doing?"

Pleased at her obvious excitement, he said, "He's announcing that the horses are about to come onto the track for the first race."

And sure enough, almost before the music finished, the horses appeared. With jockeys astride in colorful silks, they emerged from a tunnel under the grandstand. Beside each racehorse was another horse and rider, whose function seemed to be to control the eager runner. Fascinated, Nora leaned forward as the procession of ten began to walk in line along the entire length of the clubhouse before breaking rank. Some of the horses began trotting; others broke into a canter to warm up.

"Keep your eye on number six," Lane said, leaning close.

"Number six? Why?"

She didn't wait for him to answer, but started searching through the group until she found the one with six on the saddlecloth.

"Oh, Lane, he's a beauty, isn't he?" she said, thrilled. The horse, bright red in color, with a long silky tail, was cantering easily around the track, with the jockey standing in the stirrups.

"The horse's name is Speed Wagon," Lane murmured in her ear. "By a stallion called Trolley Car, out of a mare named Radio Flyer. When I saw that, I just had to buy him."

She was so intent on the horse that it was a moment before what he'd said registered. When it did, she whirled around to look at him. "You—what?"

His eyes twinkled. "You told me to invest in transportation stock, remember?"

"Yes, but I . . ."

Stunned, she looked back at Speed Wagon. The horse had reached the far side of the racetrack by this time and was moving easily along, its coat glistening in the sun. The sight awed her, and for a moment she forgot what she'd been about to say. Then she turned hastily back to Lane.

"When I said that, I meant, you know—*stock*. I didn't mean for you to buy a *racehorse!*"

Laughing at her expression, he said, "Then you should have been more specific. I just took you at your word. And the horse *is* called Speed Wagon. It seemed like fate."

Nora was speechless for a few seconds. Then she found her voice. "How can you make jokes? You know what I meant!"

"It's too late now."

"No, it isn't. You can...you can give him back, or something!"

"Give him back? Before we see how he runs?"

"But...but..."

She was still sputtering when a bell rang, and through a loudspeaker over their heads, an announcer intoned, "It is now post time!"

On the far side of the track, the horses were being led into the starting gate. As soon as the runners were all in place, a man standing to one side of the gate thrust a flag into the air. Immediately, the announcer cried, "The flag is up!"

The gate clanged open, and practically as one, all ten horses burst onto the track, their jockeys standing in the stirrups. Over Nora's head, the loudspeaker erupted with, *"And they're off!"*

Galvanized by the excitement, Nora forgot all about their discussion, and quickly began to search for Speed Wagon, who, when she saw him, seemed to be stuck somewhere in the middle of the pack. Grabbing Lane's arm, she cried, "He's boxed in! They won't let him get by!"

"Just wait," Lane said.

The sight of the horses running in a tight pack down the backside of the track before hurtling into the first turn thrilled Nora beyond belief. For a few tense seconds, she lost sight of Lane's horse; when she found him again, beginning to move up toward the leaders on the outside, she began to shout without even knowing it.

"Come on! Come on, Speed Wagon! You can do it!"

Speed Wagon proved worthy of his name. As though contemptuous of other challengers, he seemed to reach down and find extra power. Nora was delirious with joy when he flew under the wire three lengths ahead of his closest competition. She threw her arms around Lane and laughed.

"He won, he won!" she cried.

"That he did," Lane agreed.

Without thinking, she brought Lane's head down to hers and kissed him fiercely. As Lane kissed her back, pulling her into him, she suddenly realized what they were doing. Horrified, she pushed herself away.

"I'm sorry!" she said, her face turning crimson. Too late, she jerked down her suit jacket while glancing quickly around to see if anyone else had seen them. How could she have *thrown* herself at him like that? How could she have acted like this? She was mortified.

"Sorry for what?" he asked. "For getting excited? For getting carried away for once?"

"I . . . I shouldn't have done that," she said.

"Yes, you should have," he insisted. He reached for her, but when she jerked back, he didn't press her. Instead, he said, "Come on, let's go down and congratulate our winner."

She looked at him in horror. Hadn't she already made a big enough fool of herself? "No, I can't."

"Yes, you can. You have to. It's an obligation."

"Not mine!"

"Yes, yours."

Despite her protests, he dragged her down to the winner's circle. She tried to hold back, but she was stymied by fans, who had just realized that superstar Lane Kincaid owned the winning horse. He had protected his identity as Speed Wagon's owner by using the name of a corporation on the racing program. But he could hide no longer and before he and Nora reached the winner's circle, they were mobbed by excited autograph seekers. As the crowd grew around them, she hoped she'd be able to slip away and wait in the car, but Lane held on to her too tightly for her to break away. After a few minutes, they managed to shove their way through with the help of security guards.

"I really hate this," Nora gasped, trying to get her breath.

"It's all part of the game," Lane said, smiling at the people in the crowd who were chanting his name.

"Some game," she muttered.

Just then, there was a flurry of activity, and when she looked up, Speed Wagon was being brought into the winner's circle. Nora tried to get out of the way, but with half a ton of steaming horse, along with the jockey, track officials, the beaming trainer, and two grooms in the small enclosure, there wasn't much room. Before she knew it, she was being positioned with Lane and the trainer for what she thought was an award. Above them, the diminutive jockey was again perched on the back of the horse after weighing-in, and she was going to congratulate him when she glimpsed a photographer moving into place.

Oh, no, she thought, panicked. Trying to get away, she took two steps to the side. Lane saw her, and took her arm.

"Lane, I don't want to be in this picture—"

She hadn't noticed that she had moved closer to the horse's head. Curious, Speed Wagon looked around, and when he nudged her shoulder, she was so surprised that she whirled toward him—her mouth a round O—just as the flash went off.

"Hey, that was great!" the photographer said.

"You can't use that picture!" she cried frantically.

But no one heard her; they were all too busy laughing at the little joke the horse had just pulled off. As the photographer disappeared into the crowd, Nora wondered how soon she'd be able to get her resumé together. There was no way she was going to be able to explain why, despite her fervent promise to avoid publicity, somehow she'd managed to make the newspapers again.

"I THOUGHT YOU were excited about the race," Lane said as they were going back to the car after that awful win picture had been taken. Nora was leading the way, her heels clicking on the pavement. She didn't look back, and he asked, "What are you annoyed about? Is it because of that mob back there? I know I shouldn't have signed—"

Her voice shaking because she was so angry with herself, she said, "It's not that! I'm used to fans crowding around, stampeding everything, demanding someone's entire attention. I grew up with it, remember?"

"Then, I don't understand."

He looked puzzled—as well he might, she thought grimly. She knew how she must have looked during the race—screaming like a banshee, practically falling out of the box in her excitement. Then, when Speed Wagon finished first, she'd—

She didn't want to think of it. That kiss had been a mistake, a big mistake.

"What is it, then?" he asked.

She stopped and turned impatiently to him. "Look, Lane, I know you meant well, but this just isn't going to work. I don't want to get involved with anyone, I told you that."

Anger...annoyance—hurt?—flared in his eyes. "You don't mean just anyone, do you?" he asked. "You mean actors. Nora, you've told me how you feel before, but I still don't understand. It's like me saying that all money managers are alike. It isn't right to condemn everyone in the profession just because you've had a bad experience—"

"I'm not condemning everyone," she said childishly. "My mother is an exception."

"She is that," he agreed, trying a smile. When she just stared at him, he shook his head in exasperation. "Look, I'm not asking for a permanent commitment here—"

"Oh, really?" she snapped. "Well, that's good, because it would mean you'd have to be serious about something for once, and we can't have that, can we?"

He reddened. "You can't have it both ways, Nora. On the one hand, you say you don't want to get involved, and yet on the other, you're condemning me for not wanting to make a commitment. Why can't we just take things as they come? Why do we have to—''

"This is so typical!" she cried. "You don't understand me at all. I don't *take things as they come,* I plan my life! I know where I'm going and how I'm going to get there. My job means everything to me—''

"Everything?"

That stopped her for a second. Then, because she had so much riding on the fact that she'd made all the right choices, she said, "Yes, everything! I've worked hard to get to where I am, Lane. I won't jeopardize it now, not for anyone. You'll have to accept that."

"Why? It doesn't make any sense. Why would your job be at risk just because you're seeing me? What kind of people do you work for, anyway?"

The truth is, with your background you won't make the cut... It's the show-business element... It's just not the right image for the firm...

Rodney's hateful words flashed through her mind, and she stiffened. "I don't need to explain myself to you!"

He looked at her a moment. Then he shook his head again. "I never thought you were a snob, Nora."

"I'm not a snob!" she said. She clenched her hands, wondering why she was trying to make him understand. "I work for a conservative firm that shuns publicity. I was warned, in fact—''

"Warned? What does that mean? Are you saying that someone at your office *threatened* you?"

"Of course not! It's just..." She wanted to forget the whole thing, but she'd said this much; she might as well tell it all. "I'm competing for a big promotion, if you must know. It's very important to me. And these pictures in the paper don't help. My boss doesn't like it, and one of our biggest clients doesn't like it, either. First, it was that picture at my mother's party—"

He was looking at her as if she were speaking another language. "As I recall, that was a lot more unflattering to me than it was to you. I took some ribbing for it, in fact."

"Yes, well, *I* got called on the carpet, and it wasn't a pleasant experience!"

"You really got in trouble for something silly like that?"

"I could have lost my job! Money managers, especially from firms like Bullard and Sweeney, don't get their pictures in the paper, unless it's for a chamber of commerce award! We aren't caught in some embarrassing, humiliating situation like I was at that stupid party!"

"It seems to me that I was the one who was embarrassed, not you."

"We're not talking about you, don't you see?" She was really angry now. "I'm not surprised you don't understand! With your attitude toward life, I doubt anything at all embarrasses you!"

"I resent that."

"Well, resent it all you like! It's true!"

Abruptly, she became aware that they were having this loud discussion in the middle of the parking lot. With effort she lowered her voice. "I'm not going to argue about it, Lane. The point is, my boss doesn't appreciate the negative publicity. It's not good for the firm's image, and it certainly isn't good for me, not where my job prospects are concerned."

"But—"

"No! Listen to me! I know it's a novel concept for you that not *everything* in life is fun, but that's the way it is. *Some* people take things seriously!"

"But you're not like that."

She looked at him in outrage. "Yes, I am, and don't tell me I'm not! I've worked hard to be this way—"

"*Be* this way? What way, Nora? Serious and grim and never having—all right, I'll say the horrible *F*-word—*fun*. Admit it now, you had a good time today. Why are you trying to turn it into something it wasn't?"

She didn't want to answer him. Maybe she didn't know how. "Just take me back to the office, okay?"

"Look, if it will help, I'll come in and talk to—"

She whirled toward him again. "Don't you dare! You've done enough harm! Just stay away from me!"

Wanting to end this horrible scene, she looked around again, and tried to find the car. When she saw it two rows over, she started in that direction. To her fury, he didn't follow. "If you don't take me back now," she said, "I'll walk."

With a sigh, he started after her. "Nora, wait—"

"There's nothing more to say. I told you how I feel, so let's just drop it. In fact, let's forget this day ever happened."

During the return ride, the tension was so thick Nora could have cut it with a knife. Telling herself she *wanted* it this way, she sat stiffly on her side of the car. She knew she hadn't been fair, but she wouldn't apologize. It was even more clear to her now than ever. No matter how she tried not to let him, he affected her too much for her to let her guard down—even for an instant. As soon as he pulled to a stop in the parking lot behind the office, she reached for the door.

"I didn't mean to make you angry," he said. "I thought, when I bought the horse, that it—"

"I know what you thought," she said tersely. "You thought it would be a joke, something frivolous and entertaining. Well, fine. If that's how you want to live your life, you go right ahead. It's none of my business—just as it's none of yours how I live mine."

"Nora, wait. Can't we—"

She didn't want to talk anymore. She opened the door and got out before he could stop her. "You'll have to excuse me," she said frostily. "I have work to do."

She slammed the door, and marched up the walk and into the building. All she wanted now was to get to her office without having to speak to anyone, but there was that damned Rodney, coming out of the copy room. Before he could say a word, she squared her shoulders.

"Yes?" she said coldly.

Rodney wasn't stupid; he saw the look on her face and decided against making any comment. *A good thing,* she thought grimly, brushing by him. She stormed into her office and banged the door shut.

CHAPTER ELEVEN

"THEODORA, YOU LOOK enchanting," Arthur said, opening the door to his penthouse apartment on the night of the dinner party.

"Thank you, love." Theodora gave him a kiss and swept in, dramatically dropping her gold silk shawl on the back of the nearest sofa. She hoped her nervousness wasn't obvious. This party was so important. She wanted to do everything right. She pirouetted so he could admire her dress.

It wasn't black, as Nora had suggested. The gown she was wearing was one of the simplest ones she owned, a rich purple silk sheath with a plunging neckline and thousands of bugle beads. Seeing Arthur's smile of approval, she drew him over to one of the couches and pulled him down beside her.

"Now, tell me again who these people are," she commanded. "I don't want to look like a fool tonight, calling someone by the wrong name, or thinking they're in steel or something, when they're involved in stocks."

He lifted one of her hands to his lips. "Just be yourself, darling. Don't worry about anything else. I know everyone will love you as much as I do."

She wasn't quite as sure of that as he seemed to be. Dismayed to realize she was nervous again, she took a glass of champagne from a tray just as the doorbell rang. Normally she didn't drink, but tonight it seemed she needed false courage.

That flute was the first of several she had during the obligatory—rather dull—cocktail hour that followed. But when they finally went into dinner, she became determined to interject some gaiety into the evening. It was time, she decided, to shine as a hostess.

"Arthur, darling," she said sweetly when one of the male guests finally ended a long-winded conversation about brokerage houses and dummy accounts and takeovers, "I thought this was to be a social occasion, not a business meeting." She looked around the table, flashing her most brilliant smile at everyone. "You men all work so hard, I think you deserve some time off from all those dreary company details, don't you? Now, I heard the most amusing story the other day..."

And with that, she regaled them with a highly entertaining anecdote about a renowned director and the practical joke an equally famous actress had played on him. Aware of her audience, she cleaned up the details a great deal, but the tale was still funny. She was a natural storyteller, and all the men laughed, Arthur the loudest. Two of the women even smiled, but the third, a Gorgon of a creature named Minella—*Mina,* for short, of all things, Theodora thought—merely pursed her lips and looked even more constipated than she had before. Seeing that, Theodora sighed. Would the evening never end?

She did make it all the way through dessert before disaster struck. In fact, she was just silently congratulating herself on her success when Arthur announced that he and the men were going to withdraw for a short while into the library. A little business discussion, he said. Nothing "the ladies" would be interested in.

"I beg your pardon?" she said. She looked around the table for support, but when the wives seemed to take this inexplicable chauvinistic action in their stride, she looked at Arthur again. "Have I missed something? Were we transported back to Victorian times without my being aware of it?"

"I know it's an outmoded custom," he agreed. "But it won't take long."

With a paternalistic smile that immediately set her teeth on edge, he came around to the foot of the table and kissed her cheek. "Don't be difficult, darling," he whispered. "We'll be back before you know it. I promise."

Theodora was still in shock at his actions when he gestured to his male guests and the four of them disappeared into the study. She looked blankly around the table again. Everyone was staring at her, clearly waiting for her to lead them into the living room. Arthur would hear from her, she thought grimly, but right now, duty called.

"Well!" she said brightly, "it seems we're on our own, ladies. Shall we?"

She rose gracefully and led the way. She was trying to think of something to say when one of the women spoke. Her name was Olive Dunsmuir, and after a quick look at her friends, she said, "I'm embarrassed to say this, but George and I rarely go to movies. Not that we regard it as a waste of time, of course," she added hastily. "It's just that my husband is home so seldom. He spends day and night at the office."

"What a shame!" Theodora said sympathetically. "Isn't there anything you can do?"

"Oh, the situation suits me just—" Olive stopped midsentence, then she turned bright red. "I mean...er...oh, dear, please don't get the idea that I don't like George around! After all, we *have* been married twenty-six years."

"Twenty-six years!" Theodora exclaimed. "I've been married five times—twice to the same man, mind you—and I doubt I'd have that much time to my credit if I added up all five!"

There was a silence. Suddenly, everyone was busy staring into their coffee cups. Finally, another woman, who hadn't said much all evening, cleared her throat. In strained tones, she said, "I'm sorry, Theodora, but I've never seen you on stage. Are you...er...involved in a play now?"

Theodora's head was beginning to ache. Wondering where in the *hell* Arthur was, she started to answer, when suddenly she was struck with a brilliant idea. If the men were going to desert them, why couldn't they have a good time on their own? It was time to salvage this horrible evening—or at least make the last part of it *fun*.

"I'm not on stage now," she said, "but if you like, I can sing some songs from my last tour."

Now that she'd thought of it, she was elated. There was a piano at the end of the room; she rose and headed toward it. With a flourish, she sat down and dashed off a riff. Excellent, she thought, it was perfectly in tune! Smiling a little wickedly at the ladies to include them in the scheme, she began to sing.

She hadn't planned it, but when the words to one of the bawdy songs from the stage musical *I'm No Lady* came to her, she decided it was the perfect choice to get things rolling. She'd won a Tony Award for playing Prudence, the madam who had a mirror where her heart should have been; the character had swept through life larger than life, living every moment to the fullest, enjoying herself to the utmost. The show had been a smash, a number-one hit on Broadway for several years until Theodora had tired of the energetic role. The actress who had replaced her was quite competent, but by then Theodora had made the role her own.

And now she was about to show these women why, Theodora thought proudly—and a little tipsily. She began to belt out the ribald, "Aimin' to Please," and was delighted to find that she was in perfect pitch. Oh, wasn't this wonderful! she thought, congratulating herself. *Finally,* the evening was about to have a little life added to it!

She was so caught up in her own performance that she didn't realize when Arthur and the husbands had joined them. By that time, she was already halfway into the burlesque, *Life's a Fantasy, So Let's Dream On!,* and when she finally saw the men standing there, she almost squawked to a stop. But then, she thought, the show must go on, and she segued into her finale, one of her very favorite songs from the show, "Get Yourself Another Girl!"

"And I'm tellin' you, it ain't gonna last, so if you're smart, you'll get yourself another girl ... !"

She ended the song with a bang. For a moment there was quiet. Then the men began to applaud, and after a second or two, the women joined in. Arthur was last to congratulate her; when she risked a quick glance in his direction, he was looking a little stunned.

"That was wonderful, Theodora," he said when the applause had died down. "When I asked you to act as my hostess this evening, I had no idea you intended to entertain my guests, as well."

She knew by his expression that he didn't approve of her impromptu performance. Mortified, she could barely wait for everyone to leave. Fortunately, it didn't take long. Almost before the last "thank you for the lovely evening," and the "so glad to have met you" was said, she was closing the door on his guests and turning to him with a contrite apology.

"I'm so sorry," she said. "I didn't mean to ruin the evening."

"Don't be silly, my dear," he said. She couldn't be sure, but it seemed his smile was a little forced. "You didn't ruin a thing. How many other people are treated to a private show by a famous Broadway star? I think everyone enjoyed it. I did, I know."

He was being polite. But the evening was ruined for her, and she decided to forego her plans to stay the night. Arthur was putting up a good front, but she felt she had embarrassed both of them and she wanted to go home.

"Don't go," he said, when she put down the phone after summoning her driver.

"No, really, I must—"

"Are you sure I can't persuade you?"

"No, not tonight," she whispered. "But I'll take a rain check."

By the time Theodore arrived home, her headache was dangerously close to a migraine. Too late, she wished she hadn't given her maid, Maria, the night off; after the debacle tonight, she needed someone to talk to.

Stripping off the purple gown—oh, why couldn't she just have worn dull old black, and been conventional like everyone else?—she looked at herself in the mirror and knew that black wouldn't have helped. She wasn't conventional, and that's all there was to it.

Sighing, she slipped into her satin dressing gown and reached for the cold cream. But as she was opening the jar, she put it down and stared at her reflection. How was she going to handle this situation? She didn't want to make any more social blunders where Arthur was concerned. If she was going to marry him—and she was, as soon as he asked her—then she needed guidance. She had to talk to someone who comprehended people who lived lives like his... Of course! Her own daughter was the most calm and conservative and precise person she knew—even more so than Arthur was. Nora would know exactly what to do.

CHAPTER TWELVE

NORA WAS HAVING a bad morning. She'd had trouble sleeping again, and she knew why. Telling herself she was *not* going to think about Lane, she dragged herself out of bed, and into the shower. She had an important meeting with Lester Snook at his home this morning. Wishing the appointment was any other morning but this, she drank a cup of strong coffee, hoping it would clear her head.

As always, Chauncy had eagerly brought in the morning paper, a trick she'd taught him when he was a puppy—but only useful, she realized now, if one wanted to read the paper in the first place. Dreading what she might find in the sports section, she steeled herself and opened it. When she saw the photo, she grimaced.

"Film star reaps glory first time out!" the headline shouted.

And there, underneath the banner for all the world to see was the picture that had been taken in the winner's circle. Lane was there, proud and happy, the elated trainer beside him. An ecstatic groom was standing by the big Thoroughbred; the jockey astride the horse looked pleased as punch. As for her and Speed Wagon—there they were in all their glory, the horse nudging her, she looking back at him in surprise, her mouth a circle, like a comic-book character.

She couldn't look at it any longer; snatching up the paper with an exasperated cry, she threw it in the trash. This was worse than she had expected. She put her head in her hands and groaned. What was Mr. Bullard going to say? And wouldn't Rodney have a field day with this!

As always, Chauncy seemed to sense her distress. Placing a giant paw delicately on her skirt, he whined, demanding her attention. When she felt him there, she bent down. "Oh, Chauncy," she said mournfully, "what a mess!"

Fortunately, she didn't have time to dwell on it. She put the dog outside, gave him an extra pat, then gathered her things and went out to the car.

Snook lived in a section of Sierra Madre filled with beautiful estates. Since he was a recluse with more money than he knew what to do with, people came to him, not vice versa, and as she took the exit off the freeway, she started rehearsing responses in case he'd seen the sports section this morning.

"Well, it really wasn't my fault," she could say. "I was just walking by, and they grabbed me and pulled me in before I could stop them."

She could just hear the reply. "Oh, really? And what were you doing at the racetrack in the first place? Wasn't it the middle of the day? A *business* day?"

She was so anxious she almost felt sick when she finally found the address and paused before the huge iron gates. She'd never been here before, but Ginger had once delivered some papers and her description had reminded Nora of stories about Pickfair, the fairyland that Mary Pickford and Douglas Fairbanks had created during their heyday as film stars.

Now she saw that the estate wasn't like Pickfair at all. It looked more like something out of a Gothic novel. No wonder Snook was a little odd; who wouldn't be, living here? she thought, noting the towers with conical roofs, projecting attic gables and domed turrets. This wasn't Pickfair; it was the House of Usher.

But she hadn't come to judge Lester Snook's taste in period architecture; she was here to bring him up-to-date on his investments. She parked, hefted her bulging attaché case and went up a series of marble steps to the front doors. The heavy brass knob she found made such a deep reverberating *GONG!* when she pulled it that she jumped.

She was still trying to compose herself when the door swung open. The man on the threshold was dressed in a gray suit with a white shirt and crisp black bow tie. He bowed slightly, and said in a reedy voice, "You must be Miss Nora Carmichael. Do come in. Mr. Snook is expecting you."

"Thank you. I—"

He had already turned and started to walk away. Quickly, she hurried after him, and after he'd shown her to a room, he bowed again. "Please make yourself comfortable," he said. "I will inform Mr. Snook that you have arrived. He will join you shortly."

After he'd disappeared, she looked around the elegant room. In another era, this must have been a drawing room, she thought. It was decorated with tall vases, priceless Tiffany lamps on lovely inlaid tables, brocade and velvet tapestries and upholstery—in short, all the things that Chauncy could have destroyed simply by walking in. All it would take, she thought, was one sweep of his tail to reduce everything to rubble.

At the image, she was tempted to giggle. She told herself this wasn't funny—and nearly laughed out loud. Horrified, she tried to think of something boring—trusts, taxes, anything that would keep her mind off this inexplicable impulse to laugh. What would Snook think if he came in and found her collapsed with mirth?

She was nervous about making a good impression, that's all it was, she told herself, taking deep breaths. All she had to do was calm down and remember why she was here. Mr. Bullard had sent her because he believed she was good at her job.

But that was before he saw the paper this morning, she thought mournfully. What would he think of her now? Maybe next time, he'd send Rodney.

Thoughts of Rodney definitely sobered her, and she was her most solemn, businesslike self when the door opened and she turned. Seeing Lester Snook for the first time, she had to hide her surprise. Except for the age lines in his face, he looked like a small boy. Barely five feet tall, he crossed the room on tiny feet, his hand out.

"So nice to meet you at last, Miss Carmichael," he said in a deep voice that completely belied his small size. "Please, sit down."

Hoping she didn't look quite like the fool she felt, she took a chair opposite the one he chose. When she saw that his shoes barely touched the floor as he sat back, she hastily brought her eyes up to his face. He smiled, and she smiled in return.

"Before we get started," he said, "I want you to know that I saw that picture of you in the winner's circle yesterday at Santa Anita Racetrack."

That wiped the smile off her face. Now that the time had come for an explanation, all she could say was a weak, "You did?"

He leaned forward, his eyes gleaming. "Yes, I did. I didn't know you were interested in racehorses, Miss Carmichael. You should have told me. I have fond memories, myself. You probably don't know it—or might not care if you did—but I once was a jockey. Oh, yes," he said, pleased when he saw her astounded expression. "I rode all the time back East when I was young. I changed my name in case my parents found out, but of course they eventually did. Then I had to quit. My mother worried so, you see. Kidnapping, and all that."

"I'm...sorry," she said helplessly. She didn't know what else to say.

"So was I," Snook said. "I enjoyed myself until then. It was the most fun I've ever had." He leaned forward again, his eyes alight. "I haven't been to the races in years. Tell me about it, will you? Every detail. I get it on satellite, but it just isn't the same as being there in person..."

NORA FELT quite dazed by the time she left the Snook mansion. She and Lester—"You have to call me Lester, Nora. I won't hear of anything else!"—had spent the morning talking about horses. Or at least, she thought wryly, *Lester* had. She had just listened, fascinated and amazed at the same time. They hadn't discussed business matters at all; whenever she tried to reach for her briefcase, he'd wave his hand and tell her to take care of the details herself.

The morning passed so quickly that when she realized it was after eleven, she had to make her excuses. He immediately invited her to lunch, but she had to refuse him.

"You'll come back, won't you?" Snook asked, walking her to the front door. "And you'll tell me when Speed Wagon is going to race again?"

"Why don't you come and see for yourself?"

"Oh, no, I rarely go out—especially to public places," he said uncomfortably. Then he winked. "But I'll watch on the satellite—and I'll make a bet with my bookie. How's that?"

"Great," Nora replied. Her mood on the way back to work was euphoric. Who could have guessed that the dreaded appointment would turn out so well?

But her sense of well-being began to dissolve the closer she got to the office. She'd jumped one hurdle, but she still had another to face if her boss had seen the paper. She had the sinking feeling that Snook's favorable reaction might not matter to him.

She felt tense all over again as she pulled into a space behind the building. Since it was lunchtime, the lot was almost empty, so she was surprised when she started inside to hear another car pull in behind her. When she turned, she saw a late-model, midnight-blue Cadillac. She didn't recognize the car, but when a man dressed in a conservative blue suit with white shirt and red tie got out, she knew who he was. Frozen to the spot, she wondered frantically why he'd come. She'd made it clear that she didn't want to see him again. Why hadn't he listened?

WHEN LANE SAW Nora's face, he wondered that himself. In fact, he thought, as he pocketed the car keys and headed toward the building's back door where she was standing, he asked himself what he was doing here. It had seemed so logical earlier this morning. Now he wasn't sure at all.

Well, too bad, he thought, he was here. Once again, he hadn't slept well, and he'd been up even earlier than usual to study lines for a studio call later today. For some reason, that damned script of Wyatt's had caught his eye, and, unable to help himself, he'd started reading it again. It was just as good—better— than it was the last time he'd tried not to read it, and when he realized he was getting sucked in again, he angrily threw it halfway across the room and went out for a swim. He was sitting morosely on the diving board when Esperanza brought him some coffee and a copy of the morning paper. He wasn't in the mood to read, but he thumbed through the sports section until he came to... The Picture.

"Oh, no!" He jumped to his feet, the diving board rocking underneath him.

Esperanza had already started into the house, but she turned to ask, "What is it, *señor?*"

The banner headline read: *"Film star reaps glory first time out!"*

"It's a disaster!" he groaned, jumping off the board and spreading the paper on the table.

She came back to look. When she saw the photo, she smiled. "Isn't that your new racehorse, the one that won yesterday?"

"Yes, yes, but look who else is there!"

She peered at the photo again. "Is a good likeness of you, *señor.* But then, you always take good pictures. Why, what's the matter? Don't you like it?"

"No, no, the picture's fine. It's just—" He stopped. "Do I still have any suits?"

"Suits? Of course you have suits!" She shook her finger in his face. "But it's been so long since you wore one, I'm not sure where they are."

"Well, find one for me, please. And a white shirt. And a tie."

"A *tie?*"

Ignoring her sarcasm, he said, "Yes, a tie. I have a business appointment this morning—a *serious* business appointment—and I have to look the part. So, go, go—" He shooed her away with his hand, then called after her, "And please ask Cosmo to dust off the Caddy, will you? I'll take that instead of the Porsche today."

She stopped and looked at him again. "Are you all right, *señor?* I mean, are you ill, or something?"

He didn't know what he was feeling. Why *was* he doing this? Was he out of his mind? He must be, to think of going to so much trouble for a woman who had made it clear that she didn't want anything to do with him. A suit, he thought. A tie. The Cadillac.

Amazed at himself, he shook his head. Well, so be it. He wasn't going to let this go, not without giving it another try. He'd always known that there was more to Nora than met the eye. He'd suspected that the first night they'd met. There she'd been, all buttoned up in that prim business suit with the proper conservative pearls and heels and...that look in her eye. One glance had told him that, despite the modern schoolmarm facade, Nora Carmichael was not who she pretended to be.

And then there had been the dog.

When he thought of Chauncy, he grinned. That big Saint Bernard-Behemoth cross had been the clincher for him, all right. Someone else might have guessed that if Nora did own a pet, it would be a cat—an entity as haughty and apparently self-contained as she appeared to be. But he'd looked into those expressive green eyes of hers, and he knew better. She might try to deny it, do her best, in fact, to suppress it, but whether Miss Nora Carmichael wanted to admit it or not, the fact that she owned a dog like Chauncy—and the way she had acted at the races yesterday, among other clues—proved that there was a part of her personality that she could never suppress, no matter how hard she tried.

Now, as he walked across the parking lot to where she was standing, he began to wish he'd donned battle gear instead of a suit. He took a deep breath.

"Hi," he said. "Now, before you get mad, let me explain, at least. All right?"

"What are you doing here?" Nora demanded. "I thought I told you never to—"

"I know what you told me," Lane said. "But when I saw the picture in the paper this morning, I thought I'd better come down and see if you needed help explaining things to your boss."

"I told you, I don't need any help!"

"And here I made such an effort to be respectable, too," he said reproachfully. "A suit, with a tie, I might add, an outfit I don't wear for *anyone,* not even the studio. And you'll notice, instead of my sports car, the dull old Cadillac. I didn't want anyone thinking I was just another flaky actor who didn't know how to conduct himself."

He smiled the smile that had come so close to stealing her heart. Her hands clenched, she asked, "Why are you doing this to me?"

She sounded so distressed, he was sorry he'd tried to be so smart. He tried to reach for her, but she eluded him and went inside. He followed her. "I'm sorry," he said. "I really thought I could help. When I saw the newspaper this morning—" He stopped, searching her face. "You said negative publicity could cause you trouble here, and if it has, please let me talk to your boss. I'll tell him it was all my fault."

"I told you, you don't have to tell him anything," she said fiercely, glancing over her shoulder. Bullard's office door was closed, but if he heard someone out here when everyone was supposed to be at lunch, he might investigate. Quickly, she tried to push

Lane out the door; it was like pushing against a wall. She stopped. "Just go! You've done enough—"

"Oh, there you are, Nora," a voice boomed suddenly from the end of the hallway. "I thought I heard voices. When did you get back?"

Slowly, she turned to face her boss, who had just come out of his office. "I ... er ... just a few minutes ago," she said.

"How was your meeting?"

"Fine," she answered. She knew she had to introduce the two men. No matter how much she wanted to, she couldn't just pretend that Lane wasn't standing right here beside her. "I'll tell you about it later, Mr. Bullard, but right now, I'd like to introduce a...er..." She'd almost called Lane a client. "Friend" wouldn't do, either, she realized, so she finished awkwardly, "Mr. Bullard, this is Lane Kincaid. Mr. Kincaid, Orrin Bullard, the head of the firm."

While the two men shook hands, Nora tried to think of an excuse to give Bullard for Lane's presence. She was so preoccupied with this new problem, in fact, that she wasn't paying attention to their exchange of the usual pleasantries until she heard something about the races. Instantly, all her senses became acute.

"My congratulations on your racing victory yesterday," Bullard was saying when she tuned in again. "I hadn't seen it in the paper, but a client just phoned and said that the win was very impressive."

"Thank you," Lane said modestly. "It was great to win the first time out, and that's why I stopped by. I wanted to thank Nora again for advising me to buy the horse. If it hadn't been for her, I never would have known the satisfaction."

Bullard's speculative glance rested on Nora, who could feel her face turning beet red. Before she could think of a reply to that, he said, "Lester did mention that you were in the photo, Nora. But I suppose you have an explanation."

With a mighty effort, she pulled herself together. "Yes, I do—"

"I'm afraid that was my fault," Lane interrupted. "I've never owned a racehorse before, and I have to admit, I did insist that Nora watch the race with me. Then, when Speed Wagon actually won, we all just forced her to come into the winner's circle with us. She didn't want to, but...well, we insisted." He grinned that famous grin—handsome, at ease, man-to-man. "Have you ever been to the races, Mr. Bullard? When a horse, running in your name, under your colors, actually wins, well, I'm sure that you can understand how easy it is to get carried away by the thrill of the moment."

What Orrin Bullard was about to reply to that, Nora never knew. She was spared when, just then, the private line rang in his office. He was clearly expecting a call, for after a quick look at them both, he excused himself. But before he started off, he said, "It's been a pleasure meeting you, Mr. Kincaid." And to Nora, "I'll be waiting for your report."

"I'll take care of it right away," she said.

As he disappeared into his office and closed the door, Lane and Nora were left alone in the hall, where Nora, at least, had no intention of staying.

"Goodbye, Lane," she said. Without giving him a chance to say anything more, she started toward her own office.

"Wait," he said, walking with her.

Unwillingly, she looked up at him again. Wishing he hadn't worn that suit, she wondered how she was supposed to resist him when he'd gone to so much trouble for her. Why *was* he doing this? Why couldn't he just leave her alone?

"What do you want?" she asked. "No, never mind, I don't need to know. I don't have time for this, Lane. I've been gone all morning, and I have a lot to do."

"You're angry again."

"No, I'm not. I just want you to leave."

"Well, I'm not going to, until we discuss this."

"We don't—"

"Yes, we do." And with that, he took her arm and hustled her into her nearby office. When he shut the door behind them, she whirled around, intending to tell him she didn't appreciate being manhandled. Before she could get the words out, his arms went around her. Outraged, she tried to jump back, but he held her firmly. Then, looking at her red face for a long moment, he sighed and released her. "I'm sorry," he said. "I just didn't know how to get through to you any other way."

"Well, that wasn't the way!" she declared, angrily tugging her suit jacket down.

"Look, Nora, I know what you've told me, but I can't believe you don't feel something for me."

"I do feel something for you," she said stubbornly. "Right now, I feel angry, and if you do that to me again, you're going to be sorry!"

"I'm already sorry," he said. "I didn't want this to happen, either."

"What are you talking about? Nothing's happened!"

"Oh, no? Then tell me you didn't enjoy yourself yesterday. It won't kill you to confess that even you enjoy having some fun occasionally. Come on, Nora, say it for once."

"I don't have to admit anything to you!"

"Yes, you do. Otherwise, I'll just stay here all day."

Because she desperately wanted him to leave before she did something insane, like flinging herself into his arms, she reached for the doorknob. He put his hand over hers, and try as she might, she couldn't take it back again. "Lane, this is ridiculous. Let me go!"

"It's no more ridiculous than your resisting me."

Infuriated and more confused than she wanted to admit, she said scathingly, "Oh, really? Well, I know it's a blow to your giant ego that a woman—that any female on earth!—doesn't immediately melt in your arms, but let me tell you something, Lane Kincaid, I'm not one of your air-brained bimbos!"

He looked down at her. "No, you're most assuredly not that."

She knew he was going to kiss her. She could feel it even before he bent toward her. She put a hand firmly on his chest, and said, "Don't you dare kiss me!"

"Why not?" he asked. "Are you afraid you're going to have to admit you enjoy that, too?"

"I don't enjoy it! I—"

It was too late. But then, she thought, surrendering as his mouth came down on hers, it had been too late for a long while now. She'd tried to tell him she didn't like him; she'd tried to convince herself that she despised what he did for a living. But even if those things had been true—and she wasn't sure now that they were—she still found him irresistible. It wasn't his good looks, or his charm, or his suave, smooth ways. It was something she didn't know about yet, but which she had sensed from the first time they'd met. She'd seen it in the way he'd treated her dog; she'd sensed it more in the things he hadn't said, than in what he had. And she'd seen another glimpse of him today. He could have come here as a big star, a man-about-town, trying to impress her boss with his celebrity, but he'd made an effort to distance himself from all that. He'd worn a suit; he'd driven the Cadillac. Why had he done those things, if he hadn't been trying to please her?

Maybe it hadn't been an effort at all, she thought. Maybe she only wanted to believe there was more to him than met the eye because she was so enjoying this kiss. Without realizing it, she lifted her arms, her hands cupping the back of his strong neck. Sighing, she wound her fingers in his thick hair, and then felt the hard line of his jaw with her thumb. She could control her mind, but her senses seemed to have a will of their own—especially when she felt his hard body against hers. Lost in feeling, she wanted him to do more than kiss her; if they'd been alone, she would have pulled him down with her onto the carpet and—

Appalled by her thoughts, she pulled away from him. *She'd done it again!*

"You shouldn't have done that!" she said.

Smiling, he asked, "But aren't you glad I did?"

He reached for her, but she eluded him. "No, I'm not glad! This is a place of business, Lane, and—"

"Every place is a place of business to you, Nora. You should learn to relax."

"I don't want to relax!" she said ridiculously. "I'm happy just as I am."

"No, you're not," he insisted. "Not really, not deep inside."

She forced herself to look him straight in the eye. "You don't know me well enough to say that," she said. "And the fact that you *can* say it, proves that you don't know me at all."

He looked at her a moment longer, then smiled a slow, knowing smile. "Oh, I know you, Nora. You just don't want to admit it yet. But you will one day. I promise you, you will." He reached for the door and opened it.

"Oh, no, I—"

She was too late. The door closed behind him, and he was down the hall by the time she'd pulled herself together and jerked the door open again. She was about to call him back when she realized she wasn't alone. Feeling someone watching her, she turned and saw Rodney standing in the doorway of his office, a nasty smile on his face. He had obviously heard more than he should have. She glared at him a moment; then, with an effort that caused her to break into a sweat, she calmly shut the door and let Lane walk out by himself.

CHAPTER THIRTEEN

DESPITE HER own problems, Nora was anxious to find out how the dinner party with Arthur had gone. She was sure her mother would call the night after the party, but when she didn't hear anything, she phoned Theodora only to learn from the maid that Freddie Princeley had suddenly decided to take the cast and crew down to Palm Springs for some location shots. Disappointed, Nora had to wait two nights before Theodora finally called.

"Oh, darling, I'm so glad you're home!" Theodora said when Nora answered.

"I'm not the one who's been out gallivanting around," Nora said. "Why didn't you call me before you left? You knew I wanted to find out about the party."

"I wanted to, but there wasn't time! I didn't want to cry on your shoulder at work, and Freddie hardly gave us two minutes before we were careering off down to the desert for those silly location shots. Besides, I didn't want to tell you over some stupid machine."

"Uh-oh, that doesn't sound good. What happened?"

"The dinner party with Arthur was a disaster!"

"Oh, Mother, you're just being dramatic. Among other things, you always shine at parties." She thought of something and added glumly, "It's your daughter who seems to have problems in a crowd."

Theodora didn't laugh, as she'd expected. "Not this time. In fact, I made an absolute *fool* of myself. It was awful, the worst night of my entire life."

"What happened?"

"I don't want to go into it," Theodora said with a shudder, and then proceeded to do just that. By the time she got to the part where she'd begun entertaining the ladies because they'd been deserted by their chauvinistic host, Nora didn't know whether to laugh or not.

"Well," she said hesitantly when Theodora finally came indignantly to a stop, "I guess you showed him, didn't you?"

"I suppose. Oh, darling, sometimes I just don't know what gets into me. It's like a little devil takes me over, and after that, I . . . well, it's just terrible!"

Nora sympathized. After all, she'd recently had the same problem controlling her own impulses. Quickly thrusting away embarrassing memories, she asked, "What was Arthur's reaction?"

"That's just it, I'm not sure! He *says* he didn't mind, but...but I *know* I saw something in his eyes."

"Maybe you just *think* he's blaming you," Nora said.

"If he is, he's perfectly within his rights. Oh, Nora, what am I going to do? I thought I could fit into his world, but if that evening is an example of what I'll have to endure, I'm just not sure."

"But I thought you wanted to marry Arthur!"

"Well, I did. Or at least, I thought I did. Now, I don't know. I'm so muddled about this, I don't know what to do."

"It isn't like you not to know exactly what you want. Maybe you should talk to Arthur."

"I'd *like* to, darling, but he's always surrounded by people. We never go anywhere by ourselves anymore. He always invites someone else along."

"Is he afraid to be alone with you, do you think?"

"Well, not *always*, if you know what I mean," she said suggestively. "But even that hasn't happened in a while. I've been working on this damned film, and now he's going out of town for a few days."

Nora could hear the desolation in her mother's voice. "Maybe you need to plan a romantic little dinner for two when he gets back."

"Dinner?" Theodora brightened for a moment, then she sighed. "We never eat alone, either."

"Well, how about lunch? You can call his secretary and make a private appointment—just the two of you. That would work, wouldn't it?"

Theodora thought about it. "You know, it might, at that," she said, sounding enthusiastic as she began to plan aloud. "Arthur has a private dining room off his office. I could have lunch sent up, and we would have a glorious hour just to ourselves. I'm sure his secretary will help me arrange it. Oh, Nora, you're absolutely brilliant!"

"I don't know about that. I'm sure you would have thought of it eventually yourself."

"Maybe so, but you saved me the trouble. Oh, I feel so much better! And now that that's settled, tell me about you and Lane. How is that working out?"

The last thing she wanted to talk about was Lane Kincaid. "It's not," she said shortly. "And I don't want to discuss it, understand?"

"Oh, dear."

"Now, Mother—"

"I'm sorry, darling. But you know, now that I think of it, maybe that explains—"

"What?"

"Well," Theodora said thoughtfully, "Lane has seemed a little preoccupied. He's always so professional, you know. He never blows his lines or misses his marks—at least not until the past few days. Why, a couple of times he's even called his love interest in the film by your name. That isn't like him—"

"You're making this up."

"No, I'm not—I swear," Theodora said. Then she paused delicately. "But of course, it doesn't mean anything does it? After all, if you're not interested..."

"I'm not!"

"Well, really, Nora, you don't have to bite my head off!"

"I'm sorry. Let's just not talk about Lane Kincaid."

"Whatever you say," Theodora said, too agreeably. Nora thought her mother had something else up her sleeve, until Theodora added, "You've made me feel so much better that I think I'll go soak in a hot bath while I plan my luncheon strategy. Thank you so much, darling. I'll be in touch.''

Exasperated, Nora hung up, too. Before she knew it, she started to wonder if she'd misjudged Lane—and pulled herself up short. "Oh, no, you don't,'' she muttered. "You said you weren't going to think about him, and you're not. So just forget it.''

On that thought, she got up—and almost tripped over Chauncy, who had been lying patiently by her feet. While she was on the phone, he'd fetched his leash from the pegboard.

"All right, all right, I can take a hint,'' she said. "But I'm too tired to do more than go around the block tonight, understand? Tomorrow I'll take you to the park, I promise.''

A promise seemed to be good enough for Chauncy. Wagging his tail so mightily that he almost knocked her off her feet, he followed her upstairs while she changed and then led the way to the front door again. Nora bent down before they went out and gave him a quick hug.

"*You'll* always be there for me, won't you, Chauncy?'' she murmured, burying her face in his thick ruff.

As though he understood, he barked. Or maybe, she thought wryly, he was just anxious to start off. Opening the door, she allowed him to drag her down to the sidewalk.

It was a perfect evening to be out; the air was mild and she breathed in deeply. Dusk had always been one of her favorite times of day; it was such a quiet time, everyone and everything getting ready to settle down for the night.

Everything but Chauncy, that was, she thought fondly, as she was pulled along in his wake. She decided to extend her walk. The park where the dogs could be let loose for a run was a couple of blocks away, and by the time they arrived at the edge of the grass, she was a little out of breath. For some reason, Chauncy had seemed more anxious than usual to get here, and when she looked around, she was disappointed to see that someone else was already there. She'd hoped they'd be alone tonight, but even from this distance, she could see a man leaning casually against one of the trees, his hands in his pockets.

"Damn it." She didn't feel like talking to anyone tonight.

Chauncy had had his nose to the ground during their entire walk, but suddenly the dog looked up, saw the man who was still almost halfway across the park, and gave a loud, joyous bark. Before Nora could stop him, he lunged forward, breaking her hold on the leash.

"Chauncy!" she cried as he started off at a lumbering run.

Because they hadn't yet reached the special enclosure at the center of the park, she was afraid that he might run out into the street. She raced after him, and shouted his name again, but as if he'd suddenly gone deaf, he didn't even pause in the beeline he was making for the stranger, who was...

Not a stranger.

When Nora recognized the man in the growing darkness, she skidded to a stop. "Lane!" she cried. "What are you doing here?" But then, before he could answer, she held up a hand. "Never mind, I don't want to know." She glanced irritably at her disobedient dog, who was still jumping around him ecstatically, and commanded, "Chauncy, come!"

But her faithful, loyal dog who she'd been positive just moments before would always *be* there for her, ignored her order, sat down right beside Lane and began to gaze up at him adoringly.

"Chauncy!" she cried again.

Lane looked down at her naughty dog. "I think you'd better do what she says, old man," he said with a smile in his voice that made her grit her teeth. "Go on, Chauncy, go to Nora like a good boy."

"I don't need you to tell my dog what to do!" she snapped. "I can manage him perfectly well by my—"

Lane gestured again, and with a last wag of his tail, Chauncy obeyed. As though they were in an obedience trial, the dog came straight to her, walked around behind just as he was supposed to do and came to a perfect sit by her left knee, staring straight ahead. Her lips tight, she looked down at him. She could have sworn there was a twinkle in the dog's eye, and she was so irritated she was tempted to leave them both here while she turned around and marched home by herself.

"All right," she said to Lane, "you've just demonstrated—again—that you know how to make my dog behave better than I do. Is that why you're here—

to show me up? Or was it just because you had nothing better to do?"

He hesitated at her tone, but then he said, "As a matter of fact, I'm supposed to be at a fund-raiser with Delilah Miles. But, as I always seem to be doing with you, I came to apologize, instead."

She wasn't about to give him an inch. Her voice stiff, she asked, "About what?"

"About the way I handled things the other day."

Exasperatingly aware that her heart had begun to beat a little faster just at seeing him, she managed to say coolly, "Oh? And what way was that?"

"I shouldn't have come to your office before calling you first," he said. "I thought at the time that it was a good idea, but..." Seeing her stubborn expression, he shook his head and tried another tack. "I would have called to apologize, but Freddie made one of his usual spur-of-the-instant decisions and had us heading out of town before I could. I just got back and I didn't want to leave a message on some damned answering machine, so I decided I'd come and see you in person."

"At the park? Why didn't you come to the house?"

"Because I wasn't sure you'd even listen to me, never mind let me into your house to explain."

"You're right about that," she muttered. Then she thought of something. "How did you know I'd be here, anyway?"

"I didn't. But you said you always took Chauncy for a walk after work, so I took a chance..." He stopped, and she had to steel herself. Even in this darkening light, he looked so handsome he made her throat ache. "I'm sorry, Nora, I always seem to make you angry. I don't mean to, believe me. I came tonight to ask if we could just start over. I'll be as circumspect as hell, I promise."

"I'm not sure you even know what the word means, Lane," she said. "But it doesn't matter, anyway. I thought I made myself clear the other day—"

He looked at her a moment longer, then he sighed. "You're right," he said. "You did make yourself clear. Okay, if this is the way you want it, I won't bother you again. Goodbye, Nora."

And with that, he started walking away. Nora watched him, her hands clenched at her sides, her jaw clamped tight. She wasn't going to call him back; she wouldn't tell him not to go. This was what she wanted, wasn't it?

At her feet, Chauncy whined. Anxiously, he stood. Glancing from her to Lane and back to her again, he wagged his tail and then took a hesitant step after Lane before returning to her side. He whined again. Wishing she could explain things to him, she put her hand on his massive head.

"Sit, Chauncy," she said.

Ten steps away, Lane turned. "Did you say something?"

It was too dark now to see his face clearly, but something in his voice made her...

Before she could weaken, she said, "No. I was just talking to Chauncy."

"You're really going to let me just walk away?"

Chauncy whined again and started to wag his tail. He took two steps toward Lane, then bounded back to her again. At the sight, she sighed.

Lane heard it, too. "Nora?"

"I can't fight the two of you," she said, and then held up her hand as Lane started toward her and Chauncy whirled around in delight, almost knocking her down. Giving them both a look, she said sternly, "But remember, you *two,* I'm not committing to anything. We're just going to take it one step at a time...."

His eyes glowing, Lane took her hands. "Thanks, Nora," he said softly. "You won't regret giving me another chance, I promise you that."

Thinking that she was already regretting it, she looked up into those eyes. A fragment of an old song flashed across her mind just then, and she knew it could have been written for her: *Just one look, was all it took...*

That's what had happened to her the night she'd met Lane, she thought. Just one look, and everything in her life had changed. Beginning to feel a little frantic again, she said, "Remember, Lane, I'm not—"

He pulled her toward him. With a smile, he said, "I know—committing to anything. Isn't that supposed to be my line?"

"Yes, but I—"

He searched her face. "Don't worry, Nora," he said softly. "This is new for me, too. We'll do as you want, take things slowly, all right?"

She'd thought that's what she wanted, but now she wasn't sure. With their bodies almost touching, her panic was replaced by something even more elemental. She wondered if he felt it, too.

"You look—" Just then, Chauncy barked and Lane laughed wryly as he glanced down at the dog who was demanding attention. "Hey, can't you give a man a break?"

In response, Chauncy barked again. "He's ready to leave now," Nora said. "He won't settle down until I take him home for dinner."

Reluctantly, Lane released her hands. "All right— this time," he said. "Come on, I'll give you both a ride."

He'd parked the Porsche a short distance away, but when they got there and he opened the passenger door, Nora looked inside and laughed. "Where's Chauncy going to ride, in my lap?"

Lane looked perplexed for a moment, then he said, "He can straddle the console. It's only a short ride. Here, let me get this out of the way..."

He grabbed the jacket he'd thrown on the passenger seat, but as he went to open the trunk, Nora glimpsed a copy of a script stuffed down between the front seats. It was titled, *Nobody Home,* and without thinking, she reached for it.

"What's this?" she asked, beginning to leaf through it. She saw the opening monologue, but before she could do more than read the first few sentences, Lane had poked his head around.

"What?"

She held up the script. "This."

His face clouded, and he came back to where she was standing. Practically snatching it from her, he threw it into the trunk. "It's nothing. Just something my agent wants me to do."

"Oh," she said, a little taken aback by his attitude. "I'm sorry, I didn't mean to intrude."

He took a deep breath. "You didn't. It's just that... well, it's not for me, that's all."

"What's it about?"

Instantly, she wished she hadn't asked the question. Looking even more grim, he said, "It's boring—a whole lot of soul-searching. The only thing the guy does through the entire movie, until almost the end, is whine and complain." His voice had turned rough, and when he realized how he sounded, he tried to laugh. "Listen to me! I guess what I'm trying to say is that it's not my style at all. I've tried to convince my agent, Wyatt Parmalee, but he's got this agenda. Now he's started leaving so many copies of that thing around that I'm tripping over them wherever I go."

"Maybe it's because—"

"Look," he said abruptly, "can we change the subject? This is between Wyatt and me. I don't want to talk about it. Chauncy, get in the car."

As always, the dog immediately obeyed Lane. This time, though, Nora didn't mind. With Chauncy taking up so much room, she had to squeeze in herself, and as they started off, she was suddenly glad that the dog's bulk between them prevented conversation. She didn't want to admit it, but she was disturbed by Lane's response just now. She wondered why he'd reacted so strongly to his agent's simple request. Was something wrong with the script, or did the problem lie with him?

A different question came to mind when they pulled up at the house. Should she ask him in? If she did, would it lead to something she wasn't sure now she was ready for? It turned out she didn't have to make an immediate decision. Before she could say anything, the car phone rang, and after answering, Lane spoke a few terse words and then hung up.

"That was the studio," he said. "They're wondering why I haven't showed up at the fund-raiser yet. I'm going to have to put in an appearance, at least, I guess, or risk the wrath of the gods falling on my head."

Trying not to show how relieved she was, she said, "That's all right, I understand."

He looked as if he wanted to kiss her, but with Chauncy scrunched between them, there wasn't room. He reached for the car handle so he could come around to her side, but she quickly opened her own door and got out before he could.

"You'd better get going," she said. "We can see ourselves in."

He looked wryly at Chauncy, who had gotten out of the car with her and was sitting by her side. "You take care of her, boy," he said.

As though he understood, Chauncy barked. Shaking his head, Lane met her eyes and said, "Good night, Nora. And—"

"And?"

"Well, it's not that I don't love Chauncy," he said ruefully, "but do you think that the next time we see each other, we could get a dog-sitter, or something, for him?"

Despite herself, Nora was still smiling when he drove off.

OUT IN BEVERLY HILLS a few days later, Theodora awoke with a smile. The talk with Nora had encouraged her. Her daughter's suggestion about inviting Arthur to lunch was fine, as far as it went, but she could be much more imaginative than that. After all, Arthur worked so hard. He rarely had any *fun,* and one of the things he said he loved most about her was that she could always make him laugh.

"You're so unpredictable, my dear," he'd said to her fondly more than once. "I never know what you're going to say or do next."

"And you like that?" she'd asked.

"I do. I get so tired of people waiting for me to react before they respond—or worse, of having them agree with everything I say."

"You'll never have to worry about that with me," she teased. "I might not have the education or the background you and your friends do, but that doesn't mean I don't have an opinion about any subject you can name."

She had expected him to laugh with her, but when he didn't even smile, she asked, "What is it? Did I say something wrong?"

At the time, they'd been lying side by side on a double chaise lounge, out on the landscaped terrace of his penthouse. The entire space was so expertly crafted and designed that it was like being in a garden—but one that was floating twenty stories in the air. There was even a pool in which Arthur swam his fifty laps on the mornings he was there. A waterfall splashed at one end of the terrace, adding to the gardenlike atmosphere.

Arthur sat up with a frown. "I don't like it when you say things like that. A formal education isn't the only measure of worth. What about native intelligence, or natural talent, or better yet, plain common sense?"

Touched, she reached up and stroked his back. "I didn't mean anything by it, you silly man."

He looked at her over his shoulder. "Yes, you did. That's not the first time you've mentioned formal education. Does it really matter so much to you that you never went to college?"

The mood had been ruined. She'd been hoping she could talk him into doing something really daring, like going swimming in the nude, or making love right out here on the terrace. It was the servants' afternoon off, and who would see them, twenty stories up? But she knew by his expression that she'd never talk him into anything like that now, so with a sigh, she sat up, too.

"It's not so much the lack of a college education I miss," she admitted. "I guess what I'd like is the confidence it gives—"

"Confidence! But you're one of the most confident people—man or woman—that I know!"

"Thank you, but sometimes it's a facade. I *am* an actress, you know."

"We're all actors in one form or other," he said firmly. "I'll bet there's not a soul living who doesn't wear a mask at times. No, I take that back—*most* of the time."

She put her arms around him, resting her cheek against his shoulder. "You're sweet, Arthur, you really are. But you know what I mean. Sometimes one's rough edges can't all be smoothed away. They poke out at the most inconvenient and embarrassing times."

Turning slightly so that he could hold her, he murmured, "I can't imagine you ever embarrassing me."

She hadn't pursued it. Why would she? She would have been a fool to carry on a discussion of her weak points when he began kissing her and caressing her in such delightful ways. But even so, no matter what she said or did, she couldn't persuade him to discard his traditional ways along with the clothes he was wearing. They made love that day, not out in the open under the warm blue sky, but in the bedroom, behind closed doors, as was only proper and customary.

This morning, as she lay in bed, she wondered if she'd ever get Arthur to loosen up. Deciding this was not the time for negative thought, she sat up, reached for the phone and dialed his office. When his secretary answered, she said, "Edie, this is Theodora DeVere. Is Mr. Winslow going out for lunch today?"

"Going out? Well, no, but—"

"Good," she said, already preoccupied with her plans. "Would you please tell him that I'll be there at twelve-thirty sharp to take him to lunch? I know how busy he is, so I promise I'll only keep him for an hour. Thanks so much, Edie. Goodbye now."

"Wait—"

But Theodora couldn't wait. Smiling in anticipation, she hung up the phone, thought a minute and called Chan on the house intercom. Confident he would fulfill her requests, she told him what she wanted and then sat back with a satisfied sigh. Idly, she glanced at the phone again, then with an almost evil grin, she took the phone off the hook. Today was her day off; Freddie had promised it to her because she'd worked so hard the past few weeks. She didn't want someone from the studio to call and ruin everything at the last minute. Still smiling, she got out of bed and went to take a shower.

CHAN WAS as good as his word. He had Theodora's picnic basket ready by the time she came downstairs to pick it up at noon.

"Did you pack the champagne and the paté and the caviar?" she asked.

"It is all there, as you asked."

She thanked him effusively and told him to take the rest of the day off. But as she ordered her driver to take her downtown to Arthur's office building, she couldn't help thinking wickedly that if things went according to plan, food would be the last thing on Arthur's mind.

She didn't usually do this type of thing—at least, she thought with an inward smile, she hadn't for many years. But she still had a good figure, if she did say so herself—and besides, she'd worn even less in some of her films than she had on now. *Oh, won't he be surprised,* she thought with a delicious laugh. She looked down. Underneath the trench coat she was wearing was a flame-colored teddy. Those, and her red high heels, were the only things she had on.

Edie stood up when Theodora breezed in, at exactly twelve-thirty, the picnic basket over her arm. *Just like Little Red Riding Hood,* Theodora thought giddily, and said, "Did you give Mr. Winslow my message, Edie?"

"Yes, I did, Miss DeVere, but—"

Theodora didn't want to hear that Arthur had planned to work through lunch, something he did far too often, in her opinion. Sailing on by the desk, she held up a hand.

"Don't bother to announce me," she said airily. "If necessary, I'll go in and drag him away from his desk. Thanks for your help."

"Miss DeVere!"

But Theodora had already knocked on Arthur's closed office door. Without waiting for an answer, she twisted the knob and went right in.

"Darling!" she exclaimed, coming up to the desk where Arthur was sitting, a surprised look on his face. She tossed the picnic basket lightly on top of the polished surface and unbuckled the coat belt in almost the same motion. Dropping the garment to her shoulders, she gave him her most seductive smile. "I brought lunch," she said throatily. "But dessert is...me!"

With a gay laugh, she began to pirouette for him, and froze. Two men were sitting on the couch that had been hidden by the door she'd so blithely flung open; they looked as stunned at her appearance as she was by theirs.

"My dear Theodora," Arthur said calmly, standing to help her as she grabbed at her slipping coat.

"I'd like to present Ken Fujitsu and Martin Oppenheim of International Electronics. We were about to have lunch sent in, but since you have so thoughtfully provided it, perhaps you'd care to join us. Gentlemen, I'd like you to meet a dear friend of mine, Theodora DeVere."

Theodora didn't know how she escaped with her dignity—and her coat—intact, but somehow she managed. But by the time she got home again and was soaking in a bath, a glass of champagne in her hand and bubbles up to her chin, she knew it was time to face things squarely. Arthur was a dear man. He was a good friend. And, she thought with a reflective smile, a good lover.

But a husband?

Her smile disappeared as she sighed. Ah, that was the problem. No matter how much she tried—how much they *both* tried—they just didn't seem suited. What was she going to do about that?

Theodora went to see Arthur the next morning. She'd thought about what she wanted to do and she knew now it was right. Unfortunately, knowing didn't make it any easier, and as the elevator took her up to his office, she straightened her skirt, patted her hair, and, when the doors opened, went in to talk to the man she'd tried to convince herself she wanted to marry.

"...so you see, darling," she was saying five minutes later, hoping she wasn't going to hurt him *too* much, "it's not that I don't love you, I do. I adore you, in fact. It's just that we're not suited for each other. It's not your fault, it's mine. I just don't fit into your life-style. I'm too...spontaneous and you're too disciplined. I'm sorry, but it just isn't going to work."

They were sitting facing each other on one of the sofas in his office. He hadn't said anything yet, and as she looked at him anxiously, he sighed.

"I hate to say it," he said finally. "But I think you're right."

"You...do?" She had expected him to protest, to tell her he couldn't live without her—at the least, to say that *somehow* they'd work it out. What she hadn't anticipated was this acquiescence—or was it relief she saw in his eyes? She was about to tell him exactly what she thought of it when the humor of the situation struck her and she began to laugh. "Arthur, *do* try not to act so brokenhearted," she said dryly. "If you sob once more, I really will feel guilty for wounding you so deeply."

Smiling, he reached for her hand. "I'm sorry, my dearest. It's just that I've been trying to think of a way to tell you this very thing, and now you've done it for me."

Trying to muster some indignation—what she really wanted to do was giggle—she said, "Is that so! Well, you could have mentioned it before now and saved me several episodes of acute embarrassment!" She looked at him from under her lashes. "Tell me, was it the dinner party or the teddy at lunch that finally changed your mind?"

"Neither," he said, kissing her fingers. "I loved your fire and your spirit and your...er...imagination from the first, Theodora. They're what make you so very special. Please believe me, darling, it doesn't have anything to do with you. The fault is mine. I just can't keep up with you."

His answer was perfect. If he'd said anything else, she would have been insulted. "Oh, my." She sighed. "We tried, but I guess it just wasn't meant to be."

"What will you do now?"

"To mend my broken heart?" She tried to pout, but she couldn't keep the mischief out of her eyes. "I wasn't going to tell you, but since you don't seem to be *too* devastated, I suppose it's safe to let you know. I'm going to accept an engagement in Sydney. I'll fly out right after the film wraps."

"So soon?"

Basking in his obvious dismay, she smiled impishly. "No rest for the wicked, as they say."

"Does this mean we have to say goodbye right now?"

Now she *was* insulted. "Arthur, darling! Do you think I would go without leaving you something to remember me by?"

Without a word, he got up and went to his desk. "Edie," he said over the intercom to his secretary, "cancel all my appointments for the rest of the day."

With a smile, he turned to Theodora. "Shall we, my dear?"

Theodora rose gracefully from the couch and came to him. Huskily, she said, "Darling, I thought you'd never ask..."

CHAPTER FOURTEEN

WHENEVER NORA FELT restless, she put on jeans and an old T-shirt and cleaned house. Already questioning her decision about continuing to see Lane, she hoped a few hours plying mops and brooms would help her work things out. She hated being so indecisive. When they were together, it seemed Lane could talk her into anything; it was only after he'd left, and she had time to reflect, that she began second-guessing herself. Fortunately, today was Saturday; she had the whole day to wrestle with the problem while she cleaned out the closets. If her life wasn't organized, she thought grimly, at least her shelves could be.

She was deep into her task when the doorbell rang. She wasn't expecting anyone and she poked her head out of the front closet just as Chauncy got up and lumbered toward the door. That was when she noticed that he wasn't barking as he usually did for a stranger; instead, he was wagging his tail so furiously that he almost knocked over the hall table when he went by. Seeing the lamp on top begin to teeter, Nora lunged for it. With the expertise that comes from long practice, she managed to grab it just before it fell.

There was a mirror over the table, and she caught sight of herself. Her hair was straggling around her face, and her nose was powdered with dust. Brushing her hair back with both hands, she opened the door.

Lane was on the porch. Surprised, she couldn't say anything at first. Chauncy wasn't so reticent; surging by her, he jumped up on Lane in one of his exuberant greetings, and at that, she found her voice. "Chauncy, you get down this instant!" she commanded.

Needless to say, the dog ignored her. She was just reaching for his collar when Lane scratched Chauncy behind the ear a last time. Calmly, he said, "Chauncy, sit."

To Nora's annoyance, the dog did just that. *I should have known!* she thought with a glare in Chauncy's direction. But then she wondered if this was why she'd given Lane another chance. How could she resist a man who was so good with her dog?

"Hi," Lane said, now that the canine was controlled. Immediately, he held a hand up. "Now, I know what you're going to say, Nora—but really, this time I did try to call. Your phone was off the hook."

"It was?" She didn't believe him until she went to check. Sure enough, she'd tossed something out of the closet during her cleaning frenzy, and it had jiggled the receiver off the hook. Vindicated, Lane grinned.

"See? Now do you mind if I come in?"

"Please do. *And,* since my dog seems to forget I exist whenever you're around, would you mind putting him out in the backyard?" She glared again at the unrepentant Chauncy before adding, "Then, if you like, we can have some coffee."

"Coffee sounds good, but it will have to wait. We don't have time for that."

Warily, she looked at him. "Time? What do you mean?"

Instead of answering, he snapped his fingers at Chauncy, who *of course* got up and followed him down the hall to the back door. Muttering to herself about disloyal dogs who obey virtual strangers while ignoring their owners, she took the opportunity to wash up. When Chauncy finally tired of the ball game he and Lane were involved in, and threw himself down, tongue lolling, Lane came back inside. Nora was waiting for him.

"That ought to hold him for a while," he said.

"Good. Maybe now you'll have time to pay attention to me."

It was the wrong thing to say. His eyes suddenly glowing, he started toward her. "I'll be glad to give you all the attention you need."

"I didn't mean that, and you know it!" They were still in the service porch, a tiny space filled with her washer and dryer and the fifty-gallon garbage can in which she stored Chauncy's kibble. The room suddenly seemed even tinier, and she started edging her way toward the kitchen. "You said you tried to call. What did you want to talk to me about?"

"Oh, that. Well, it's my birthday today—the big Four-O. I wanted to spend it with someone special, and naturally I thought of you."

"H-happy birthday," she stammered, still not sure she was ready for all the complications of a relationship with him. She left the service porch and walked as calmly as she could to the safety of the kitchen.

"So," Lane said, following her, "now that we've agreed to start over, I thought maybe we could spend the day together. If you don't have any other plans, that is. We could do lunch, or something—whatever you like." He grinned. "After all, it's not every day that a macho superhero hunk like me turns forty. Don't you want to be there to see it?"

She pulled herself together. "I don't know. What do you think will happen? Do you break into a million pieces? Turn into a pumpkin right before my eyes?"

He laughed. "Who knows? Why don't you come with me and find out?"

It was the laugh that did it. After all, she told herself defensively, she *had* agreed to give him another chance. A simple lunch and maybe a glass of champagne would be a good beginning, a way to start slow. "All right," she said. "Just give me a minute to change."

"Oh, you don't have to change. You're fine as you are."

She looked down at her jeans and ancient T-shirt. "I can't go to lunch like this!"

"Oh yes, you can."

Before she could protest further, he grabbed her arm and started hustling her toward the door. "Wait! Let me get my purse, at least!"

"You won't need it. It's my treat."

"What about Chauncy?"

He stopped, glancing over his shoulder. From this position, they could see the sliding glass doors off the living room, and sure enough, Chauncy was there, peering in at them. He couldn't have looked more forlorn if he'd tried.

"He can come next time," Lane said. Raising his voice so the dog could hear, he shouted, "I promise!"

With that, he propelled Nora out the front door, down the walk and into his car. Feeling hurried and flushed, she grabbed her seat belt as he climbed in beside her—and then remembered he hadn't told her where they were going.

"Where are we—"

"You'll see," he said, starting the car with a roar.

"Lane," she shouted over the noise, "I don't want my picture in the paper again!"

He grinned. Leaning across the seat, he kissed the tip of her nose. "Don't worry, where we're going, no reporter can follow."

What did that mean? "Lane!"

He made a show of cupping a hand to his ear. "Can't hear you," he shouted. "I guess you'll just have to sit back and enjoy the ride!"

The ride was brisk. With the powerful car throbbing underneath them, they shot onto the freeway and headed east. As the miles whipped by, the endless tracks of houses began to give way to some open space, and when Lane finally zoomed off the freeway and Nora saw a tiny sign indicating an airstrip ahead, she turned to him.

"If you wanted to watch planes land and take off," she shouted as they roared down a dirt road and came to a rocking halt beside a hangar in the middle of nowhere, "why didn't we go to International?"

"Because we're not going to *watch* them, that's why," he said into the sudden silence as he stopped the car.

"What? But you said we were going to have lunch—" She stopped and looked at him suspiciously. "You did mean *here* in Los Angeles, didn't you? I mean—you aren't thinking of *flying* someplace to eat!"

"Not to eat, no," he said with that grin. He started to get out of the car, but she lunged across the seat and grabbed his arm.

"Lane, tell me what's going on!"

He was about to answer, but just then, a man in coveralls emerged from the hangar. Seeing them there, he shouted, "Hey, what's up?"

"We are, if the plane's ready," Lane shouted back as he came around and pulled Nora effortlessly out of the car. "Did you get my message?"

"She's all gassed up. We're just waiting for you."

"You're losing time, then, because we're here. By the way, this is Nora. Nora, meet Dailey Farwell, one of the best pilots in the business."

Feeling somehow as though she were in the twilight zone, Nora tried to remember her manners. "Hello, Mr. Farwell—"

"Oh, hell, call me Dailey, everyone does," the pilot said. He squinted. "You going to dive, too?"

"Dive?" she echoed. "What do you mean, *dive?"*

Daily glanced at Lane. "Oh, hey, man, I'm sorry," he said. "I didn't know it was supposed to be a surprise."

"No problem," Lane said. "She had to know sometime. It might as well be now."

"Know what? What are you guys talking about?"

Dailey backed away. "I'll leave this to you," he said to Lane. "I'll just go and check the chutes, like a good friend should."

"Chutes?" Nora said.

Lane couldn't have looked more innocent if he tried. "Didn't I tell you? I always skydive on my birthday. It's just something I do."

Nora's eyes widened, and she stumbled back a step. "Sky*dive?*" she said, her voice rising as she realized just what he intended. Wildly, she shook her head. "Oh, no, not me!"

"Come on, you're going to love it."

"No. No, I won't. I'm not going to... You can't..." Realizing she was stammering, she looked around, searching for—what? Escape? It was too late. With a laugh, Lane took her arm and started toward the hangar. She tried to dig her heels in, but it had no effect. "Lane, I'm not going up in any plane, do you hear me?" she cried. "And I'm *not,* repeat *not,* going to... to..." She couldn't say it. She couldn't believe this was happening. "Lane! Listen to me! I can't do it! I never have, and I never wanted to, and I won't!"

He stopped. "You're not afraid, are you?"

"Afraid? Me?" She tried to sound indignant, but she wondered just what she was feeling. Quickly, she looked out at the airstrip. A plane was sitting there, and Daily was walking around it. It seemed obvious that it was the one they intended to take up. It suddenly looked very small. "I don't know," she said, still staring at it. "I've never done anything like this before."

"Then it's about time, don't you think?"

Again, she looked at the plane. It seemed to have shrunk. "No, I—"

"Are you afraid to fly?"

"Don't be silly, I fly all the time! But I...but I don't jump out of the things! I sit there, like everybody else does, until we get where we're going."

"But Nora," he said softly, "you're not like everybody else, are you? You want to do this, I know it. And I'll be with you, every step of the way. Daily is a great pilot. You won't even know you're up."

"Well, I—"

"Come on, Nora—let yourself go," he said, encouraging that damned little devil inside her that she was having such a hard time controlling lately. "Look around. There's nobody here but us. Not a reporter in sight. Who's going to know?" He bent a little so he could look into her face. His eyes were very blue. "Except me... and you?"

Biting her lip, she looked at the plane again. It *was* a beautiful machine, she had to admit. She didn't know much about planes, but this one was painted white with red-and-blue stripes and it looked...it looked as though it were just waiting for the chance to dash down the runway and leap into the sky. And when she thought of herself and Lane in that plane, how free it would feel, how—

She tried to bring herself up short, to get this wild feeling that was surging inside her under control, but she couldn't manage it. Despite herself, her eyes began to sparkle, and her face took on a glow. Right now, it didn't seem to matter that she didn't *do* crazy, impulsive things like this. Who cared that she had schooled herself all these years to be always in control? How could she *not* respond to that look in Lane's eyes; how could she ignore that beautiful little plane sitting on the runway, just waiting to take her up into the experience of a lifetime?

"All right," she said before she could think about it anymore. Inside her, she was sure she could hear the little devil shouting a cheer. She felt like cheering herself. "I'll do it!"

Lane didn't question her. Instantly, he turned to Daily and shouted, "Two to go!"

"Then let's do it!" Daily shouted back, thrusting his thumb into the air.

Thirty minutes later, wearing a jumpsuit that was so big she'd had to roll up the cuffs, Nora tried to climb into the plane, but she couldn't manage it. As though her body had just realized what she was about to do, her legs started shaking so much she couldn't get up the ladder. With a laugh, Lane boosted her up and she landed in the belly of the plane with a thump.

Dailey was already up front at the controls, a copilot beside him; they both looked back with a grin as she stumbled in. Then Lane followed, and before she could swallow over the sudden dryness in her throat and tell everybody she'd changed her mind, they were rolling out to the runway, picking up speed...airborne.

True to his word, Lane was beside her as the plane bounced into the sky, and Nora looked down with amazement. Far below already, the ground was falling away, and if she pressed her face against the window, she could see a tiny little building and an even smaller little car beside it that were the hangar and Lane's Porsche. Her eyes widened.

"We're up so high!" she exclaimed.

He grinned at her expression. "Isn't it great?"

It was—more than that. Now that they were aloft, the churning in her stomach settled down. She'd never been in a plane this small; it almost seemed as if she were flying herself. For a thrilling moment or two, a hawk soared below them, then, too soon, it drifted out of sight underneath one of the wings.

"I... I never knew it could be like this," Nora breathed, glancing at Lane, who was sitting right beside her, his arm casually over her shoulders. When she realized that he'd been watching her and not the scenery outside, she blushed and looked out the window again.

He leaned toward her. "Now, aren't you glad you came?"

She couldn't imagine why she'd been afraid of this. It was wonderful, she thought, and turned to tell him so. But just then, Dailey called something out over his shoulder, and when Lane began to get up, she looked at him in alarm.

"What are you doing?" she asked. "Where are you going?"

Smiling, he reached down and pulled her up. "Now we're *really* going to fly," he said.

She'd forgotten all about jumping out of the plane. It seemed a crazy thing to do—crazier now than it had on the ground. Panicked, she cried, "No, I can't! I've... I've changed my mind!"

It was too late to change her mind. The copilot had already left his seat and had made his way to the back of the plane. He was crouched beside the door, waiting for who-knew-what. Suddenly terrified, she looked around, saw Dailey still sitting up front and said, "I'll stay with Dailey! We'll all meet you on the ground!"

Lane laughed. "You don't really mean that."

She looked down. The ground seemed awfully far away. She had to be crazy, she thought. How could she even *think* of jumping out of this plane?

"I don't know what to do!" she wailed.

"You don't have to do anything," Lane said calmly. "Remember, I told you we'd be strapped together?"

She had forgotten that. They were both wearing a harness affair; Lane's had a bulky pack on the back that she just now remembered held the parachute. Even so, she had to be sure.

"What if something goes wrong?" she asked tremulously.

"Nothing's going to go wrong," he assured her. "I have an instructor's license and I've done this a thousand times—"

"It's not enough!" she cried, but it was a token protest, and they both knew it.

"All right," she said unsteadily but determined to go through with it, after all. "But I'm so scared that I've completely forgotten what I'm supposed to do. Tell me again—and make it simple!"

He made it as simple as possible. Turning her around so that her back was to his front, he clipped them together with the harnesses. The copilot, seeing they were ready, checked the leather caps and plastic goggles they were both wearing, tugged at the rig and the straps to make sure everything was working and nodded. He opened the door and Lane stepped forward, taking Nora with him.

"Wait, I'm not ready!" she screamed as the wind hit her in the face.

"You're going to love it," Lane said in her ear. Then he stepped out into open air.

Nora was too terrified to scream again. With her eyes squeezed shut, she prepared to die. But nothing happened except that they started to...float. Dimly, she heard the roar of the plane's engines recede as the aircraft sped away, then there was only the sound of the wind rushing by.

Cautiously, she slitted her eyes, then quickly shut them again when she glimpsed the ground so far below. But wait, she thought: what was that panorama she'd seen?

Bit by tiny bit, she opened her eyes again, until she forgot her fear and was staring with wonder. She'd never seen anything like this! Below them, the earth spread out as far as she could see. The sight was so incredible that she gasped. Now that she wasn't so afraid, she could even feel the warmth of the sun on her face, could hear the wind whistling in her ears and feel the buoyancy of the air. Flying in a jet, she thought, had never been like this!

"Oh, Lane!" she cried. She tried to turn her head to look at him, but he was right behind her, and all she could see was the side of his helmet. She didn't realize until then that he was guiding them with his arms and legs, spreading both wide so that they floated on an invisible tide. She thought she heard him laugh, but she couldn't be sure, for she was smiling like a fool herself by then. She loved this! Why hadn't she ever done it before?

"Hang on, we're going up," he said in her ear just before he pulled the cord that opened the chute.

The multicolored square chute unfurled behind them, filling with air so rapidly that it took them on a wild ride up, making her gasp. The feeling was so much beyond anything she'd ever experienced that she cried, "This is great!"

In answer, Lane put his arms around her and held on tight. This time, she was sure she heard him laugh, and she joined in. Oh, she never wanted this ride to end!

All too soon, of course, it did. Long before the ground started rushing up at a dizzying speed, she'd forgotten she'd ever been scared. She even remembered what she'd been told about taking the shock of landing in her knees and ankles. Then it was over. She was on her feet in a second, turning to Lane after he'd unsnapped the harness that bound them together. Laughing with pure delight, she launched herself right into his arms.

"I want to go again!" she cried. "I've never experienced anything so wonderful in my life!"

Fortunately, it wasn't as windy on the ground as it had been on high. If it had been, the parachute and lines that he dropped so that he could kiss her would have tangled up and carried them away. His lips were cold at first from the jump, but Nora didn't care. Holding him tight, she kissed him again.

"Oh, Lane, I'll never forget this!"

"I knew you'd love it," he said when they finally pulled back to catch their breaths. "You, Nora Carmichael, are not what you pretend to be, or what you try to seem."

"Oh, yes, I am!"

He stopped her protest with another kiss, and for a while neither of them realized they were no longer alone. Still wrapped up in the thrill of the moment and in each other, they didn't notice Dailey landing the plane and then trotting over to the big field to see what was keeping them. Even when she realized he was there, Nora wasn't embarrassed, as she normally would have been. When she saw him grinning at them, she grinned back and gave him a smart salute.

"Hey, Dailey!" she called. "That was great! When are we going up again?"

There wasn't time to go up again, not today, anyway. On the way back to the hangar, Lane put his arm around her and said with a laugh to his pilot, "I think we made a convert."

"Happens every time," Dailey said, and then stood outside to wave as they drove away.

Lunch seemed anticlimactic after what Nora had just experienced. She was sure she was too excited to eat...until they stopped at a little out-of-the-way place Lane had found where people knew who he was but still minded their own business. Despite her protest, he ordered them both huge sandwiches, and then chuckled when she immediately attacked the ham on rye with gusto.

"I thought you weren't hungry," he said with a twinkle in his eye, between bites of his own roast beef.

Nora glanced down at her spotless plate with a wry smile. "I didn't think I was." She looked up again, her eyes glowing. "But I couldn't help it. I've never done anything like that before. It was...out of this world!"

He reached for her hand. "And so are you," he said softly.

Remembering the scene out in the field after they'd landed, she felt herself grow warm. "Lane, I—"

Quickly, he motioned for the check. "Oh, no, you don't. You're not going to start backpedaling on me now. Remember, it's still my birthday, and we have to do whatever I want."

"Whatever *you* want?" She looked at him indignantly to hide the excitement she felt at the thought that this day wasn't over yet. "I didn't agree to that!"

"Oh, I'm sure you did," he said, throwing down some money for the check.

"Where are we going now?" she asked as he bundled her into the car. "What can we possibly do now that will top that jump?"

With an unmistakable light in his eyes, he turned to her. "Guess," he said.

CHAUNCY GREETED them with a joyful bark when they got home. Lane had pulled her into his arms the instant they unlocked the door, but after a kiss that left her breathless, she extricated herself reluctantly and said, "I have to let him in. If I don't, he'll start to howl."

"Let him in, then," Lane growled in mock impatience. Quickly, he kissed her neck, and then he released her. "But can't he stay down here?"

"*You* try to convince him," she said despairingly. "He never pays any attention to me."

"No problem," Lane said confidently. "I'll just explain things to him, man-to-man."

Wishing him success, Nora gratefully left him to the task of subduing the eager Chauncy, and went upstairs. She didn't have time for a shower, but she hurried into the bathroom to dab some of her best perfume behind her ears. As she did, she saw herself in the mirror and recoiled. Oh, Lord, what a mess. After that wild ride, her hair was tangled, and she had a smudge of something on her cheek. She was just reaching for her hairbrush when Lane appeared behind her.

"You look beautiful," he whispered.

"How can you say that? I—"

He turned her around to face him, and stopped whatever she'd been about to say with a look that made her forget her appearance. His gaze held hers as he took her hand and turned it faceup. His mouth seemed to burn when he kissed her palm, and when he touched the inside of her wrist, her breath caught. Still holding her hand, he moved to the inside of her elbow, and then he put her arm around his neck and, just like a hero in a movie, effortlessly lifted her and carried her into the bedroom where he gently set her on her feet. Then he placed both hands on her waist and slowly drew her to him again.

When they touched, she could feel his body's reaction, and something essential in her responded. With a soft sound, she pressed more tightly against him.

"Lane, don't you think we should—"

He stopped her midsentence by winding his fingers gently in her hair and turning her face up to his. He gazed deeply into her eyes for a long moment, then slowly lowered his head to kiss her again. This touch of his lips released the desire she'd been trying to hold back, and all she could think was that she wanted more of him, all he had to give. She forgot everything else—promises, hesitations, reservations—wrapped her arms around his neck and returned his kiss with all her heart.

Her response rocked him, and they clung to each other, trembling with emotion, until finally they had to break the contact or be swept away utterly.

Gasping, Lane raised his head. He looked as dazed as she felt, his eyes so blue they appeared almost black. "I want you," he said hoarsely. "I want you like I've never wanted anyone or anything ever before."

She wanted him, too—wanted to feel his skin under her hands, wanted to feel the bunching of his muscles as she caressed him, wanted to feel every inch of his body. Pulling his shirt out from his pants, she slid her hands up his belly to his chest. His skin was smooth and warm under her touch, and she put her cheek next to him for a moment, luxuriating in the feel and scent and power of him.

With a groan, he reached for her. She was still wearing her closet-cleaning jeans and T-shirt, but when he put a hand on her breast, the material felt like armor, and she wanted to fling her clothes off so she could feel his hands on her. Quickly, she reached for her shirttail, but he anticipated her and gently pushed away her hands.

"No," he whispered. "Let me..."

Slowly, they undressed each other. As each garment fell away, her desire mounted until she was almost shaking with the urge to fling herself upon him and beg him to make love to her. But every time she lost control and reached for him, he held her gently away, until finally, they had unsnapped the last snap, unbuttoned the last button, pulled down the last zipper, and were standing naked before each other.

The look on Lane's face made the excruciating wait worthwhile. Never had a man looked at her as he was doing now, and never had she felt so desirable as she did when he finally brought his eyes back to her face and whispered, "You...you're so...beautiful..."

With a smile, she lifted her arms and pulled him to her. The feeling of his body next to hers made her draw in a breath, and she closed her eyes, luxuriating in the sensation. With their arms around each other, they stood still for a long time, enjoying this moment so they could prolong the next. But finally, with one thought, they moved to the bed.

She wanted to make the wonderful, tender moment last, but in the instant they lay down together, it was as though a storm rose up and swept them away. Nora tried to step back, to slow down and take her time, but her body wouldn't allow it. Lane's touch stirred the fire inside her, and when she caressed him until he could no longer control his own desire, she was more than ready for him. By the time he entered her, they didn't have time for slow kisses or gentle touches; passion had become a throbbing, living entity of its own, demanding release.

"Oh, Lane," she said, her breath against his cheek, "I can't wait—"

He couldn't wait, either. Hunger, once liberated, wouldn't be denied, and they clutched at each other, straining to know each other in a union as old as Time. His mouth was hot on her breasts, his tongue a tease on her nipples, his hand an exquisite agony that moved ever so slowly to caress her until, unable to bear the exquisite torture any longer, she wrapped her legs tightly around him and guided him inside.

Pure sensation took them over, and suddenly they were in the midst of a whirlwind, their bodies no longer their own, passion hurling them into a place where pleasure began to build and build until Nora had to bite her lip to keep from screaming. As sensation spread through her like welcome fire, she renewed her efforts to bring Lane with her, until finally, at the same joyous instant, they reached the apex and cried out together. As Nora strained upward, Lane's name on her lips, his cry joined hers. Holding tightly together, they exulted in shared sensation until at last, they laughed in sheer release ... and collapsed like leaves in a spent wind.

A LONG TIME LATER, Lane lifted his head. "What's that noise?" he asked.

Nora had been drifting in some dreamworld she couldn't explain. She hadn't heard a thing, but when he asked, she lifted her head and tried to listen. It was a . . . scratching sound.

"What?" she muttered.

She was about to sit up when the door to the bedroom burst open and a hundred-plus pounds of dog launched himself across the room. Nora only had time to fling the tangled bedclothes over their naked bodies to protect them before Chauncy landed at the end of the bed like a giant cannonball, rocking not only the bed, but practically the entire room.

"What the hell?" Lane shouted, his voice muffled. In her haste, Nora had thrown the covers over his head, and he was trying to fight his way out from under them and Chauncy's heavy weight at the same time. When he finally succeeded in pulling the bedspread off so he could look around, Nora started to laugh. "Welcome to Chauncy's world," she said, trying not to giggle.

Lane's hair was standing on end. Scrubbing at his face, he muttered, "What's the matter with that dog? I told him to stay in the kitchen!"

"He was worried about me," Nora said, doing her best to look solemn. "I guess we made a little too much noise, and he thought he should investigate."

"Investigate!"

She laughed at his expression. "You should know by now that he won't stay where he doesn't want to."

Lane threw off the covers, and got up. He looked down at the dog who had wormed his way up to a place beside Nora. "Didn't we talk about this, old man?" he demanded.

As dejected as could be, Chauncy whined and got down off the bed. Practically crawling, he came to sit in front of Lane, his ears dropping, and the whites of his eyes showing pitifully as he peered up at the man.

"Oh, for heaven's sake!" Lane said, trying not to laugh. "He should have been in pictures, Nora. What a ham!"

Nora would have answered, but she was too busy staring at Lane. Standing there without a stitch on, he was enough to take her breath away. She was about to reach for him when the phone rang.

"What now?" Lane said, exasperated. "Is this Grand Central Station? Whatever happened to privacy? Chauncy, you stay down," he added as Nora laughed and pulled him back into bed. "We'll discuss this later." To Nora, he said, "Aren't you going to answer that?"

"What are you, the conductor?" she asked, nibbling on his ear. "Don't worry about it. I'll let it ring."

Distracted by the sensations she was arousing in him, he forgot the phone, which rang two more times before the answering machine by the bed clicked on. By then, with Lane's hands roaming over her, Nora had completely forgotten it, too. But as soon as she heard her mother's voice, she lifted her head. Beside her, Lane threw himself back on the pillow and groaned.

"Darling, are you there?" Theodora asked on the machine. "Oh, if you are, please answer. I have to talk to you. You'll never guess what's happened!"

Nora sighed. "I have to answer," she said to Lane, who by this time had thrown a dramatic arm over his eyes.

"Go ahead," he muttered. "The next thing will probably be the Salvation Army Band wanting to march through the bedroom."

"Shh," Nora said, reaching for the receiver. Sitting up, she clutched the sheet around her and said, "Mother, I'm here. What is it? What's happened?"

"Oh, darling, thank goodness," Theodora exclaimed. "I wanted to tell you before you found out some other way. Remember when you advised me to take Arthur to lunch? Well, it was a disaster..."

Although she tried to signal him to wait, Lane got up and dressed during Theodora's tale of the picnic-lunch debacle. Nora knew he was going to leave if she didn't stop him so she interrupted her mother in the middle of a sentence, and promised to call her back as soon as she could. Throwing on a robe, she followed Lane downstairs.

"You don't have to go!"

"Yes, I do. It's late, and the mood is gone. What did your mother want?"

"Oh, to tell me about something silly she did where Arthur was concerned."

He looked intrigued. "What was that?"

Because she didn't want him to leave just yet, Nora found herself relating the embarrassing story of her mother's attempted seduction at Arthur's office.

When she got to the part where Theodora dramatically threw off her coat to reveal the fact that she was wearing nothing but a teddy underneath, Lane laughed.

"Trust Theodora to do something like that!"

Nora tried not to be, but she was annoyed at his reaction. "It's not funny, Lane!"

"Yes, it is," he insisted, still amused. "Oh, I can just picture the scene!"

So could Nora. And the more she thought about it, the more irritated she became. How could her mother have done something so... so outrageous? And how could Lane think it was funny?

Her hands clenching, she demanded, "Tell me what's amusing about a woman—about my mother, for God's sake!—showing up at a place of business and interrupting an important meeting wearing nothing but a... but a..." She was so outraged that she couldn't even say it. Just *thinking* about it made her embarrassed. How *could* her mother have done such a thing?

"Hey," Lane said, obviously just now realizing that she wasn't laughing with him. "It was just a joke."

"A joke! Can you imagine what Arthur felt? And what about the two businessmen?"

He looked taken aback. "It was all in fun—"

"Fun! Is that all you think of?"

"Why are you so mad?"

Why couldn't he understand? Lifting her chin, she said, "I should have known you'd stick together. Actors always do!"

"What do you mean by that? I'm not taking sides—"

"Oh, yes, you are!" She knew she was overreacting, but she couldn't seem to stop herself. "I can't tell you how many times I've seen my mother sailing into complete catastrophe on a whim! It happened all the time when I was a child. Neither of my parents ever gave a thought to the consequences of their actions. They just acted on the spur of the moment and did whatever the hell they wished!"

"Hey, you don't have to get upset—"

"I'm not upset!" she shouted. Realizing how she sounded, she made an effort to control herself. Her voice cold, she said, "I don't want to discuss this anymore. I think you'd better go. Didn't you say it was late?"

"Nora, why are you doing this?"

"I'm not doing anything!" she cried. "I just want you to go!"

He looked at her a moment longer, then he nodded. "All right, if that's the way you want it."

"That's the way I want it."

"Fine. Good night."

"Good night!" she snapped. Then, after she'd seen him to the door, she couldn't resist. "Oh, yes—happy birthday."

"Yeah, right. Happy birthday," he repeated bitterly. Without another word, he turned and strode down the walk.

Just barely preventing herself from slamming it, Nora shut the door and leaned against it. When she heard the Porsche start, she closed her eyes and sank down until she was a little heap on the floor. Chauncy, who had been quiet during the fierce argument, came and sat beside her. Tentatively, he gave her cheek a lick. That was all she needed. With a sob, she burst into tears and buried her face in his ruff.

"Oh, Chauncy!" she wept. "How could things have gone so wrong so fast?"

CHAPTER FIFTEEN

WHEN NORA CAME to work Monday morning, her office was filled with roses. Transfixed by the sight, she was standing on the threshold when Ginger came up and said with a grin, "They've been coming ever since I got here. Bunches and bunches of them."

"If any more come," Sherrie said behind them, "we won't know where to put them all."

Nora knew how to remedy that. Her face set, she handed two of the closest vases to each secretary, and asked them to take the others and put them around the outer office.

"Oh, I think it's *so* romantic," Ginger said with a sigh.

"Imagine, sending *dozens* of roses," Sherrie said. She looked slyly at Nora. "It must have been *some* weekend!"

"It was," Nora said in a tone that indicated she didn't wish to discuss it. "But not in the way you think."

The two secretaries glanced at each other, then wisely took their bouquets and went away. As soon as they were gone, Nora went to her desk and called the studio. She intended to tell Lane that it wasn't going to do him any good to inundate her with flowers, but a secretary informed her that everyone was in an all-morning production meeting and couldn't be disturbed, so she had to leave a terse message, instead. She was just hanging up when she saw Rodney standing in the doorway. She thought he'd come to make some smart remark about the roses, but then she saw the newspaper folded under his arm.

Not again! she thought, and said coldly, "Yes?"

Smirking, he came into her office and held out the paper. "I thought you might be interested in this. I've already marked it."

He had indeed: in red. When she saw the article, she tried not to cringe. The item began:

Rumor has it that superstar Lane Kincaid was seen at a certain airfield this weekend, wrapped up with a mystery woman who's said to be giving him financial advice. If money matters were being discussed, we'd like to be let in on the deal. Seems they were sealing it with a kiss...

It took all her willpower to fold the paper casually and give it back to Rodney. "And your point is...?" she said.

His eyes glinting spitefully behind his round glasses, he said, "Come on, Nora. It's obvious that *you're* this mystery woman."

"And why would you think that? Mr. Kincaid is a star. He knows hundreds of people."

"I'm sure he does. But how many of them are supposed to be giving him financial advice?"

Nora thought of a dozen things to say to this hateful little man, all of them calculated, she could bet, to send him running even faster to Mr. Bullard than he already intended. She had to content herself by saying, "I don't have any idea how many people give Mr. Kincaid financial advice. If you'll excuse me, I have to get back to work."

"You were warned about this," he said, ignoring the hint. "Now, I know you pulled a fast one last time with that fiasco at the racetrack, but we're both aware it's not going to work again. Tell me, Nora, how are you going to get out of this?"

Nora reached pointedly for one of the folders in front of her. "I don't have to explain anything to you. So, you do what you have to, Rodney." She looked up at him, her gaze direct. "But I'll tell you one thing— your pitiful attempts to discredit me aren't going to work. Mr. Bullard might not like unwanted publicity, but he likes your kind of behavior even less."

Her bravado lasted until he left. When she was alone, she slumped at her desk. It didn't take a genius to figure out what he was going to do. Rodney was probably on his way to Bullard's office right now. No doubt she could expect a summons before the day was out, so she'd better start thinking of an explanation—fast. This time, the promotion wasn't on the line; it was her job that was at stake.

THE SUMMONS CAME late that afternoon, just when she'd lulled herself into believing she might escape. She still hadn't a clue about what she intended to say; she'd just have to trust her instincts.

Five minutes later, she was glad she hadn't agonized over a speech. The newspaper was on Bullard's desk when she went in, and when she saw the item circled in red, it was obvious that her nemesis hadn't wasted any time. Before she could think of what to say, the boss spoke.

"I'm disappointed in you, Nora," he said. "I thought we had an understanding."

"We did," she said, outwardly calm while inside she was shaking like a leaf. "As far as I'm concerned, we still do."

"You've seen this?" he asked. At her nod, he demanded, "Then how do you explain it? Are you this 'mystery woman'?"

Just when she needed all her poise, she could feel that little devil inside struggling for expression again. Already irked at Bullard's attitude, she told herself she was going to remain in control no matter how tempted she might be to tell him exactly what she thought.

"I can't explain it, Mr. Bullard," she said. "Furthermore, I don't think I should have to."

He looked at her as though he hadn't heard right. "I beg your pardon?"

Recklessly, she went on. "I thought you called me in here to ask about some aspect of my work. Have I disappointed you in that capacity? Have I failed to live up to your expectations at the office?"

He reddened. "Your work is not the issue here! You know exactly why I wanted to see you. I demand an explanation!"

"And I can't give you one. My personal life is my business."

"Not when it affects this firm!"

She couldn't believe they were having this conversation—or that she was behaving in this outrageous manner. What was happening to her? She didn't know, but she couldn't seem to stop herself.

"How has it affected the firm?" she heard herself ask. "As far as I know, the 'mystery woman' is just that. Why do you think it was me? Does it matter if it was? My work has been satisfactory. And to my knowledge, none of our clients have made any complaints."

By this time, Bullard was clearly trying to control his temper. "Nora, I'm aware that you've been working very hard these past few months, but I will not tolerate this . . . this insubordination. You know how I feel about publicity, and—"

Suddenly, the only thing Nora knew for sure was that she was tired of catering to this man, tired of tiptoeing around so she wouldn't offend him, weary of apologizing and explaining and *demeaning* herself because she'd wanted a promotion she was no longer sure she desired, anyway.

Not want the promotion? Was she out of her mind? She must be, but if she was, she suddenly felt freer than she had in years. She had no doubt she'd probably regret this wild impulse, but as she looked at her red-faced boss again, she didn't care. For once, she was going to do what she should have done long ago, and think about the consequences later.

"I'm sorry, Mr. Bullard," she said. "But it seems we don't see eye to eye here—"

"We certainly do not! Now, you listen to me, young lady—"

That did it. If there was one thing she'd always hated, it was to be called "young lady," as though she were a schoolgirl who needed a good talking-to.

"No, I'd like you to listen to me," she said before she could think it through any further. "It seems to me there's only one solution here. You'll have my resignation on your desk before close of business today."

He couldn't have looked more shocked if she'd taken out an ax and started hacking away at his antique desk. "You can't quit!"

She had already started toward the door. At his exclamation, she turned around. "Yes, I can," she said. "I just did."

"You'll be sorry!"

She already was.

BY THE TIME she got home, she was exhausted. She knew the news would spread fast in that small office, but she wanted to avoid explanations for as long as possible, so she'd typed her resignation and placed it on his desk herself after everyone had gone. It was after six by the time she arrived at the house; her steps dragging, she was just letting Chauncy in when the phone rang.

At the sound, she sighed. She hoped it wasn't her mother; she hadn't called Theodora back last night after that horrible scene with Lane, but they'd had a brief conversation around noon when Theodora called to finish the story about breaking up with Arthur. Nora was sorry about that; she'd liked Arthur Winslow. But she couldn't muster much sympathy when she had so many problems of her own, and besides, her mother hadn't sounded devastated, just a little wistful.

To her dismay, it wasn't her mother on the phone; it was Lane, and as soon as he heard her voice, he asked, "What's wrong?"

She didn't want to go into it. Nor did she want to talk to him. She needed time to think about what she had done; a few days—maybe a few years—to adjust to the fact that she had just sabotaged her entire career.

"Nothing's wrong," she said tersely. "What do you want?"

He hesitated a moment, then asked, "Did you get the flowers?"

"Didn't you get my message?" she countered.

"Yes, I got it, but I couldn't call you back. Nora, can we talk?"

"Lane, it's been a long day, and I'm not really—"

"I don't want to leave it like this, Nora," he said. "I'm sorry we had that…misunderstanding last night, but I'd like an opportunity to explain. Or at least," he added, "to understand what the hell happened so that I can make it right. Will you give me the chance?"

She hated herself. When he was like this, she had no resolve at all. "The last time you said that," she reminded him, "I found myself strapped to a parachute."

"Which you enjoyed," he said. "Are you free this weekend?"

"This weekend?" she repeated. Then she realized that, at the moment, with no job prospects lined up, every day of her life would soon be free. Trying not to cry at the thought, she said, "Don't tell me you've found another investment."

"Well, as a matter of fact, you *did* advise me to look into utilities, remember? And as far as I know, water and power qualify."

"Lane, I'm not in the mood to joke around—"

"No, I can see that," he said, instantly sober. "All right, then, let me put it like this. Our slave driver of a director has ordered us all back down to Palm Springs for more location shots, and in spite of the fact that I threw myself on his mercy, he won't let me out of it. We're leaving tonight, which is why I'm calling instead of camping on your doorstep. As much as I'd like to see you sometime—any time—this week, that's out. So I thought... I hoped...I could talk you into coming up to Lake Arrowhead with me next weekend. Just for the day if you want," he added hastily. "I'd like it to be the whole weekend, but I won't push my luck."

"Lane—"

"No, please listen, Nora. I have to go up, anyway. I've got a little place there that I haven't visited for a while, and I should check things out." Pointedly, he added, "It has two bedrooms."

"Lane, I don't think that's a good idea—"

"Please, Nora? I can't believe you'd condemn me for a little insensitivity."

It was more than his reaction to her mother's debacle, she thought: it was a lifetime of choices that each of them had made.

Be firm, she told herself. She'd already gotten herself into enough trouble because of him, and she couldn't let him sway her. Where was her backbone?

Turned into a noodle, apparently, she thought as she answered, "Even if I wanted to, I couldn't leave Chauncy. The last time I had to board him, he was so depressed he started losing his coat."

"No problem," Lane said without cracking a smile. "Bring him along."

"I can't—"

"Yes, you can." He sensed that she was weakening and went on quickly. "Now, listen, Freddie promised us faithfully that he'd have us all back by Saturday morning, so we'll go up then. You won't have to do a thing. I'll drive, I'll cook, I'll even walk the dog if you like. All you have to do is relax."

It was tempting, she had to admit. And it certainly seemed to beat the prospects of lying around the house wondering if she had a future or not. Even though she knew she should refuse, she heard herself agreeing to come—only for the day.

"Whatever you say," Lane said quickly before she could change her mind. "I'll see you Saturday morning."

Was she doomed never to stand up to this man? she wondered as she hung up the phone. Hoping the coming weekend would give her some answers, she looked down at Chauncy. The big dog was sitting patiently at her feet with his leash in his mouth. Her world had just crumbled, but he was ready for his walk.

THE REST of the week was a nightmare. Nora knew that she couldn't keep her resignation secret, but she hadn't expected everyone to know the next morning. Both secretaries were almost in tears, and even Rodney Jones was too shocked to gloat—especially when Orrin Bullard informed him that he'd decided to table the matter of the promotion for anyone—indefinitely. Tight-lipped, Bullard had asked Nora to stay on until he found a replacement, and she agreed—if he wrote a letter of recommendation for her in return. Coldly, he said he would.

About midweek, she took Ginger and Sherrie out to lunch. She felt she owed them some kind of explanation, but after she'd told them what had happened, she had to talk them out of quitting, themselves.

"But it's not fair!" Sherrie said.

"I had my choice," Nora reminded them. "And I don't want either of you doing anything rash just because of me."

"But what will you do when you leave?" Sherrie asked plaintively.

"I'll find another job," she said more confidently than she felt.

"You're not even going to take a vacation?" Ginger asked.

It hadn't even occurred to her. The upcoming weekend—the upcoming *day trip*—with Lane was all the time she intended to take, and she wasn't even sure right now that she should do that. With her career derailed, she shouldn't be wasting time. She needed to get her life back on track again.

Still, when Saturday arrived, she and Chauncy were ready. Just in case. Of what? she wondered. A hurricane? An earthquake? Some other natural disaster that would keep them at the lake overnight? She'd packed a small duffel with a few things. Chauncy's accoutrements took more space, but Lane didn't even change expression when he saw the two bags on the porch. In fact, she thought, he looked even more tentative than she felt as he came up the walk. As though unsure of his welcome, he gave her a circumspect kiss on the cheek when she answered the door, but Chauncy wasn't so reticent. The dog jumped up on Lane in his usual expansive greeting, and as she watched them play for a moment, she wondered wistfully why things couldn't be so simple where she was concerned.

She still wasn't sure she'd made the right decision about this, and when Lane finally gestured to the dog to get down, and saw her expression, he asked, "You haven't changed your mind, have you?"

She wanted to say yes, close the door and pretend none of this had ever happened. Instead, she shook her head. "No, I haven't changed my mind. It's just—"

"Can we enjoy the drive? When we get to the lake, we can talk . . . all right?"

He was right, she thought. It was too beautiful a day to start fighting, especially over something she wasn't even sure about. "All right," she agreed. "But when we get there—"

"We'll go to the mat, if you like," he said, crossing his heart.

"You seem quiet," he said after a few minutes of driving. "Are you sure everything's okay?"

"Everything's fine."

"Well, *you* don't seem fine. Did something happen while I was gone?"

Now was the time to tell him, but she couldn't make herself do it. "Nothing happened. I told you, it was just a . . . long week. Leave it alone."

"Hey, I was just asking."

"Well, you had your answer."

"Why are you acting this way?"

"Does it matter? We both know that I view things more seriously than you do. But then—" she glanced out the side window "—you don't take things seriously at all, do you?"

"Why should I take things seriously? Life can be dreary enough at times without my being grim about it."

"Well, *that's* an interesting attitude."

"I just don't believe in going around preparing for the worst to happen," he said between clenched teeth. "I've found that it usually does, anyway."

"And what bad things have happened to you?"

"I wasn't talking about me. I meant, people I know. Like some of those older actors at the studio, for instance. They're the ones you should have as clients, not all these rich old coots who really don't need any help at all."

She turned angrily to him. "How did we get from you not taking things seriously to my not doing the right thing with my work?"

"I'm not criticizing you. I just wonder if you realize how many people in the business made money in the past and yet have nothing to show for it today."

"Can I help it if they haven't planned for the future?"

"Yes, you can," he said, irritating her even more. "Or, you could, if you wanted to."

"I can't believe you even care about this! Isn't this one of those *serious* things you avoid like the plague?"

He reddened, but persisted, "Well, usually, I have to admit. But I can't avoid this, not after talking to some of these guys. Zane Whittacker, for instance."

That got her attention. "I don't know what you mean," she said stubbornly. "I talked to him at Mother's party, and he said he was doing just fine."

"Well, he would, wouldn't he? He's hardly going to tell you that he didn't manage his money very well, not when you used to look up to him as a child."

"But that's ridiculous! Zane is a friend!"

"He *was,* Nora. Now he's just a used-up old actor. There are a lot of them around who could use your help, you know."

Obstinately, she crossed her arms. "If they need help, all they have to do is make an appointment with someone."

"But not where you work. They wouldn't even get in the door, would they?"

She had no answer for that. If she'd had any doubt about the kinds of clients Orrin Bullard wanted to cultivate, she'd had a stinging lesson just this week, hadn't she? Feeling guilty because she still hadn't mentioned her resignation, and even angrier because he was making her feel this way over something she couldn't do anything about, she said, "That's not my fault!"

He looked as though he wanted to push it, but then decided against it. "You're right," he said. "Look, I don't want to fight. I guess it just affects me so much because I wonder if that will be me in a few years."

Still annoyed with him, she muttered, "It won't be you."

"You don't know that. You keep telling me I don't take things seriously. Maybe I'll spend all my money and end up a bum."

"Maybe you will," she agreed just to irritate him. "But you're right about one thing," she added. "I don't know you. I wonder if anyone does. You never talk about yourself. Why is that?"

"It's no big secret. There's nothing to tell."

"Everyone has a story, Lane."

"Not me," he insisted. "I'm just an ordinary guy who happened to get an extraordinary break. It wasn't anything I did. I was just in the right place at the right time."

"In other words, you're saying that talent had nothing to do with it."

"Talent? As I recall, you're the one who's said— more than once, I might add—that talent isn't required for what I do. According to you, all I have to do is say what they tell me, go where they point and stop when they say so. Any idiot can do that."

She flushed. "I didn't say that at all. Or if I did, I didn't mean it—exactly that way. Besides, if you recall, I also said I thought you were capable of more."

"I don't remember your saying that."

"Well, I did. And since you brought up the subject, I never said, or believed, that real acting was just a matter of mugging on command or being able to repeat lines you were supposed to memorize."

"I'm sure your mother will be glad to hear that," he said. Tentatively, he reached for her hand. "Let's not quarrel. Just forget everything I just said, all right? I don't want to ruin this by saying or doing something stupid."

As his hand covered hers, she knew she should tell him about her week. But they were just driving into the town of Lake Arrowhead, and since the time wasn't right, she said, "I don't want to fight, either. Let's pretend it never happened."

He gave her fingers a squeeze, and looked at her. She smiled, and quickly glanced away. Through the window she saw a little store. To change the subject, she asked if they should stop, but he shook his head.

"I'll come back later if I have to," he said. "I called ahead and had the caretaker stock up on a few staples. We can get settled, figure out what we need, and I'll drive back in."

She was about to remind him that they were only going to stay the day when he turned onto a private driveway. At the end was a beautiful cantilevered home built of cedar logs, and when she saw it, she exclaimed with surprise.

"Is that yours?"

"Mine and the bank's," he said, stopping the car in front of the garage. "Do you like it?"

"Like it! It's magnificent!"

It was even more gorgeous inside. A huge living room-family room combination boasted high-beamed ceilings and clerestory windows, while a massive stone fireplace bisected the front windows and made the lake seem almost part of the house. Overstuffed couches and chairs were scattered around, and the floor was covered by a rug with long fringe. Floating above it all was a loft bedroom that looked down on the living room and out over the water.

Nora was hastily looking away from the bedroom when Chauncy bounded in. He wasn't accustomed to hardwood floors, and when he tried to stop, he got tangled up in the rug and started to skid. Uttering a frightened howl, he went sailing by, and she made a frantic grab for him, thinking: here we go again. She missed by an inch. Momentum carried him across the room before he finally fetched up against the hearth.

"Chauncy!" she cried, rushing over to him. He looked at her so sheepishly that she had to give him a hug. Just then, Lane came in.

Seeing the path the dog and the rug had made across the room, he smiled. "I see Chauncy's made himself at home."

"I'm sorry," she said helplessly. "But I tried to warn you how it would be."

"Don't worry about it," he said, dropping the bags and coming over to her. "He can't hurt anything in here. And if he does, I'll just replace it. It's no big deal. Now, what do you want to do first? Take a walk down by the lake?''

Until he had come to stand by her, she'd wanted to do just that. But suddenly, the last thing on her mind was taking a walk, and as she looked at him, she saw the same longing in his eyes that she felt herself.

''Or,'' he said hoarsely, ''the lake can wait...''

The loft was warm from the afternoon sun, the bed invitingly covered with an old-fashioned quilt. Nora reached for him as they lay down side by side, but instead of kissing her, he began to whisper of the feelings she'd caused in him, and the ways he wanted her. His hands began to roam over her body, gently at first, and then with increasing passion, until every touch burned through her clothes and she wanted to rip them all off.

She'd worn jeans and a blouse for the long drive, and when he finally started to unbutton her blouse, she moaned and tried to hurry him. He wouldn't be rushed. He slowly unfastened her buttons one by one, and then, just as slowly, pushed the garment away so that he could look down at her. She was still wearing a bra, her breasts rising and falling with each labored breath; when he ran a finger inside the lace, barely touching her nipple, she moaned again and reached for his hand.

Gently pushing her hand away, he bent down and brushed his lips across the swell of her breasts. Then he turned her slightly so that he could undo the bra's clasp.

She'd thought she would feel self-conscious when he lifted up slightly and looked down at her. But his expression banished her shyness, and when he bent down to caress her bare breasts with his lips, she put her hands in his hair and arched her back.

It was too much for him. He pulled his shirt over his head, and got up to kick off his pants, but she sat up and reached for his belt. Tugging him toward her, she pressed her face against the warm skin of his belly, unsnapping his jeans and pulling them, with his shorts, over his hips. Groaning, he kicked both garments away, and took her into his arms.

"I never thought I would feel like this with any-one—ever," he said as he looked into her eyes. "I never thought I'd get the chance to feel like this again...with you. Oh, Nora, I'm so sorry...."

"So am I," she whispered. "Oh, Lane, so am I...."

She hadn't thought anything could be better than the first time, but it was. She'd never felt so free and uninhibited, and as she drew him back down onto the bed and straddled him, she knew all that mattered was the feel of his body, the touch of his hands, the sensation of his mouth on her, pulling her up to him and kissing her all over. They waited as long as they could, but finally desire overtook them. Lane took her to heights she'd never dreamed about before, and when she finally cried out with pleasure, he was right with her. They held on to each other, and rocked back and forth until the intense feeling gradually abated, but even then, when Nora was finally able to look up at him, his eyes looked like stars.

"Oh, Lane," she said with a sigh, as he fell down beside her, breathing hard. "I never dreamed it could be like this...."

A long time later, when she was almost asleep, she heard a whine. She lifted her head, and listened. The long afternoon had drifted to twilight, and shadows were thick in the loft. But even so, when she saw a lonely silhouette in the doorway, she had to smile. After the last episode, it seemed that Chauncy had learned to wait his turn.

"Come on," she whispered, patting the bed. "You've been a good dog, and now you can get up."

The springs protested loudly when the dog jumped up beside her, but Lane barely moved. Nora thought he was sound-asleep, but after Chauncy had turned around twice before finally throwing himself down, Lane sleepily reached down and gave the big dog a pat.

"Good boy, Chauncy," he murmured sleepily. "Thanks for giving the other guy a break."

Then he turned over and put his arms around Nora, drawing her close to him. She was about to say something to him when his breathing evened out and she realized he'd fallen asleep. Smiling, she snuggled against him and drifted off, herself.

NORA OPENED her eyes to bright sunshine and the welcome smell of coffee. She sat up quickly, trying to think where she was. Then she remembered, and looked at the clock on the bedside table with horror. It was almost nine...in the morning! She couldn't believe she'd slept the entire night without waking. She threw off the covers, and jumped up before she noticed the note on the pillow. It seemed that Lane hadn't been as lazy as she; the note said that he and Chauncy had gone into town for supplies.

Lane hadn't mentioned when they'd left or how soon they'd get back, but when she went downstairs, she found that he'd been thoughtful enough to leave her a fresh pot of coffee. After pouring a cup, she went back upstairs to get dressed. She was just making the bed when she accidentally hit the chair where Lane had tossed his duffel bag. The chair began to tip over, and when she grabbed it, a copy of a script slid out of the bag and dropped to the floor.

"What's this?" she murmured, reaching for it. With a start of surprise, she realized it was the script she'd glimpsed in Lane's car. She knew she should just put it back, but curiosity got the best of her. It was just a script after all, nothing sacred.

There was a note from Wyatt on the title page. It read:

Lane, don't be mad about this. I told Esperanza to tuck this into your bag before you left. I know if you read it again, you'll agree it's the perfect breakaway vehicle for you. We'll talk when you get back.

Even more intrigued, she sat down on the bed and opened the script to the first page. She'd only had time to read a few sentences before, but as she finished the first paragraph of the monologue by Tyler Dane, the protagonist, she was hooked. The character leaped off the page, the pain and bitter longing Dane had carried from his childhood cut like glass with every sentence. Reading on, Nora pictured Lane in the role, and with each word, she became more excited. It would be the role of a lifetime!

She couldn't turn pages fast enough. Every word drew her on, and whenever the lead character came on scene, it was as though even the air shimmered around him. It was one of the most powerful, most eloquent male roles she'd ever read. It would take everything Lane had to give and then some, she knew, but she was sure he was capable of doing it justice. Tyler Dane would prove that Lane was what he aspired to be: an *actor,* not just someone who appeared on screen.

"What are you doing?"

She jumped violently. She'd been so absorbed that she hadn't realized Lane had returned. Surprised, she looked around. He was at the head of the stairs, and when she saw the expression in his eyes, she wondered briefly what Chauncy had done to upset him. She didn't dream he was angry because she'd read the script, and she waved it at him as he came all the way up into the loft.

"I know I shouldn't have, but I couldn't help myself!" she exclaimed. "Once I started, I couldn't put it down. It's wonderful! Why didn't you tell me? When are you going to start shooting?"

"I'm not," he said as he grabbed the script from her and tossed it into the duffel bag.

Blankly, she looked at him. "I... What do you mean?"

"It's simple enough, don't you think? I'm not going to do it."

"Not do it! But... but why? Any actor would *kill* for a part like that!"

"Not me," he said, his voice cold.

She couldn't believe it. Grabbing his arm, she said, "Talk to me! Are you serious?"

He jerked his arm away. "I don't want to discuss it anymore. Come on, let's go have breakfast."

"Breakfast!" She looked at him uncomprehendingly. "I don't want anything to eat! I want to talk about this!"

Obviously, he didn't. He walked away from her, and started down the stairs. She stared for a moment, then she rushed after him. By the time she caught him, he was in the kitchen.

"Lane—"

He looked at her so fiercely that she stepped back. But she couldn't just let it go, and so she said, "I don't know what's wrong, Lane, but—"

"Nothing's wrong. I just think you should mind your own business."

"Mind my own business!" Shocked and angry, she said, "Well, you didn't feel that way yesterday, when you were talking about *my* work!"

"That was different."

"Different! How?"

Suddenly, he slammed a fist down on the counter. "I don't know!" he shouted. "It just was, okay? It just was!"

She hadn't noticed before, but he'd left Chauncy out on the deck. The big dog, always so protective of her, had heard their raised voices, and was standing by the screen, whining to get in. Without thinking, she opened the door, and when Chauncy came in, he pressed close to her side. It was clear that the dog didn't know what was going on, but that was okay, Nora thought: neither did she. Controlling her temper with an effort, she said, "I'm sorry, Lane, but that's not good enough."

"Too bad. It's going to have to be."

"I just don't understand—"

"You don't have to understand, all right?" he raged. "This is my business, and I'll handle it the way I see fit!"

"Well, the way I see it, you're not handling it at all!" she accused. "For heaven's sake, think about it! If you're lucky, roles like this come along once in a lifetime! You'd be a fool to turn it down!"

"And what would you know about it, Miss Comfortable-and-Secure," he demanded. "*You* never take chances...oh, no, not you! You live your life being as predictable and *safe* as you can be!"

It flashed through her mind that she still hadn't told him about her resignation. Now that it was too late, she cried, "We're not talking about me! We're talking about your career!"

"And what do *you* know about my career!" he roared. "You don't know me! Nobody does! I'm the only one who knows what I can do, and I'm telling you for the last time, forget it! I do what I do, and that's the way it is. Now let it go, damn it! Just let it go!"

"You know what I think? I think you're *afraid* to do it! Yes, *afraid!*" she cried. "You'd rather just walk through all those stupid action films because that's so easy! You've said it yourself, you're not up to a serious challenge! Oh, no, not Mr. Take-Life-As-It-

Comes! And you dared to criticize me! You . . . you make me sick!''

"I think it would be best if I took you back."

"Yes, I think so," she said, and went up to pack the duffel bags.

The ride home was the longest in her entire life. They didn't speak a word until the car stopped in front of her house and Lane turned to her. Before he could speak, she opened her car door.

"Don't say anything," she said. "I think we both know now that this...this *attempt* at a relationship was a giant mistake. Obviously, you're not the man I thought you could be, and since I seem to have disappointed you, too, I don't think we need to see each other again."

He started to say something, but she gave him such an angry look that he gave up. He got out of the car, and opened the trunk for her bags. She took them without a word; then, she turned and marched up the walk toward the house. Chauncy looked at Lane for a moment, whimpered softly, then, his tail dragging, he followed his mistress.

Lane watched them until they'd disappeared inside the house. Slamming the trunk with a curse, he got back into the car.

"Great," he muttered savagely to himself as he drove off. "Just *great*."

CHAPTER SIXTEEN

"Darling," Theodora said over their salads at Al Frescoe's, a tony place near the studio, where she and Nora were having lunch. "It's obvious that something went wrong. You've been miserable for a week now. I've never seen you like this."

Nora put down her fork. "I told you, Mother, I don't want to talk about it. Now, may we please change the subject?"

Theodora sighed. "All right, dear, whatever you wish." She eyed her daughter covertly. Nora *had* told her that she'd quit her job over some dispute about policy, but since she didn't know much more than that, she asked tentatively, "Perhaps you'd prefer to discuss work? Have you applied for a new job?"

Nora's face clouded even more. "I've set up several interviews, but..." Frustrated, she shook her head. "Nothing seems right. I don't know what I'm going to do."

Theodora put her hand over her daughter's. "I know that whatever you decide, it will be the right thing for you."

"I wish I could be as sure of that."

Surprised, Theodora said, "But, darling, you always plan well." Her expression turned wry. "Not like your mother, I'm afraid."

"Are you having second thoughts about this new engagement in Sydney?" Nora asked. "Or about Arthur?"

"Oh, no—neither. It's just that I . . . well, I think I could have handled things better."

"You're not the only one," Nora said gloomily. Then she squeezed her mother's fingers. "I'm going to miss you."

Thinking that they were getting dangerously near to a teary scene here, Theodora tried to be more cheerful. "Well, it won't be forever," she said. "I'll be back. And then, there's always the telephone. We can call each other . . . as soon as I get the time difference straightened out in my mind, that is!"

Nora smiled. She knew she could look forward to telephone calls at all hours of the night because her mother wouldn't be sure what time it was here. "Still," she said fondly, "a long-distance relationship isn't the same as having you here."

"Yes, I know. I used to feel the same way about your father."

"My father?" Nora repeated. "You never talk about him."

"I know. But I've been thinking lately that was a mistake. You know, I realize now that I was partly to blame when your father and I couldn't make it work."

Nora sat back. "What? On the rare occasions we've talked about Dad, you always said that his drinking was the reason for the failure of your marriage . . . marriages."

"Well, yes, I *said* that," Theodora admitted, toying with her glass. "But what was I *supposed* to say?

How could I tell my own daughter that my pride got in the way of my love for her father—just as his got in the way of his love for me?''

Nora didn't know what to say. She had never heard her mother talk this way. ''Why are you telling me this now?''

''Oh, I don't know. I guess I felt too guilty before. You know, I've never told you this—I've never told anyone, in fact—but when Patric begged me to give it one last try, I refused. I was proud and hurt, and I didn't want to give him another chance when I felt I'd already given him so many. What could he prove to me, I wondered, after he'd failed so often? By the time I realized how foolish I'd been, it was too late.''

Nora thought of Lane, but before she could start second-guessing herself, she hardened her heart. It wasn't the same, she told herself. Her parents had been in love, while she and Lane . . .

''I wish you'd told me this before, Mother,'' she said.

''I know. I wish it, too, but the time never seemed right. Now, it does.'' Suddenly, Theodora leaned forward. ''Don't make the same mistakes I did, darling,'' she said intensely. ''I know you say you don't love Lane, and that even if you did, it wouldn't work out. But I let the love of my life slip away and I've regretted it ever since. Please don't let it happen to you.''

They parted soon after that, Theodora giving her daughter a fierce hug out on the sidewalk, which Nora returned. While her driver waited to help her into the car, she turned to Nora one last time. ''The *Time and a Half* wrap-up party is tonight, darling," she said. "Are you sure you don't want to come?"

Nora looked at her with fond exasperation. "You'll never give up, will you? No, I don't want to come, Mother. I know Lane will be there. But thanks for the invitation. And...have a good flight out. Will you call me as soon as you get there?"

"The instant I set foot on Australian soil," Theodora promised. Then she blew a kiss and disappeared into the luxurious interior of the limousine, a thoughtful look on her face.

BY THE TIME Theodora got to the party, the place was in full swing, and as she accepted a glass of champagne from a passing waiter, she glanced around, looking for Lane. She finally spotted him lurking by himself in a corner, nursing a drink. She watched him for a moment, debating. But she knew there was no way she could leave the situation as it was; she had to make one last attempt to fix things.

But after she'd worked her way across the crowded room and just "happened" to end up standing beside him, Lane was unresponsive. "I don't want to talk about it," he said sullenly after she'd casually mentioned Nora. "It's over and done with, and that's all there is to it."

She sensed there was much more to it than that, but all she said was, "All right, darling. Whatever you say. I just thought I could help."

"No one can help," he said fiercely. "Your daughter is the most impossible woman in the world."

"Oh, I agree that Nora can be inflexible," she said with an inner smile, "but I warned you about that right from the beginning, didn't I?"

He turned away. "Yeah, well, I should have listened. If only she hadn't found that damned—" He stopped. "Never mind. It doesn't matter."

"You know, you and Nora remind me so much at times of myself and Patric."

"Oh, really? And just how is that?"

Ignoring the sarcasm, she said, "Well, we loved each other, too—"

"*Too?* I never said a thing about love!"

You didn't have to, Theodora thought with another secret smile, but all she said was, "All right, let's just say that Patric and I loved each other, but we couldn't make it work." She sighed. "It *was* a shame. Even though we couldn't get along, Patric used to tell me that I had an infallible instinct about what roles he should take, and I felt the same way about him. All the quarrels in the world couldn't change that."

Lane looked interested for a moment, then his handsome face closed down again. "It's not the same thing. You and Patric were married."

"Yes, twice, as you know. The problem, I guess, was that we didn't try hard enough either time. For some reason—" she glanced sideways at him "—our pride always got in the way. When I think now that I let the love of my life get away because I couldn't admit I was wrong, well, it breaks my heart. We could have been so happy, and yet..."

She'd timed it perfectly, for just then, Freddie came up to remind her she had promised to pose for photographs. As he led her away, she looked back. Lane was still standing where she'd left him, but when she saw his expression, she was satisfied. Smiling brilliantly, she stood beside the director while the flash bulbs went off. When she had time to look again, Lane was gone.

AT HOME that night, Nora couldn't stop thinking about what her mother had said that afternoon at lunch. *Was* she making a mistake where Lane was concerned? Should she give him another chance? Maybe she should call and apologize...

No! she thought. Theodora had the best intentions in the world, but she just didn't understand the situation. She and Lane were too different. They didn't have a chance. Her head in her hands, Nora tried to hold back her tears. It wasn't just that Lane was an actor. Somewhere along the line, she'd accepted the fact that she'd fallen in love with someone in the business. She could have handled that. No, the problem was Lane's attitude toward life—toward anything serious. After her tumultuous childhood, wasn't she entitled to some stability and a sense of being able to depend upon someone besides herself? How could she ever depend on Lane when he insisted on never growing up?

Abruptly, she got up. This endless soul-searching wasn't doing any good; it was just depressing her more. She'd distract herself with mundane things, like getting Chauncy's dinner.

But once she had mixed the kibble and put it down for him, the dog sniffed the bowl indifferently, and walked away. He'd never done that, and as she watched him in surprise, he went to his corner of the kitchen and threw himself down on his bed. His head between his paws, he looked at her with sad eyes.

"What is it, Chauncy?" she asked. "Are you sick?"

But of course he couldn't tell her; all he could do was give a pathetic little whine. Alarmed, she was wondering whether to call the vet when the phone rang. Her mind still on Chauncy, she answered without thinking. It was Lane. As soon as she heard his voice, her heart began to pound.

"Don't hang up," he said. "At least not until you hear what I have to say."

"What do you want, Lane?"

Out of the corner of her eye, she saw Chauncy lift his head at the sound of the name. She watched him sit up, his head cocked, and thought: he wasn't sick— he was just...depressed?

Telling herself that was ridiculous, she turned back to the phone just as Lane was saying, "...ask if you'll go somewhere with me. Don't say no," he went on hastily, anticipating her refusal. "I wouldn't ask, but a friend of mine is giving a piano recital tonight, and I promised her I'd come. I thought—hoped—that you'd come with me. She's very talented, so I know you'll enjoy the music. But even more, I think it will explain a few things."

Explain a few things? What did that mean? Did she want to find out? For an instant, she was tempted, but then she realized that if she agreed to go, she'd be opening herself up to the hurt she'd been trying to heal ever since that disastrous trip to the lake last weekend. She was about to refuse when something her mother had said at lunch flashed across her mind.

My pride got in the way of my love for your father... Don't let the same thing happen to you....

She bit her lip. It wasn't the same thing, she tried to tell herself, but she asked, anyway, "Why are you asking me, Lane?"

"Because if you'll listen, Nora, I've got some explaining to do, and this will be part of it."

As always where he was concerned, she could feel herself wavering. "I don't know—"

"Please, Nora."

It was the simple plea that did her in. Surrendering, she said, "All right, I'll go."

"Thanks," he said quietly. "I'll make sure you won't regret it."

EXACTLY AN HOUR LATER, the doorbell rang. Chauncy nearly fell down in his rush to get to the door. Things were so simple for Chauncy. He liked Lane and had no problem showing his feelings. It was only people who complicated their relationships, Nora thought as she watched man and dog greet each other.

When he had finally given Chauncy enough attention and the dog sat down obediently at his command, Lane turned to her. "You look beautiful," he said.

She hadn't known what to wear, but for once, her usual uniform of black dress, pearls and conservative pumps seemed hopelessly dull and conventional. Some time ago, her mother had given her a silk suit in a vivid shade of teal, and on impulse she'd pulled it out. She wasn't quite brave enough to wear the jacket without anything underneath, so she added a stretch lace blouse her mother had also given her, and then, feeling reckless, added heels and a necklace and earrings of silver links. When she was ready, she hardly recognized herself; panicked, she raced back to the closet to drag out the black dress again, but just then, Lane had arrived. Now, seeing his expression, she was glad she hadn't had time to change.

"You look nice yourself," she said.

Tonight, he was wearing slacks and a sport coat, a blue long-sleeved shirt casually open at the throat. As always, he looked so handsome her breath caught.

"Thanks," he said. "Are you ready?"

Wondering if she'd feel this awkward all night, she said, "Almost. Just give me a minute and I'll put Chauncy out back."

"Oh, let him come."

"To a recital?"

"He can wait in the car. It's not a formal affair. And I brought the Cadillac."

Nora didn't know what Lane had in mind, but when Chauncy realized he was going along, there was no stopping him. He streaked by them both, bounded out to the car and jumped in almost before Lane had the back door open. Nora climbed into the front, and once they were on their way, she had to ask, "What's this about?"

"Have patience," Lane said. "You'll see."

A while later, when they turned off the freeway into a poorer suburb of Los Angeles proper, she wasn't sure she wanted to find out. The run-down area made her nervous, and she put her hand on Lane's arm.

"Where are we going?"

"Don't worry, we're almost there. It'll be all right."

"Why are you being so secretive? Why won't you tell me what's going on?"

"Because I want you to see for yourself. Look, we're here."

When he pulled over, she glanced around. They had parked in front of a lighted building that had a sign identifying it as a teen club. Puzzled, she asked, "Is this where the recital is being held?"

Before he could answer, there was a commotion at the door. A group of teenagers came bursting out, and as they ran toward the car, a tiny girl in a miniskirt led the pack. She had a cloud of black hair, huge black eyes and a mouth crimson with bright red lipstick. She reached the car just as Lane got out, and grabbed his arm.

"You came! Lane, you came!"

With a smile, he bent down and gave her a quick kiss on the cheek. "Hey, Anita," he said. "I told you I'd be here."

A tall blond girl elbowed her way to the front of the little group. "Hey, Lane," she drawled, "aren't you going to introduce us to the chick?"

Before Lane could reply, one of the boys stepped forward. With a flourish, he opened Nora's car door. "Hector Saldano, at your service," he said, bowing as he helped her from the car.

"Guys, this is Nora Carmichael," Lane said. "Nora, this is Anita, the star of the show, and

LeeAnn, and Hector, and—'' He paused, glancing over Hector's shoulder to a boy who was hanging back. ''Is that Jesse?'' he asked.

A boy wearing boots and a leather jacket ambled forward, his hands in his pockets. ''It's me, all right,'' he mumbled. ''How's it hang—''

''Jesse!'' LeeAnn said with a quick glance at Nora. ''Remember your manners!''

Jesse looked at the blonde. ''Oh, yeah, right,'' he said. Then, ''How're ya doin', Lane?''

''Just fine. How's it going with you? Is that family you're living with now treating you right?''

Obviously trying to be casual, Jesse brushed back his long hair. ''They're all right,'' he said. ''A little strict, but I can't complain.''

''I'll say not,'' Hector put in with a grin. ''Three squares a day and his own room. He's never had that.''

Lane nodded, his eyes still on Jesse's face. ''And the grades?''

''Not bad, not bad,'' Jesse said, smiling. Nora, who was watching but not understanding a word of the conversation, saw that when he smiled, Jesse was a handsome young man. LeeAnn apparently thought so, too. Moving over to his side, she put a proprietary arm through his.

''His grades are the pits, but not for long,'' the girl said. ''We're working on it.''

''Sounds good,'' Lane said. He looked at Anita. ''Well, when does this shindig start?''

Anita smiled impishly. ''Any time, now that you're here.''

"Well, if you're waiting on me, you're losing time," he said. "Come on, let's go in."

Before they could all start inside, Hector looked into the car. "Hey, Lane, is this your dog?"

Lane looked back. "No, Chauncy belongs to Nora, I'm afraid. He's quite a specimen, isn't he?"

The teenagers crowded around. "Man, that's the biggest dog I've ever seen!" one of them said.

"You never would have known it when he was a puppy. He was a tiny little thing," Nora said.

Jesse smirked. "Sucked you in, did he?"

"Just like you did with me, Jesse," Lane retorted.

Everyone laughed, but as they all started inside again, leaving Chauncy to guard the car, Nora held back until Lane took her arm. "I'll explain later," he said. "For now, let's just enjoy the recital."

Enjoy it, they did. A grand piano had been set up at one end of the room, and the chairs around were filled with parents, teenagers and other children. The place was noisy when they entered, but when people saw Lane, there were shouts of greeting and a smattering of applause. Looking pleased and embarrassed at the same time, he gestured back and shook his head. Anita had saved two seats for them in front, and as Nora sat down, she glanced at Lane. How did he know all these people? she wondered. What was going on?

She didn't have time to ask, for just then, the miniskirted Anita came up to the makeshift stage. The audience quieted, and in the sudden silence, she said, "I'd like to dedicate this night to the man who made the music possible—my friend, my man. Lane Kincaid."

As Nora turned in astonishment to look at Lane again, Anita sat down at the piano. For the next forty-five minutes, no one in the audience, not even the children, moved. Transfixed like the others, Nora listened as Anita filled the room with glorious sound. Her head bent over the keyboard, her eyes closed, she played like a virtuoso—which was just what she was. When she finally took her hands from the keys and stood up and bowed, Nora was on her feet with the rest of the crowd. The applause was thunderous, and when Anita caught Lane's eye, she shyly smiled.

NORA DIDN'T GET a chance to talk to Lane until the small reception was over and most of the people had gone home. Over punch and cookies that had been carefully set up on the battered counter at one end of the room, he congratulated Anita on her performance, and reluctantly—and with renewed embarrassment—accepted the heartfelt gratitude of her parents. After that, other parents came up to praise him for things he had done for them and their children; finally, when he was occupied by yet another group of teenagers, who were eagerly telling him about their grades, Nora couldn't stand it any longer. Drawing Hector aside, she said, "Lane didn't tell me, so I'm asking you. What's all this about?"

Hector looked at her. "You really don't know what the man has done?"

"No. Tell me."

He thought a moment. "Well, I guess you could say that he gave us a different way of looking at things," he said. "He took a bunch of delinquents from the barrio and showed us there was another way—just like the one he'd found."

"Like the one he'd found," she repeated. "What do you mean?"

"You didn't know that he's from the neighborhood, that he grew up around here?" She shook her head, and he gestured. "Yeah, two streets over, where his grandmother lived. He came to live with her after his mother dumped him for the last time."

"His mother...dumped him? I don't understand."

His eyes went to Lane, then back to her face. Suddenly uncomfortable, he said, "Hey, look, I probably shouldn't have said anything. If he wanted you to know, he would have told you."

"Yes," she said slowly. "I guess you're right." Across the room, she looked at Lane. As though he sensed her eyes on him, he turned just then and glanced her way. Seeing her expression, he excused himself from the group that surrounded him and came over.

"Lane, I think we should talk," Nora said.

"Uh, I'll be seeing you," Hector said quickly. "It was nice meeting you, Miss Carmichael. And if you're in the neighborhood, drop in anytime. Lane doesn't allow any booze or brew, but we've always got soda. We'll play a few games of pool, see how—"

"She gets the picture, Hector," Lane said.

"Oh, yeah, right," Hector said. With another grin, he took off.

When he was gone, Lane said, "You want to go for a drive?"

"Yes, I would. How about a couple of streets over, to see where your grandmother used to live?"

He grimaced. "Hector has a big mouth."

"A good thing. I found out more about you from him in one conversation than I have talking to you for weeks." They started out to the car, but halfway down the walk, she halted. "Why didn't you tell me? Why did you keep something like this a secret?"

He hesitated, but finally he said, "I didn't know how to tell you. Every time I tried . . ." He shook his head. "It wasn't anything I could take credit for, Nora. It was just something I did."

"Something you did!"

"Look," he said abruptly. "Let's get Chauncy and walk a bit. Maybe I can explain."

Chauncy was only too happy to be released from the car. Lane snapped on his leash and held it as they started out. For the first few minutes, Lane was so quiet that Nora wondered if he'd changed his mind about an explanation.

"I never knew my father," he said at last. "But my mother was—" his mouth twisted "—the euphemism they use now is substance abuser. But what she was, was a drunk and a drug addict. She had a lot of problems, my mom. When I was about five or six years old, I remember thinking it was my job to help her back to the apartment where we lived. If she didn't come home by about two in the morning, I'd go out looking for her. I knew where she'd be. If she wasn't at the local bar, she was down along Firestone, trying to score. Sometimes, when I couldn't find her, I stayed with her friends. But they had problems of their own, and in the end, my grandmother took me in."

Nora felt numb. "I didn't know. I never imagined..."

"Why should you? I didn't want to look back, and I certainly didn't want anybody else to know about my past. I was just sixteen when my grandmother died, but I didn't tell anyone at school because I knew if the authorities found out, they'd put me in some foster home. I'd heard stories... Well, it doesn't matter. Then, after I graduated—"

"But... but your mother, Lane. Where was she?"

He shrugged, but even on the dark street, she could see the pain in his face. "Who knows? She disappeared somewhere along the line, and I never saw her again."

"Oh, Lane, how awful!"

"Yeah, well, that's the way it was. Anyway, after I got out of school, I traveled around for a while, worked odd jobs, saw some of the country. I didn't have any money, and what with one thing and another, I never even thought about college. I was working at a gas station down by the beach when that talent agent spotted me. The rest, as they say, is history."

"Not quite," Nora said softly. "You said that you didn't want to look back, Lane, but you did. You came back, in fact, to help these kids. You started the Teen Club."

He looked embarrassed again. "Well, I remembered how lonely I was when I was their age. I didn't have anyplace to go. It was a miracle that I didn't get into serious trouble, and I figured that since I'd escaped, I'd do what I could to help other kids who needed a hand."

She looked down. "And here I thought you were never serious," she said.

"I can't blame you for thinking that," he said. "I've worked hard at projecting a shallow personality. When you've seen the things I have, the last thing you want to be is serious. It's too painful, I guess."

She hardly knew what to say. "I'm sorry, Lane," she said. "I misjudged you."

He stopped and took her hand. "It wasn't your fault. You saw the Lane I wanted you to see. I did everything I could to blot out my childhood... But I need to know—can you forgive me for not telling you before now?"

"If you can forgive me for hiding a few things from you."

"Such as?"

"I didn't experience the tragedy you did, Lane, but what I saw when I was growing up affected me, too. You see, I was terrified of the insecurity I felt."

"Insecure? You?"

She smiled bitterly. "Oh, yes, me. My parents loved each other, I know, but they were both so volatile. One of my most vivid memories as a child is the sound of a door slamming, shaking the house. Sometimes they'd even fight each other to be first to get out." She looked up at him. "I didn't know if they were serious about the threats to leave or not, but I was scared, anyway. When you're a child and you don't understand, everything is terrifying, it seems. I was constantly afraid that one of them would leave for good and I'd never see him or her again.''

''Oh, Nora.'' His hand tightened on hers, but she wasn't finished.

''And then, one day, my worst nightmare came true. My father left and never came back. After that, I vowed that when *I* was old enough, I'd control every aspect of my life. I'd be so serious that nothing bad could ever happen to me again.''

''Oh, my darling,'' he said as he gathered her into his arms. ''If only you'd said something ...''

She buried her face against his chest. ''What about you? We were both hiding from each other, Lane— and from ourselves.''

He pulled her tightly to him for a moment, then he held her away again. ''How can I make it up to you? What can I do to prove how serious this relationship is to me?''

''I think I'm the one who has something to prove,'' she said shakily. She took a deep breath. ''And I guess I could start right now. I quit my job at Bullard and Sweeney last week.''

''Last week? Why didn't you tell me?''

''Well, that's the point, isn't it? I was going to, but I ... couldn't. I felt so silly at the time. After complaining bitterly about *your* impulsiveness, how could I confess that I'd done something so rash? Even now, I'm not sure what happened. Instead of meekly agreeing with my boss when he intimated that I shouldn't see you again, I told him it was none of his business what I did in my private life.''

''You did that?''

"Yes, I did."

He stared at her a moment. Then he smiled broadly and whirled her around. "I was right! *That's* the Nora I knew was hiding all this time! Oh, my lady, I'm so glad you finally let her out!"

Seeking reassurance, she asked, "You don't think I was foolish?"

His eyes twinkled as he reached into his back pocket and pulled out an envelope. "No more foolish than I've been."

"What's that?"

"Oh, nothing," he said, holding it out of her reach. "Just an agreement between me and a couple of producers to do that damned screenplay you liked so much."

She looked at him blankly. Then comprehension dawned, and she tried to snatch the envelope from him. "You signed to do that film? Oh, Lane, let me see it!" She made another grab, but with a laugh, he held it higher. "I don't know," he said, pretending to rethink things. "Since you've apparently forgiven me, maybe I don't have to go this far. Maybe I should just tear up the agreement and keep on doing those super-stud films you admire so much."

"Don't you dare!" she cried. Then, too happy to dissemble any longer, she threw herself at him. "Oh, I love you," she said. "I'm so proud of you I could cry!"

Looking a little emotional himself, he reached for her hand and put the envelope in it. He curled her fingers around it, and stared deep into her eyes. "Kiss me, instead," he said. "But first, tell me you'll be my wife."

"Your wife!"

Nora was too overcome to answer, so Chauncy did it for her. Sitting on his considerable haunches, he looked up at his two most favorite people in the world and barked. There was no doubt in either of their minds that he was saying, "Yes!"

"Well, I guess we have *his* answer. What about yours?" Lane said.

Nora smiled. "I have to ask one question first."

"What?"

She looked at him mischievously. "Are you being serious?"

Lane gathered her to him with an expression she couldn't mistake, as he whispered fervently, "Are you kidding? I've never been more serious in my life!"

EPILOGUE

EVEN BEFORE Lane Kincaid's new film opened across the country, word was that his characterization of the angst-ridden Tyler Dane was certain to gain him an Academy Award nomination—if not the actual statuette. His performance was outstanding. As the troubled and tortured but ultimately triumphant protagonist, Lane had electrified test audiences. With that one role, it seemed he'd left his "beefcake" image behind forever.

In Los Angeles, where the premiere was held, powerful searchlights pierced the black sky on a perfect spring night, while red velvet ropes on either side of the main entrance to the theater held the crowd back. A hush briefly ensued with each limousine that pulled up, followed by a cheer when yet another celebrity emerged and waved to the crowd before going inside.

But no one received such a roar of welcome as did the star of the film himself. When the white stretch limo stopped at the curb and Lane stepped out, girls screamed and fainted; even the men in the crowd cheered. As he stood in the spotlight, Lane was even more handsome in person than he was on screen. A lock of sun-streaked blond hair fell onto his lean face, and his gray-blue eyes were amused as he scanned the throng.

"Hey, my man, Lane!" cried an accented voice from the crowd. It was a special group from the Teen Club, who had all been given a place of honor inside. Lifting his hand to wave, Lane grinned as he helped his new bride out of the car.

Nora emerged into the glare of the lights, and smiled at her devoted husband. Her daring red-sequined dress shot sparks into the night, and a few whistles of admiration resounded throughout the crowd. The noise caused a third member of the entourage to peek out from the back seat. When the fans spotted him, they laughed and cheered again.

Chauncy was a familiar figure to them by now. There had been pictures in the paper of him and Nora strolling on Rodeo Drive looking at wedding gowns. When he attended his mistress's much-publicized wedding to one of filmdom's handsomest bachelors, even jealous females had to smile at pictures of the dog walking proudly down the aisle, gingerly carrying the ring pillow in his massive jaws. In interviews afterward, the newlyweds admitted that the ceremony wouldn't have been the same without him, but they were more cagey when they were asked if the dog was going to accompany them on the honeymoon. That was when the bride's mother, dressed in electric blue, and fresh from a smashing success in Sydney, had indicated, somewhat warily, that she and Chauncy were going to stay with an old friend at his penthouse while the bride and groom were out of town.

Tonight, Chauncy had to stay in the car. But he was waiting patiently when the crowd poured out of the theater after the premiere a few hours later. As at the advance showings, the film had been a triumph; few left dry-eyed. Greeting his family with a bark when they climbed inside to go on to yet another celebration party, he settled down and listened to the conversation with one ear cocked attentively.

"Well, what did you think?" Lane asked as the limousine pulled smoothly away from the curb.

"What I always think when I see that film," Nora said. "You were brilliant. If you don't sweep the awards, it will be a travesty." She put her arm through his. "I'm so proud of you!"

He put his arm around her shoulder and drew her closer. Tipping her head up, he kissed her briefly on the lips. "If you're proud of me," he said, "that's all the reward I need."

With a smile, she traced his jaw with one finger. "But a few statuettes on the mantel wouldn't hurt, would they?"

He looked wry. "I guess not. But *if* I should get so lucky, I think I'll reserve a special shelf in your new office. That way, when you're working, you'll be reminded of your wonderful husband."

"I don't need any awards to be reminded of that," she teased. "Sherrie tells me how lucky I am every day."

"Ah, she's a good woman," he said. "I knew she'd be the perfect secretary."

"I just wish I could have seen Orrin Bullard's face when she quit to come work for me," Nora said. "In fact, I wish I could have seen him when he found out that I was starting up my own office and taking on all those—'' her eyes gleamed ''—undesirable types...like actors.''

''Not to mention Lester Snook, whom you seemed to charm like you do everyone else,'' Lane said. ''I wish I could have been there to see Bullard digesting *that!*''

Nora laughed. ''Lester was quite a coup, wasn't he? But they all seem to be happy, and Zane and the others are doing well. I've put them into some stock-and-bond issues that—''

When she stopped suddenly, Lane said, ''What?''

Nora had leaned forward to stare out. ''Is that—'' she stopped speaking, and shook her head. ''No, for a minute there, I thought I saw a puppy by the side of the road.''

''A puppy?''

''Yes, but I must have—'' She stopped again, reaching quickly for the window. ''It *is* a puppy, Lane! Look!''

Sure enough, just ahead, they could see a small young dog shivering in the gutter. In moments, the car would be past it, and as Nora looked at it, she thought, *Again?*

''Nora?'' Lane said.

They were about to go by. All she had to do was roll up the window and pretend she hadn't seen anything. But now, as though he sensed that something momentous was about to happen, Chauncy had sat up. His head was cocked in her direction, and when he saw her looking at him, he barked. How did he always seem to know? she wondered.

Chauncy's approval was one thing; Lane's was another. Quickly, she turned to her husband. "Lane, would you mind—"

He started to laugh before she could finish. It appeared that he, too, sensed what she was about to ask.

"I always thought Chauncy needed a companion, but it's up to you."

Her eyes gleaming with the mischief that being in love had brought out in her, she made her decision. With Chauncy wagging his plumed tail, and Lane smiling indulgently, Nora raised her voice and said, "Driver, we have to pick up another passenger. Please, pull over!"

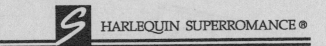 HARLEQUIN SUPERROMANCE ®

COMING NEXT MONTH

#582 MOONCALLER • Patricia Chandler
Logic told Whitney Baldridge-Barrows to hate Gabriel Blade. He
was planning to turn the Havasupai village at the bottom of the
Grand Canyon, where she worked as a doctor, into a posh tourist
resort. But logic had nothing to do with Whitney's response to the
man....

#583 IF I MUST CHOOSE • Lynda Trent
After her divorce, Lacy Kilpatrick wanted nothing to do with
romance—but she hadn't counted on sexy Austin Fraser showing
up. Nor had she counted on her family calling him "the enemy" and
forbidding her to see him.

#584 McGILLUS V. WRIGHT • Tara Taylor Quinn
Never mind that sparks flew between them—Tatum McGillus and
Jonathan Wright should never have said hello to each other. The
timing was wrong, and they couldn't agree on anything. As if that
weren't enough, they stood on opposite sides of the law. This was
one relationship that would need a miracle to survive.

#585 DIAL D FOR DESTINY • Anne Logan
The last thing Lisa LeBlanc's sister Dixie said before she disappeared was that she was going to meet a man named Gabriel
Jordan. Lisa managed to track Gabriel down, but the man denied
ever speaking with Dixie. Somehow, Lisa was sure he knew more
than he was telling. To uncover the truth, she had to stay close to
Gabe. An idea that was not altogether without appeal.

AVAILABLE NOW

#578 THE LAST BUCCANEER
Lynn Erickson

**#579 THE DOG FROM RODEO
DRIVE**
Risa Kirk

#580 SIMPLY IRRESISTIBLE
Peg Sutherland

#581 THE PARENT PLAN
Judith Arnold

**Fifty red-blooded, white-hot, true-blue hunks
from every State in the Union!**

Look for MEN MADE IN AMERICA! Written by some
of our most poplar authors, these stories feature fifty of
the strongest, sexiest men, each from a different state in
the union!

Two titles available every other month at your favorite
retail outlet.

In January, look for:

DREAM COME TRUE by Ann Major (Florida)
WAY OF THE WILLOW by Linda Shaw (Georgia)

In March, look for:

TANGLED LIES by Anne Stuart (Hawaii)
ROGUE'S VALLEY by Kathleen Creighton (Idaho)

You won't be able to resist MEN MADE IN AMERICA!

If you missed your state or would like to order any other states that have already been published, send your name, address, zip or postal code along with a check or money order (please
do not send cash) for $3.59 for each book, plus 75¢ postage and handling ($1.00 in Canada),
payable to Harlequin Reader Service, to:

In the U.S.	In Canada
3010 Walden Avenue	P.O. Box 609
P.O. Box 1369	Fort Erie, Ontario
Buffalo, NY 14269-1369	L2A 5X3

Please specify book title(s) with your order.
Canadian residents add applicable federal and provincial taxes.

MEN194

My
Valentine
1994

Celebrate the most romantic day of the year with
MY VALENTINE 1994
a collection of original stories, written by
four of Harlequin's most popular authors...

MARGOT DALTON
MURIEL JENSEN
MARISA CARROLL
KAREN YOUNG

*Available in February, wherever
Harlequin Books are sold.*

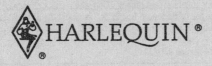

◆ HARLEQUIN ®

®

VAL94

HARLEQUIN SUPERROMANCE ®

Women Who Dare will continue with more exciting stories,
beginning in May 1994 with

THE PRINCESS AND THE PAUPER by Tracy Hughes.

And if you missed any titles in 1993
here's your chance to order them:

Harlequin Superromance®—Women Who Dare

#70533	DANIEL AND THE LION by Margot Dalton	$3.39	❏
#70537	WINGS OF TIME by Carol Duncan Perry	$3.39	❏
#70549	PARADOX by Lynn Erickson	$3.39	❏
#70553	LATE BLOOMER by Peg Sutherland	$3.50	❏
#70554	THE MARRIAGE TICKET by Sharon Brondos	$3.50	❏
#70558	ANOTHER WOMAN by Margot Dalton	$3.50	❏
#70562	WINDSTORM by Connie Bennett	$3.50	❏
#70566	COURAGE, MY LOVE by Lynn Leslie	$3.50	❏
#70570	REUNITED by Evelyn A. Crowe	$3.50	❏
#70574	DOC WYOMING by Sharon Brondos	$3.50	❏
	(limited quantities available on certain titles)		

TOTAL AMOUNT	$
POSTAGE & HANDLING	$
($1.00 for one book, 50¢ for each additional)	
APPLICABLE TAXES*	$ _____
TOTAL PAYABLE	$ _____
(check or money order—please do not send cash)	

To order, complete this form and send it, along with a check or money order for the
total above, payable to Harlequin Books, to: **In the U.S.**: 3010 Walden Avenue,
P.O. Box 9047, Buffalo, NY 14269-9047; **In Canada**: P.O. Box 613, Fort Erie, Ontario,
L2A 5X3.

Name: _____

Address: _____ City: _____

State/Prov.: _____ Zip/Postal Code: _____

*New York residents remit applicable sales taxes.
Canadian residents remit applicable GST and provincial taxes.

WWD-FINR

NEW YORK TIMES Bestselling Author

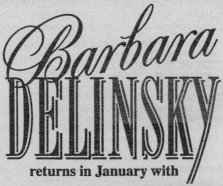

Barbara
DELINSKY

returns in January with

THE REAL THING

Stranded on an island off the coast of Maine,
Deirdre Joyce and Neil Hersey got the
solitude they so desperately craved—
but they also got each other, something they
hadn't expected. Nor had they expected
to be consumed by a desire so powerful
that the idea of living alone again was
unimaginable. A marrige of "convenience"
made sense—or did it?   BOB7

 HARLEQUIN®

HARLEQUIN®

Don't miss these Harlequin favorites by some of our most distinguished authors!
And now, you can receive a discount by ordering two or more titles!

HT#25409	THE NIGHT IN SHINING ARMOR by JoAnn Ross	$2.99	☐
HT#25471	LOVESTORM by JoAnn Ross	$2.99	☐
HP#11463	THE WEDDING by Emma Darcy	$2.89	☐
HP#11592	THE LAST GRAND PASSION by Emma Darcy	$2.99	☐
HR#03188	DOUBLY DELICIOUS by Emma Goldrick	$2.89	☐
HR#03248	SAFE IN MY HEART by Leigh Michaels	$2.89	☐
HS#70464	CHILDREN OF THE HEART by Sally Garrett	$3.25	☐
HS#70524	STRING OF MIRACLES by Sally Garrett	$3.39	☐
HS#70500	THE SILENCE OF MIDNIGHT by Karen Young	$3.39	☐
HI#22178	SCHOOL FOR SPIES by Vickie York	$2.79	☐
HI#22212	DANGEROUS VINTAGE by Laura Pender	$2.89	☐
HI#22219	TORCH JOB by Patricia Rosemoor	$2.89	☐
HAR#16459	MACKENZIE'S BABY by Anne McAllister	$3.39	☐
HAR#16466	A COWBOY FOR CHRISTMAS by Anne McAllister	$3.39	☐
HAR#16462	THE PIRATE AND HIS LADY by Margaret St. George	$3.39	☐
HAR#16477	THE LAST REAL MAN by Rebecca Flanders	$3.39	☐
HH#28704	A CORNER OF HEAVEN by Theresa Michaels	$3.99	☐
HH#28707	LIGHT ON THE MOUNTAIN by Maura Seger	$3.99	☐

Harlequin Promotional Titles

#83247	YESTERDAY COMES TOMORROW by Rebecca Flanders	$4.99	☐
#83257	MY VALENTINE 1993	$4.99	☐

(short-story collection featuring Anne Stuart, Judith Arnold, Anne McAllister, Linda Randall Wisdom)
(limited quantities available on certain titles)

	AMOUNT	$	
DEDUCT:	10% DISCOUNT FOR 2+ BOOKS	$	
ADD:	POSTAGE & HANDLING	$	
	($1.00 for one book, 50¢ for each additional)		
	APPLICABLE TAXES*	$ _____	
	TOTAL PAYABLE	$ _____	
	(check or money order—please do not send cash)		

To order, complete this form and send it, along with a check or money order for the total above, payable to Harlequin Books, to: **In the U.S.:** 3010 Walden Avenue, P.O. Box 9047, Buffalo, NY 14269-9047; **In Canada:** P.O. Box 613, Fort Erie, Ontario, L2A 5X3.

Name: _____

Address: _____ City: _____

State/Prov.: _____ Zip/Postal Code: _____

*New York residents remit applicable sales taxes.
Canadian residents remit applicable GST and provincial taxes.

HBACK-JM